UNREQUITED

A DARK MAFIA AGE GAP ROMANCE

BRATVA KINGS

JANE HENRY

SYNOPSIS

He was never supposed to touch me.

I was never supposed to love him.

But some lines don't stay drawn.

I live in a world of rules and expectations, where obedience is survival and love is a liability. I was the innocent one. The youngest sister. Sheltered by my brothers and kept far away from the family's darker affairs.

Until him.

He's dangerous. Nameless. Obsessive.

Mine for one stolen hour a week, and every time he leaves me, he takes a piece of me with him.

But when I find out his true identity, my world implodes.

They call him the Undertaker.

The man who buries problems no one else can
solve.

Loving him means betraying my family.

Choosing him means choosing war.

But he's already chosen...me.

PROLOGUE

Present day

ZOYA

It all feels like a dream.

A strange, hot, fevered dream I can't wake up from.

"I'm ready."

Any second now, I'll open my eyes and realize none of this happened. That my brother never offered me up in marriage. That I'm not marrying someone who despises me.

No.

Any second now, I'll wake up and just be little Zoya. Homemaker. The girl who makes meals for her family, who takes care of her nieces and nephews, who lives month to month, year to year, without even questioning her own needs. Zoya. Just... little Zoya.

But now, it's time.

My brothers' wives are all here. Every one of them is so beautiful. So poised. So infuriatingly supportive. So kind.

Ember wears emerald green, and her eyes glint like gems under the overhead lighting. Hard, fierce... alive. Anya offers me a soft, solemn smile, a touch of sorrow just behind it. And Polina, Rafail's wife, the only one who dares to touch me, squeezes my hand gently.

"Come, Zoya," she says with a smile that doesn't reach her eyes. "We're ready for you downstairs."

I'd asked for no procession. No standard fanfare.

I wanted it quiet. Small. Nothing traditional or ceremonial.

Because this isn't a marriage I ever dreamed of. It isn't a love story but a sentence. So why dress it up?

When the massive double doors open into our living room, something immediately feels wrong.

I can't place it. Not at first. It's in the air. Something about the stillness. A pallor. A hush.

Rafail smiles at me, and even Semyon, cold, removed, practically carved from stone, seems alert, aware, and alive.

Rodion comes straight to me and presses a kiss to my cheek. "If he ever treats you bad, sister," he murmurs low, "you know who to call."

And I know he means it, every word, but it seems like too little, too late. Shouldn't his protection come before we made it this far?

And where are the Morozovs? Weren't they supposed to

bring witnesses? I'm marrying into their family, and they're not here.

It's strange. Wrong.

"Where are they?" I ask Rafail, my voice small, trembling in the space between us.

"He's here," Rafail says, frowning. "I saw him ten minutes ago. He's all we need."

I nod. "Okay."

Music plays. It echoes off the walls and into the hollow of my chest.

Even now, a part of me still expects Seamus to come and rescue me.

From what? From this? He's not the knight in shining armor. He's *The Undertaker*.

And now I understand why.

The one who's done unspeakable things. The one even my brothers fear.

Untouchable.

Unquestioned.

The one they all obey.

And he's not coming to rescue me.

I sigh and stifle the need to cry.

My life isn't a fairy tale. It never was. It never will be.

I turn my face away when the music begins to play.

It's time.

CHAPTER I

ZOYA

I STARE at the narrow space in the hedges, hardly able to believe my luck.

Is this really happening?

I've been lonely. Restless. Half-wild from being overprotected by my family. I know I'm the baby, but how long does that title last? Will I still be the baby when I'm twenty-five? Thirty? Forty?

I'm tired of being told what to do. Tired of being the good girl.

I don't want to be the good girl anymore.

I've watched my brothers get married, one after the other. All three of them. And my older sister has been married for years now.

It's like everyone's next season of life has started... except mine.

So tonight, it's time. Something has to change.

If nothing else, I need to prove to myself that I can carve out a private pocket of freedom, one that nobody else knows about.

I wait until everyone is distracted. I made a beautiful dinner tonight and served it with a smile, like I always do.

They call me Little Zoya. The caretaker. The one who likes to cook and clean, and take care of everyone.

And I do love taking care of all of them.

My oldest brother, Rafail, and his wife, Polina. My nieces and nephews. Rodion and his fierce, brilliant wife, Ember. And now Semyon, who's clearly falling hard for Anya. They're not married yet, but it won't be long.

A sliver of moonlight catches the path ahead of me. It's early summer just outside Moscow, and the crickets chirp a quiet chorus.

It's beautiful. Desolate. And the rising heat adds to the thrill of doing something I shouldn't.

No one will find me tonight.

I've planned this too well. In my bedroom, there's a fluffy tan teddy bear, age-worn and well-loved, propped on my bed. And hidden inside is the small monitor my brothers use to track me. I've tested my little decoy three times now.

Once during a quick trip into the city.

The second time, I stayed inside but crept around the house to see if they'd notice.

The third? I snuck out for ice cream at a local street fair.

No one ever noticed.

We have guards at every exit and entrance, of course. My brothers monitor everything. They're not just overbearing but militant.

I've never been out like *this* before, not without a bodyguard trailing close behind.

Even at school, someone was always watching. Nobody dared approach the Kopolov family's precious little princess. They knew if anyone tried *anything,* my brothers would kill them.

Literally.

No one took the risk. So I stood alone at school dances while the shadows of my guards hovered nearby like grim sentinels. I went shopping alone, to the bookstore alone, and spent more than my fair share at restaurants, eating solitary meals.

I was lucky to have one friend outside of my family. Just one. Mia, the only one who's ever helped me bend the rules.

"Zoya?" Mia's voice hisses from just ahead.

"I'm here," I whisper back.

My heart pounds. I rub my clammy palms against the thighs of my fitted jeans. I'm nervous tonight, more than usual. But I'm also resolved.

Tonight, I'm doing something that would make my brothers lose their ever-loving minds.

I'm going to a club.

I'm going to have a *drink*.

Unsupervised.

And god help me, I'm going to get kissed. I've already made it my mission.

"You ready, baby?" My best friend Mia grins as she peeks around the corner of the tall hedges. Her eyes widen when she takes me in.

"Zoya... you look *gorgeous*," she praises. "No one would ever know who you are."

Tonight? I've pulled out *all* the stops.

I'm wearing a fitted, low-cut, red halter top with a vee that dips nearly to my navel. The color pops against my pale skin, bringing out my blue eyes and dark-brown hair. My jeans hug every curve. Red heels give me just enough height to feel bold, and a tiny clutch completes the look. I've practiced walking, practiced my smile.

I give her a small, nervous grin as hope surges in my chest. I sigh. How I wish I could live my life without anyone knowing who I am. My name, the title, the connections, the weight of all that entails... I'm *over* it. I need something more.

With a deep breath, I step out through the hedges, just as I rehearsed. They're covered in ivy and nestled into the old stone wall behind the estate. Hidden. Secret. Though it's not my first attempt at escape, this is the first one that feels real.

The dusky air wraps around me. Moonlight filters through the trees, and the buzz of crickets fills the silence. For a moment, I feel like Cinderella on her way to the ball.

And then... *I'm free.*

I'm shaking with nerves as Mia chatters in the driver's seat of her hand-me-down car about some guy she's meeting tonight.

"Are you sure your cousin isn't coming?" she teases with a wink.

"Matvei?" I snort. "Are you serious? He's terrifying. Unhinged."

"And the only one of them who's single," she replies, waggling her eyebrows. "Your brothers are *so* hot."

"Ew. Gross, Mia. *Stop.*"

She laughs, and I shake my head, still filled with nerves. But I'm not turning back now.

She parks her car alongside the curb in the way back. Her nondescript black Kia doesn't catch attention like my brothers' flashy, sleek cars. I like that.

Still, I feel exposed. Unprotected.

I remind myself, I need to try. I *have* to try.

With a deep breath, I follow behind Mia, well aware of the eyes of the men following the line of my cleavage and the sway of my ass as I walk in.

Mia orders me something that's like dessert in a glass over ice, creamy and sweet, and it goes down real easy.

I'm cautious. I don't accept anything from strangers, and I don't leave my drink unattended. I'm not stupid. So I just tentatively sip, like I belong here.

I let my gaze wander, with one eye glancing at the door as if expecting Rafail to storm in here and drag me home.

But no one comes.

No texts even ping my phone.

I let out a breath.

I'm getting away with it.

My eyes settle on a man at the bar. Attractive. Older than I am. Longish dark hair curls around his ears. Warm brown eyes. A dimple flashes when he gives me a wolfish grin. A warning bell clangs in my head, but I tell myself I'm just nervous about being discovered.

"Hello, beautiful," he says in a low voice. "Don't you look stunning tonight? Let me buy you a drink."

I smile shyly. "Thank you."

Mia's already in the corner, tangled up in someone else's arms and tongue. God. Seriously? She's left me all alone. I signal to her, but she doesn't even look my way.

I think of the house, imagine curling into my favorite chair with a hot cup of tea and a book.

That actually sounds better than this. Is that lame?

"Are you alone?" the man asks.

Is that a normal pickup line, or should I be worried?

I shrug, noncommittal, and let the conversation carry us forward. He's friendly and easy to talk to. Probably in his mid-twenties, so younger than I thought but older than I am.

After a while, he leans closer.

"It's loud in here," he murmurs. "Let's go for a walk."

I hesitate. Definitely more dangerous.

Still, I want to be kissed. I decided I would be. Secretly. Recklessly. Like I'm a woman someone wants, and not just a girl someone wants to protect.

I glance toward Mia, trying again to signal her, to reassure myself she's got my back, but she doesn't look up.

I clench my fists. It *is* hard to hear in here, and it's awkward to have a first kiss at a *bar*.

"Maybe."

I'm considering. I look to the door, half-decided, when I feel the weight of someone's gaze on me.

At the far corner of the bar, hidden in shadow, a man sits with a drink cradled in his large, rough hand. I can't make out his face, just the broad, tense set of his shoulders. Stillness, like he hasn't fidgeted a day in his life.

And he's watching me. He isn't even pretending not to.

And I can feel his eyes burning through me.

Me.

Why?

I look down again and note how big and thick his hands are, wrapped around what I can now see is a full pint of Guinness. Condensation rolls down the side of the glass, but it looks untouched. A prop? He just stares, like he's lost in thought, or maybe pretending to be.

I swallow hard, watching him.

Does he know Rafail? Does he know *me*?

I *want* to believe that this is only in my head, that I'm safe, and that no one recognizes Rafail Kopolov's baby sister.

But I know better.

"It's going to get busy in here soon," the guy next to me pushes. I don't even know his name.

If Rafail could see me now, he'd lose his shit. My oldest brother has always been more father than sibling. He became my guardian when I was just a child, and I've never disobeyed him.

Well. Until I started sneaking out.

Until I started feeling crushed under the weight of expectation.

I grit my teeth and nod, then push myself to standing and turn my back on the man in the corner.

We walk hand in hand down the quiet street, making small talk about the last movie we saw. Turns out he doesn't like thrillers the way I do, and he definitely doesn't read the romance novels I inhale, but we have a few things in common.

Still, this is boring the fuck out of me. Is this what women like? He's hot, he's nice enough, I guess… but I'm disinterested. He's too nice, too eager to say things he seems to want me to hear, and for some reason, I keep staring at how soft his hands are.

We're approaching a streetlight when I suddenly realize I don't have my phone with me.

"Where's my phone?" I mutter, patting my pockets. "Strange. I always have it on me." I sigh. "I have to go back to the bar," I tell him. "I think I left my phone."

He grins and winks. "You didn't. I've got it right here."

He opens his palm and shows me my phone, resting there like a prize.

A chill of unease slides down my spine. How did he get that? I never let it out of my sight, the one concession to Rafail that makes sense to me.

I swallow hard.

"That's mine," I say, trying to keep my voice steady. "Can I have it back, please?"

"I'll give it to you," he says with a wink, "in exchange for a kiss."

My heart jumps hard. I'm not sure if it's excitement or fear. I *wanted* a kiss.

Didn't I?

But now that he's closer, everything shifts. His teeth are slightly crooked. He smells faintly of garlic and onions. My attraction drains away fast.

Have I been that protected? That sheltered? Is this what it's like, meeting a man in the wild?

Am I broken?

"I'd like my phone back, please," I say again, softer this time. "I'm not ready to kiss you."

He crowds me suddenly, pressing me into a darkened doorway. Above us, the clouds shift, moonlight breaking through in a silvery wash across the sky.

"I bought you a drink," he says, with a tinge of annoyance. "And you won't even give me a kiss?"

Don't guys buy girls drinks? Was that some weird expectation I didn't know about?

He leans in, mouth slightly parted, and for one crazy, wild second, I'm convinced he's a werewolf. That he's about to bare his teeth and bite me, or throw back his head and howl into the night.

I shiver.

I've read too many books.

"No," I say more firmly. "Not now."

My voice leaves room for a maybe, but that doesn't matter. Not now. Not like this.

I put more force in my tone. "Give me my phone."

But he doesn't. His eyes flash at me, and I realize even though he's not *that* much bigger than I am, I'm small and alone, and I'm not sure I could get away that easily. And where would I even go?

Panic claws at my chest.

Fuck.

Shit.

Fuck.

Why did I do this? Why did I want to be alone? Why did I have to leave my brothers? Why did I have to prove anything to anyone?

I won't scream. I can't panic. My pride won't let me. But I'm cornered. Vulnerable. And this man is too close.

"Come here," he murmurs, his voice low and greasy. "Don't be afraid. I'll make sure you like it."

"I said *no*," I snap, louder this time, clearer. Goddamn it, I'm Zoya Kopolova, and I knew how to shoot a gun before most of my peers knew how to drive a car. Why didn't I think to bring a weapon? They're as readily available in my house as a pair of shoes.

His face twists with anger, and he lets my phone fall to the ground. It hits hard, and I wince.

"Give me a fucking kiss," he growls and shoves me back against the door.

My brothers taught me self-defense. They taught me how to shoot. But right now, every lesson vanishes. My mind blanks. I could get away from him, but without a weapon, a phone, or any idea of where I am...

He grips my chin and pushes me again when a voice cuts in.

"You'll leave her the fuck alone now."

The voice comes from behind us. Thick Irish accent. Cold. Dangerous.

"You do what I say by the count of three, or I'll slice your feckin' throat. Try me. It's been too damn long."

The man holding me jolts and spins. "Who the fuck are you?"

The stranger steps into the light. Late twenties, maybe early thirties. At least ten, twelve years older than I am. Tall. Still. Radiating power and calm like a storm waiting to break.

Even in the dim moonlight, his blue eyes glint like cut sapphires. A five o'clock shadow shades his jaw, and a scar cuts through one eyebrow. Ink curls around his collarbone and disappears beneath his shirt.

The man watching me from inside the bar. He followed us?

Did Rafail put him up to this?

He steps forward, anchoring his hands on his hips. Broad, solid, capable hands.

I swallow.

"You heard what I said," he murmurs in that accent, then blows out a breath. "I don't repeat myself. I've already exercised what little patience I have."

There's a weight to his presence, a quiet confidence that says he's used to being recognized. Obeyed. Feared even.

He wasn't just watching. He was waiting.

When the man doesn't back off fast enough, the Irishman strikes like lightning. He grabs him by the collar and swiftly delivers one solid, brutal punch. A growled word in what might be Gaelic?

"I don't know how you Russians do things," he says coolly. "But where I come from, we don't kiss a woman who says no."

His grip clamps on the guy's collar, slamming him into the wall. I wince.

"Now, are you going to leave the poor lass alone, or do I need to teach you a lesson?"

His tone isn't raised, but it slices through the air.

"You stay the hell out of this."

Slam.

A punch to the jaw. One to the gut. Another to the temple. The creep crumples to his knees.

The Irishman stands over him, blood on his knuckles and not a single hair out of place. He frowns as if looking down at discarded rubbish on the pavement. He isn't even winded.

"Aye, so you see," he says with unnerving calm. "The chance for another choice is now gone. Get the fuck out of here before I end you."

I can't breathe. My chest is tight, and my legs won't move. My brothers would react like this, *exactly* like this, before they beat the creep beyond recognition. No one fucks with a Kopolov woman.

But this... doesn't feel the way it would if my brothers were the ones delivering justice and protection.

The creep staggers to his feet and runs. A sensible choice.

The Irishman turns to me.

His voice gentles, his blue eyes glinting.

"You all right, lass?"

Lass. Mmm. I like that.

I swallow and nod. "You didn't have to save me," I whisper.

He smiles, and a dimple appears in his cheek. My god, he's hot and definitely Irish. Ruddy cheeks and dark-brown curls around his ears. Those bright, terrifyingly blue eyes.

Something in them makes my stomach twist.

"I suppose I came here for nothing, then, eh?" he says, cocking a grin. "Should've at least had the stupid feckin' Guinness."

Then he reaches for my hand.

I flinch, but his touch is gentle. Soothing. The warmth of his rough hand over mine is reassuring.

Wordlessly, he lifts my hand and presses a kiss across the knuckles.

Old-fashioned. Arresting.

"Thank you," I whisper, my heart pounding.

"Now, little lass," he says, his voice dropping low. "I don't know why you're here, but something tells me you *probably* shouldn't be, eh?"

He bends and picks up my phone. Miraculously, it's unharmed.

He taps something into the screen. "This is my number," he says. "I'll be around a bit. Not from around here, you know. Ireland. But I'm not heading back just yet."

He holds the phone out to show me. "You get into trouble, you call this number. See?"

Why is he protecting me? Why does he care?

I nod. "Okay," I whisper.

He flashes a grin—bright and devastating. My belly melts.

"Good girl," he says softly. "That's a good girl."

Then he leans in, hooks a finger under my chin. "Now go back inside. Find whoever you came with. Go home where it's safe, eh?"

I nod again and swallow hard.

Safe. Funny word, coming from him.

Because somehow, I know...

I've never been in more danger in my life.

CHAPTER 2

SEAMUS

SHE'S SWEET. Innocent.

And I don't *do* sweet and innocent. Never have.

I don't know what the hell it is about her, why she's gotten under my skin like this, but she has. I can't get the sweet, pretty lass out of my feckin' head.

Every time I close my eyes, I see her face, those wide, dark-blue eyes, the little smattering of freckles across her nose that makes her look like something out of a fairy tale. Like something pure. Untouched. Precious.

The way she looked at me... It wasn't just curiosity but something else. Like... hero worship? The way her gaze clung to mine after I saved her from that asshole who thought he could corner her. Who thought he could own her.

Feck my life.

No.

Feck my life *all* the fecking way. Because I don't have time for girls like her. Especially not in the form of a sweet, naive little Russian.

Girls like her need to be protected. Kept safe. Cared for.

Cherished.

And that's not *my* job.

I don't have the space for that. The time. The fucking energy.

Not now. Not ever.

So I leave.

I make sure she's safe, tucked away like something breakable behind glass. I tell myself I'll never see her again.

But then I saw the little tat on her shoulder I should've heeded. It should've sent me running, told me to stay away.

Instead, it felt like a brand.

Like she was already mine.

And I knew exactly where we'd met. I clocked the time, made note of it without even meaning to.

Thursday, eight p.m., Wolf and Moon.

Late enough for privacy. Quiet enough that no one would suspect anything. Just enough time between then and the weekend that it wouldn't draw attention. No reason for anyone to be watching too closely.

I should go back to Ireland.

But I tell myself there's still work to do here in Russia. Still unfinished business. The Kopolov family fucked us over, and I'm here to make sure it doesn't happen again.

So I show up. Next Thursday. Eight o'clock sharp. Back at the same place.

A quiet challenge to the universe.

Keep her away from me. Keep her safe.

And a stupid, reckless part of me hopes she comes back.

God, I hope she doesn't. I hope she knows better. That she listens and stays far the fuck away from me and everything I bring with me.

But that image... her sweet, luscious body, the way her cheek dimples when she smiles, those soft pink lips that look like they were made to whisper secrets into the dark.

Is she a virgin?

Has she ever been with a man?

Not a boy. A *man*.

Does she even know the difference?

I could show her.

I clench my jaw, close my eyes, and mutter a curse under my breath.

Fucking hell.

I can't. I won't.

And then she's there.

Like I conjured her with my thoughts.

My sweet little angel, wide-eyed and curious. She meets my gaze across the room, and my breath fucking stalls.

She shouldn't be here.

I *told* her not to come back.

I narrow my eyes at her in warning.

She should've listened. She ought to know better.

But she doesn't look ashamed. Doesn't look nervous.

She looks... defiant.

That stubborn little chin of hers tilts up like a challenge, and something sharp and electric slices through me.

So I crook a finger at her. A command, plain and simple.

Is she going to obey me? My god, if she does.

Sure enough, she whispers something to her useless feckin' friend, gets to her feet, and walks that short, dangerous distance across the room to where I sit.

"I told you not to come back here," I say. It's barely a whisper, but it hits like a threat.

Everything I say to her feels like foreplay. Like teasing. Like temptation.

And I shouldn't be doing it.

I *know* that.

"I told you," I repeat.

"And I'm telling *you*," she says with a smile, "that you're not in charge of me."

Oh. Brave little lass, eh?

But her eyes betray her. There's a flicker in them. Uncertainty, maybe?

Need, *definitely*.

A silent, unspoken thought: *I want you to be.*

Aye, sweet lass. You and me both.

"Have you stayed out of trouble?" I ask her, gentler now.

I pull the chair beside me out for her. She slides into it without a word, her body tense but eager.

"Yes," she says. But it sounds more like a question than an answer. There's hesitation in her voice that makes my brows draw together.

"Why does that sound like you're lying to me?" I lean closer.

I nod at the waitress to bring drinks.

And then it hits me. Feck, is she even old enough to drink? "How old are you?"

"Twenty-two," she says, too fast, like she's rehearsed it.

Little liar.

I growl under my breath. "Aye, try that again."

She blinks. "Twenty?"

That might be a lie too. But I decide it's good enough. Barely. She's old enough to drink. Old enough for more than that, but still...

She's twelve years younger than I am.

Good luck, bad luck? Which is it again?

"You have a keeper?" I ask.

She frowns. "A *keeper*? What is that supposed to mean? Tell me that's something Irish and not chauvinistic."

I lean back a little. "A *keeper*. Someone who watches over you. Protects you. Keeps you in check."

She pauses, like she doesn't want to answer. Then she sighs and gives me a small nod.

"I guess. I have brothers," she admits. "*Too many* fucking brothers."

I growl again. That filthy word doesn't sound right coming from her mouth. Her lips are too soft, her face too fucking pretty.

"You ought not curse like that," I tell her.

Her cheeks flush pink. Embarrassed, and slightly flustered.

That adorable little chin juts out again. "Why the fuck not?"

I lean forward, push her drink toward her, and take her hand in mine.

I run my thumb slowly over the top of it, watching her squirm in her seat.

"Because I told you not to."

She doesn't pull away.

She meets my gaze and then looks away again, her eyes wide and lips slightly parted.

Sweet trouble, I think.

Then, "Sir," a voice breaks in behind me.

I don't even look.

I'm here mapping out the Kopolov family. I've got guards stationed in every direction. Eyes everywhere. Spies. Plants. Watchers.

I hold up a hand, wordless, signaling to give me a minute.

"*Sir*," the voice says again, more insistent now.

A clearing of the throat. Another warning.

What the actual fuck?

No one interrupts me. I don't allow it. And now he's risking his fucking life by interrupting me.

"Wait," I say over my shoulder, before I turn to her.

"You shouldn't be here, babydoll," I whisper. "This isn't a place for a girl like you. Someone could hurt you. Someone could take advantage."

But I don't say the rest out loud.

Someone like me.

"Protect me, then," she whispers quietly, without really asking. "Just like you did before."

And fuck, I will. I fucking will. But I don't know if that's the right thing here.

What the actual fuck am I doing?

"Sir," comes the voice again from behind me, more insistent this time.

I turn and level him with a look. "Interrupt me one more feckin' time," I growl. I don't need to finish the sentence.

He blanches, bites his lip, then takes a step back.

"It's urgent, sir," he croaks, nervous now.

"I'll be with you in a minute." I turn back to her. She's watched the exchange with interest.

"What's your name?" she asks softly.

"James," I tell her.

It's not exactly a lie. James is a version of my real name. Close enough. Even if I told her the full thing, she wouldn't know who I was. I'd have to tell her my nickname, too, and I'm not doing *that*.

"That's a lie," she says, a hint of a smile teasing the corners of her lips. "But it's nice to meet you, James. Where are you from?"

She's a sharp one.

"Ireland," I say, watching her carefully.

She snorts. "I'd have to be dumb to not realize you're Irish with a brogue like that. What *part* of Ireland, James the Liar?" She smiles. "The powerful, scary Irish liar."

I can't help it. I smile.

I *never* smile.

So why the fuck am I smiling at her?

"The part near the water," I say evasively, grinning at her, knowing full well I haven't narrowed it down at all. I wish I didn't have to hide. I'd love to tell her I'm from Ballyhock, the most gorgeous little coastal village just outside of Dublin.

And I miss it. I miss it so much, my heart aches.

"A better answer, I guess. What brings you to Moscow?" she asks sweetly.

"What gives you the impression I'm about to tell you anything true about me?" I shoot back across the table.

She leans toward me. There it is again, that faint, floral smell. Subtle, addictive. And her gaze is locked on mine.

"And what's *your* name?" I ask, expecting her to lie like I did.

"Zoya," she says. For some reason, I know she's telling me the truth.

And just like that, my entire world comes to a screeching halt.

Fuck.

"That's a beautiful name," I tell her, trying to keep my poker face, trying to make sure she doesn't hear the record screech in my head.

"*Sir*," the voice behind me says again, louder now.

But now I know what's so urgent.

She's *Zoya feckin' Kopolova.*

The youngest daughter of my enemy.

And she's walked straight into my trap.

I've never wanted to let someone go so badly in my life.

"Would you like a drink, James?" she asks, dragging out my name like she knows exactly what she's doing to me.

"I like to stay alert," I tell her with a wink. "I don't drink."

"An Irishman who doesn't drink?" Her eyes go wide. "Is that for real?"

"Of course it is. I used to like Guinness, used to get plastered. But I like to be in charge of all my senses, my reactions. That gives me the edge. Especially over someone who's drunk or high."

She raises a brow, teasing. "Are you telling me you're drinking soda?" She points a slender finger at my glass, smirking.

"It's a prop." I smile. "How old are you again?"

She looks old enough to drink, barely, but I needle her just to see how she reacts.

She doesn't disappoint.

She sits up straighter, squares her shoulders, and gives me this haughty little look, cheeks flushed pink. And I can already picture how I'd make her whole body flush like that, pink and breathless under me.

The tension between us spikes.

"Twenty," she repeats. "You?"

"Too old for you," I say with a sigh, as if it's her goddamn age that makes her forbidden. "What's *your* drink, lass?"

"I'm not sure yet," she says with a shrug. "I like lots of things. Beer. Wine. Mixed drinks. You know."

I do know. And I'm not sure I like her drinking.

"You do realize," I murmur, "that every time you take a drink, you let your guard down, don't you? You become a little more vulnerable."

"Yes," she says softly. "I do. But it also helps me relax... a little." She exhales a shaky breath. "My family is... intense."

"I bet they fucking are," I mutter. "I know what that's like."

"Do you?" She cocks her head to the side with genuine interest.

"Aye. I'm the oldest," I tell her. "The one with the most to carry. Now that my dad's getting up there, he looks to me. He's lost a bit of cognition in recent years, you know? Lived a hard life. It's taken its toll."

I run my finger down the side of my glass, gathering condensation. Why am I telling her this?

"I'm going to have to step up. No question about it."

"And to get away from it?" she asks, tilting her head. "What do you do?"

"Work out. Go for walks. Read." I look away. "Where I come from, it's beautiful."

I can picture the blue-green sea crashing against the rocks. Quaint shops. Flowers lining every path. God, I miss it.

"Where'd you go just now?" she asks gently.

How the fuck does this woman, who barely knows me, see right through me?

"Just imagining being home," I admit, the nostalgia thick in my voice. "I want to be home."

Fuck, I really do. But I promised my father I'd scope the Kopolovs.

I guess in some strange way I never planned... I'm doing what I said I would.

CHAPTER 3

ZOYA

WE MEET EVERY SINGLE WEEK.

James the Liar and little Zoya.

Every week.

For *six months*.

Six whole months, same time, same place. A little hidden world carved out just for us. I start planning everything around our Thursday night secret rendezvous.

It becomes the highlight of my existence. I live for my Thursday nights.

The only reason I get away with it without my brothers finding out or at least suspecting that something's amiss is because they're damn busy. Traveling, marriage, children, growing our small circle into something larger, more powerful. Sometimes I pretend I'm with one of my friends, but mostly I hide my tracker.

And maybe it has something to do with the fact that no one would ever expect Zoya Kopolova to be a sneak.

Every Thursday, I bring pastries and stories and questions.

And he listens.

He watches more than he speaks, his gaze heavy and thoughtful, like he's memorizing me piece by piece. His piercing blue eyes don't leave mine as he listens.

I'm fully aware of how hard I'm crushing on him. Just seeing him with those rolled-up sleeves, his tanned, muscular forearms as he leans forward and holds onto my every word... I can't be immune to him, no matter how hard I try.

And I do try. A few months in, I gave up and fully owned my crush.

It's just a crush... right? And somehow, I started building my life around those meetings. Around him.

My Mr. Thursday.

There's something inside me that whispers warnings I don't want to hear. That I should be wary. That I should be afraid. That I *can't* have this man and shouldn't allow myself to be vulnerable around someone like him. Someone so dark, so still. So dangerous.

But I can't stop.

The more I try to pull away, the more I crave his presence. His voice. His steadiness. The way he calms the chaos in my mind. He has this way about him.

"Aye," he'll say, just listening, nodding. "Go on, little lass."

Go on, little lass.

And I do go on. Go on talking. Go on trusting. Go on falling in love with a man I barely know.

He understands the things I've never told anyone, and worse, I do tell him everything. Every dark little corner, every secret I've never dared speak out loud.

And he just listens.

With that non-judgmental calm that feels like an anchor in a storm.

But the more I talk, the more I *want*.

I want him to touch me.

To hold me.

To kiss me.

And still, after six months... all he does is buy me a drink. Walk me out. Keep his distance.

He's always there.

Always watching.

I tell myself that I'm safe with him. It's okay that I'm sneaking around without a guard because James wouldn't let anyone touch me.

Sometimes he asks questions, so casually that it almost slips past me.

"Did your brother get married?"

"Then what happened?"

"And after that?"

And I answer him. Because I don't know who else to talk to. So I talk to him.

I tell him about Anya and Semyon. About how Rodion went to the States and met Ember. How they fell in love and how she betrayed my brothers' trust. How he was forced to marry her after, but it's worked out for them.

I tell him about Rafail and Polina, and how they have children now. I tell him how things have shifted. How the rules keep changing.

And I tell him what it's like being raised by men like my brothers.

"Do you think I'll ever get free of them?" I ask, shaking my head.

He gives me a little smirk. "You're here now, aren't you?"

"Yes," I say, "but it's tricky. If this were years ago, before they were married and traveling and all, I never would've gotten away with it."

He raises a brow. "And yet, every single week, you make it. Seems to me you've got a bit more freedom than you think."

"True," I admit, smiling despite myself.

One night, he brings me a small gift. A delicate little trinket —a stunning gold ring, looped and swirled with intricate flourishes. It's so pretty it nearly takes my breath away.

"It's beautiful," I say, as he slides it onto the index finger of my right hand.

"Like you," he says with a soft smile.

Later, Ember asks where I got it.

I tell her a friend gave it to me. I don't offer details.

But now... now I wonder.

Who *is* this strange Irishman?

Why is he here, every week, without fail?

I've even started dreaming of a future, which is ridiculous.

It's all fantasy. Delusion.

We never go anywhere, never even leave the pub. Our little private world, as if it's safely cocooned in this quasi anonymity. I know that I can never be with a man like him, or any man my brothers don't choose for me. That's the way of the Bratva and always has been.

And something tells me it's a similar situation for him. If it wasn't, he would've made a move on me by now, wouldn't he?

But I can't give in to this fantasy. What am I going to do, marry him in this pub? Raise children between booths and whiskey glasses?

Right.

One day, I ask him, gently, hesitantly, "Can we ever meet somewhere else?"

He doesn't answer right away. He just shifts the subject.

Eventually, he says, "I don't think it would be safe. And I don't think your brothers would approve, would they?"

There's sincerity in his voice, like it's not just about me getting in trouble. It's about him *putting* me in danger.

"You have to understand, lass," he says quietly, "I can't."

"I don't."

He sighs and blows out a breath. "Let's go for a walk," he says, low and quiet. It's a move I didn't expect.

I go with him.

We've never been alone before. Not really. We're always in the pub, surrounded by people, noise, and shadows.

But this time, it's just us.

He's so much taller than I am. So broad-shouldered and powerful that when he walks beside me, I feel small. Protected.

He takes my hand, and it fits perfectly in his. Strong. Steady.

His dark curls sweep around his temples, soft and unruly. His eyes are a piercing blue that see right through me, clear and deep like the Irish sea he talks about. Craggy cliffs. Wild ocean. The way he said it made it sound like poetry.

He smells masculine and sharp, like the edge of something old and untamed.

When we walk together, it's clear people fear him.

God, do they fear him. They step back when he approaches, lower their voices, and avert their gazes.

And I start to realize... I *like* that people fear him. I feel safe with him, like I've tamed this wild thing that grown men fear. I have the lion eating out of the palm of my hand.

Truthfully, I'm used to being around dangerous men. But he's different. The way he carries it, calm and controlled.

When we exit the pub, we round a corner. The air is cold and bright with the smell of impending snow.

He stops walking and takes my hand. My breath catches as he turns to me.

"I want to kiss you, Zoya," he says, and I remember the night months ago when he saved me from an unwanted kiss.

This is very, *very* different.

I want to ask him to say my name again.

My heart stumbles in my chest.

Of course I want to kiss him... more than anything. But the words catch in my throat.

"Well," I manage to say with a shaky laugh, "that's convenient. Because I would actually like to kiss you too."

God, how lame am I?

My cheeks flush. I feel embarrassed, like a girl who doesn't know what she's doing.

Because I really *don't*. I've become complacent with our Thursday night chat sessions, comfortable around this much-older, forbidden man, that I've always forgotten how naive and inexperienced I am.

I swallow the lump in my throat.

I want him. I want this, so damn bad.

"Come here," he murmurs. My heart beats impossibly faster, my body instinctively responding to his command.

What would it be like if I were *fully* under his command? My insides whir with excitement and nerves.

He pulls me a little closer. Not roughly. Gently, like I'm something precious he doesn't want to break.

He smells like wind and danger and salt. Like something primal. And under that? Warmth. Comfort. Need.

"I've never been kissed," I whisper. My voice trembles. I wish it didn't.

He stiffens slightly and then tips my chin up to meet his gaze, rough fingers under the thin, vulnerable skin. "Never?"

I shake my head. "I told you I've been sheltered, remember?"

"Aye, lass," he says quietly. His voice drops, rough with feeling. "My fucking god. I can't believe I have the privilege of being your first. Come here."

My heart squeezes. Thumps. Warmth spreads across my chest and dips lower.

I love the way he talks. The way every word feels like a promise.

And I know, before his lips even touch mine, that this is going to be beautiful. Memorable.

Everything I've ever wanted.

"I said come here," he says again, even softer.

I step toward him, incapable of anything but obeying him.

"When a man kisses a woman he cares for," he murmurs, "he needs to make her feel safe."

His hand brushes the hair out of my eyes.

"It's not just about taking, you know. That's the mistake men make. They take and they take, but this?" His fingers trail down the side of my face. "This is about giving too."

I swallow and nod. I don't trust my voice.

Just kiss me already.

"You're so beautiful," he says. "So fucking beautiful." He shakes his head. "Got a flat here outside of Moscow, you know. So I could show every week."

He did?

He blows out a breath and holds my gaze. My nerves and fears meld together. A man can't seduce a woman for six months, right? If he were trying to take advantage of me, trying to somehow use me, wouldn't he have already played his hand?

"Zoya. When I close my eyes, you're the first thing I see. When I open them, there y'are again."

I swallow hard. "Okay," I say, breathless.

He chuckles softly. I love that sound. My cheeks heat.

He's Mr. Tall, Dark, and Handsome in the flesh. And all mine, if only for a moment.

"I'll tell you what to do," he says. "Close your eyes, if you want to."

I look at him, wanting to remember every second. I want to burn the image into my mind.

But I close my eyes.

I tip my head back and feel his breath against my lips.

And then, finally, *finally*, his mouth meets mine.

It's electric.

A shock of something pure and wild and aching floods me, lightning in my veins.

I stifle a moan and grip his hips.

And I kiss him back.

His hands settle on my hips like he owns them, with a branding touch that sends fire straight to my core, like he's been waiting his entire life just for the chance to touch me properly. There's no hesitancy in the way he holds me, no gentleness. Just possession.

I can't breathe. I can't think. The kiss deepens until it steals the air from my lungs and the thoughts from my head.

I love the feel of his fingers digging into my hips, grounding me. I love the heat of his mouth on mine, the way our breaths mingle like we've been doing this forever.

I've wanted him. God, I've *needed* him. I've fantasized about him while lying beneath my sheets in the dark, desperate and aching, touching myself as I pictured exactly this, just a kiss. But this is no gentle dream. This is wildfire and hunger, coiled so tight in my gut it explodes through me like a dam breaking.

And then he lifts me. Just lifts me like I weigh nothing, and my legs wrap around his waist on instinct. One hand cradles the back of my head, protective and sure, and he shifts until his back hits the brick wall with a thud that reverberates through both of us.

I'm pressed against him, his chest solid, my heart pounding so hard I'm sure he feels it through the thin fabric of his shirt. I've never felt more alive, never felt this real. Every single time I thought about him, every time I touched myself in the dark, it never even came close to this. This feeling. This drugging, dizzying taste of him.

"This," he growls into my mouth, his voice raw, desperate. And I love that I did this to him, that I'm the one who made him come undone like this. "This is the only time I get to be selfish," he says. "I want you."

I don't understand what he means. Not fully. But some part of me already does. Some part of me knows.

This kiss we're stealing? It's borrowed time. It doesn't belong to us. We're not supposed to be doing this, and we both know it. I don't know what chains he wears in his life, but I know every link in mine. Still, I want it. I fucking want *him*.

His hands grip my ass, fingers flexing, and I tighten my legs around him in response. My body answers his call with primal instinct. He kisses me like he's starving, like he's been dying for this moment. Passion, fire, desperation, all of it.

And when we finally pull apart, breathless, we stare at each other like we've just survived something catastrophic or discovered something sacred. He's looking at me like he's trying to memorize me, like I'm a prayer he'll say over and over again once I'm gone.

"We shouldn't have done that," he whispers, his voice rough and laced with regret. "You don't know what you're doing to me, lass."

But I do. I feel it. Every inch of him is tightening with restraint. He's holding himself back with an iron will, like it's taking everything not to take me and walk me into the nearest bed, lay me down, and take my virginity like he owns it.

And the scariest part? God, I would *let* him. I would open myself to him in an instant, without hesitation.

Then, slowly, reverently, his hand skims up my back, fingers gliding until they find my bra strap. I'm trembling. My breath stutters. Is he going to unfasten it? Is he going to take me some place where we can be alone?

But instead, he exhales, heavy and conflicted, and closes his eyes. His forehead rests against mine.

"We can't," he murmurs. "We shouldn't. I'm sorry," he adds, his voice breaking.

And this time, I know, I *know*, he means it. He's not playing. Not hiding. Not being evasive or cryptic. He wants me.

This beautiful, dangerous man, who's far too old for me, wants me.

Me. Zoya Kopolova. The youngest daughter in the Kopolov family. Innocent, untouched, gangly, awkward Zoya.

My god.

He bends down and presses his lips to my collarbone like it's holy ground. Like he's worshiping, not taking. And when he kisses his way up my neck, I shiver and moan, my head falling back, my spine arching.

I'd give myself to him. No doubts. Not a single question in my mind.

Soft, reverent kisses along my jaw, then his mouth finds mine again, and I surrender fully.

"I want you," I whisper. "Please."

"Tell me," he murmurs into my ear. "Please, sweet lass. Tell me what you want. I want to hear you say it. I couldn't say no to you, even if I tried."

His voice is rough, breaking me down with every syllable.

"*You*," I whisper. "I want you. I want to be yours, James. I want... more."

What am I asking for? Why would I say such a thing, knowing full well I can't have it?

There's a pause. A heartbeat. Then he whispers, "Then I don't want to lie to you."

I nod.

"Seamus," he says softly, so softly it barely registers. "My name is Seamus."

I wait for a click of recognition, but none comes.

I don't know the name, not really. But it fits. It feels right. And I know in my bones he's telling the truth now. Seamus is the Irish form of James.

"Call me Seamus," he says. "No one else does. Nobody else fucking does."

"What do they call you then?" I ask, a small smile tugging at the corners of my lips.

He hesitates for a beat before he whispers, "Boss."

A jolt vibrates through my hips. My pulse kicks into overdrive.

Of course they do, don't they?

Then he slides me slowly, sensually down the length of his body, and his erection presses hot and hard against my stomach. I want him. God, I want him so bad it hurts.

"Seamus," I beg. He stifles a groan when I say his name. "Please?"

But he shakes his head, his jaw clenched.

"No. Not now. We can't. It's too dangerous." He takes a deep breath. "If only you knew who I was..."

His forehead meets mine on an exhale. The way his face is contorted like this, like nothing short of torture, tells me all I need to know.

But how could he possibly be more dangerous than my brothers? Than the men I've grown up around?

Yes, I know the Kopolovs are at war with the Irish syndicate, but this *can't* be the man they're fighting. Matvei said just this morning that the Irish syndicate is operating out of Dublin. They're not here, not in Moscow, and I've heard all the names thrown around, and no one's ever said Seamus.

Just because he has an Irish accent doesn't mean he's the enemy.

Panic and desire claw at me. I don't want to leave. I don't want to go back to the cold safety of home. I want to go with him.

I have to voice my fear.

"You don't want me?" I ask, the desperation leaking out before I can stop it.

He curls his fingers around the back of my neck and pulls me against his chest. His arms wrap around me like a shield, warm and solid and protective.

"I want you too badly," he whispers. "That's the problem, sweet Zoya. I want you *so* fucking badly, I don't trust myself."

He presses a kiss to my forehead.

"But you know you have to go home," he says, his voice thick. "Be a good girl for me."

I nod, though it breaks me.

"I'll see you next week," he says. There's something boyish in his tone now, some tender hope that doesn't match his hard edges.

"You have my number," he adds. "If you need to call... if you need *anything*, lass... *call* me."

And then we part, slowly, like tearing fabric. And with every step I take away from him, it gets harder to keep walking.

I don't make it seven more days.

I stare at his number over and over, thumb hovering, wondering what would happen if I just called. Or even sent one text. But I don't.

It feels wrong somehow, like I'd be taking advantage of him. And I can't do that. Not to him. Not to this man I'm falling so desperately in love with.

Can it even be love? It's too soon, too wild, too unknown. I don't even know his last name or where he really comes from.

Well, I know he's from Ireland. Okay, *that* much I know. A small, coastal village, he said. And I believe him. I feel that truth in my bones.

But still. I don't know his history. I don't know who he is when he's not looking at me like I'm his salvation.

What I do know is this: I definitely have a crush. A dangerous, consuming, heart-in-my-throat crush on a man who is everything the boys Mia hangs around with, who drive fast and get shitfaced with cheap beer, are *not*.

But I *have* to move on with my life.

So I try.

There has to be life beyond a man I can't have.

So when Mia invites me to a football game, I say yes because I'm trying. Trying to feel normal. To *be* normal.

But the boys she introduces me to? That's all they are. *Boys*.

They don't have rough stubble that scrapes your skin in the best way. None of them have hands that could grip your waist like it's sacred. None of them carry danger and devotion in their eyes.

Not like Seamus. *My* Seamus.

The boy who sits next to me talks about video games. His statistics class. How hard midterms are. I stare at him and blow out a breath.

He doesn't know how hard life is. His mother still gives him an *allowance*.

I wonder if this boy has ever held a gun. If he could aim it steady and shoot someone right between the eyes to protect someone he loved.

Nah.

Sigh.

Sitting there, surrounded by kids playing at adulthood, I realize I don't belong in this world. Maybe I never did.

I was born and raised in the Bratva.

And the thought of staying there forever with the old rules, the silent codes, the bloodshed and loyalty, terrifies me.

But not as much as this emptiness does.

I know what I need. I need someone who knows. Who understands. Someone who's already counted the cost of a life like mine. Who doesn't flinch at consequences.

I'm so wrapped in my thoughts and longing that it all happens too fast.

One second, I'm laughing at a joke I didn't hear, pretending to care about the score, or some professor's weird haircut, while someone presses me for manicure and G-string opinions for an upcoming trip.

My drink sloshes in my hand. I'm thirsty and gulp the whole damn thing.

My vision's blurry, then somehow... I'm alone, separated from the others in the crowd.

My head throbs. My gaze is unfocused. I stare down at my phone, trying to remember what happened.

What the hell is going on? Why does my body feel wrong? Why do I feel like I'm floating away from myself?

Oh my god. Did somebody—?

What did I drink?

How did I get here?

I stumble forward, trying to turn back toward the stadium seating, when a hand snatches my wrist.

"Hey, gorgeous."

It's someone I barely know, a guy from earlier. I don't even remember his name. He wasn't even the dumb one who kept whining about his statistics grade. I barely register him, one of the guys sitting behind us. I think?

He smiles at me like he's owed something.

"What did you do to me?" I ask, my voice shaking. "My head—did you give me something? You fucking gave me something, didn't you?"

Anger surges through me. I'm Zoya fucking Kopolova. My brothers would slit his fucking throat and tear his limbs from his body. Hell, my sister would.

I slap at him, but my limbs feel heavy. I'm floating. My voice wobbles. "Leave me alone."

My skin is burning, too hot. My heartbeat is a frantic, uneven mess. I don't have enough strength to get away from him.

What kind of a fucking loser drugs someone's soda?

He steps closer. I go to scream, and his hand clamps over my mouth.

"No," he growls. "Uh-uh. You're not gonna make a scene."

"Leave me alone," I try again, louder this time. "Don't touch me."

I fumble for the phone in my pocket, my fingers trembling. I could call Rafail, Rodion, Semyon. Any of my brothers would come.

But if I do…

That's the end of pretending. School? Gone. Freedom? A memory.

Instead, I smile through the panic. "Alright, alright. Let's take a selfie," I say sweetly. "You want proof, don't you? Sex under the bleachers? Sounds hot."

He scowls. "Put that away."

I hear voices. Distant, echoing.

"Hello? Zoya? Where'd you guys go?"

He stiffens and takes a step back. "Don't move," he hisses. His breath reeks of stale beer. "You stay right fucking here."

The moment he turns away, I don't even think about what I do. I text Seamus, my fingers trembling. I don't have a lot of time.

> Help. Under the bleachers. Bobola Stadium. Drugged. Can't fight.

My hands tremble.

Will the text go through?

I don't know. *I don't know.*

Seconds later, a reply bubble pops up. Relief surges through my veins.

> **Seamus**
> Fucking hell
>
> stay there.
>
> I'm on my way.
>
> Whatever you do DO NOT LEAVE
>
> STALL

How? How do I stall a man who's trying to hurt me?

He comes back, and I force myself to smile. My voice wobbles, and my thoughts are scrambled. "What did you tell them?"

"I said we needed a minute alone," he says.

I force a giggle. "All you need is a minute?"

My knees buckle.

I collapse like my legs have given out. I gag. And then I vomit, right there.

On the cement.

"Oh, gross," he groans, backing up.

"It's your fault," I spit, wiping my mouth, retching again for effect. "You put something in my drink. What'd you think was gonna happen? I'd fall in love with you?"

He snarls and then shoves me. I fall, cracking my head against the underside of the bleachers.

Blood trickles into my eye.

My god.

This is *exactly* what Rafail warned me about, exactly what I am supposed to avoid.

And yet—here I am.

Under the bleachers. With children.

And I'm done pretending. I'm only twenty, but *I* am not a child.

I was born into war, raised by criminals, and lived through the brutal assassination of my own parents. I don't belong in this fake-normal world.

I fumble for the blade in my boot, but I don't trust myself to use it. He's too big. Too fast.

If I slice him and he catches me, the price will be too high.

I always bring a knife because I can't carry a gun on campus. They'd find out, and I'd be done. But a knife is tricky and hard to handle in situations like this.

The screech of tires.

He's here. I don't know how I can be filled with relief and dread simultaneously, but I am.

We aren't far from the pub, but he must've flown like the wind.

Footsteps... fast, controlled, *heavy*.

And then he's there.

Seamus.

All black, from head to toe.

His eyes are murderous.

He doesn't speak. He moves.

"What the fuck?" the guy blurts—seconds before Seamus is on him.

No warning. No words.

Just violence.

One punch, then two.

Bone cracks, then screams.

This isn't a fight but a sentence.

He drags the idiot to his feet. A blade gleams in his hand, pulled from somewhere I didn't see.

"You don't get to scream through this," he growls. "No one's finding you tonight. How fucking *dare* you touch her?"

As I turn away, there's a sound. A stifled scream. A cry. A gargle.

Then silence.

Oh god, oh god.

When I turn back, my attacker is a crumpled mess. Bloody. Still. His eyes are vacant as he bleeds out onto the gravel.

Seamus kneels, then wipes the knife clean. Taps something into his phone like it's routine, as if he's placing a goddamn food order.

Then he looks up at me, stormy blue eyes *blazing*.

He cleans his hands on his pants, and the black fabric soaks up the blood.

"You alright, love?" he asks, his brows knit over the concern in his eyes.

Love.

Not girl. Not baby. Not even my name. Just—*love*.

My heart stutters.

"I'm fine," I whisper.

But it's a lie.

I'm not fine.

I'm in too deep.

And for the first time in my life...

I don't want out.

He's kneeling on one knee. So gentle. So tender. "You sure yer okay?"

I don't know what to do with myself. How can someone be so harsh, so violent—and then suddenly shift into this? It's disorienting. Unnerving.

And yet something warm unfurls in my chest, spreading like molten honey.

"Yeah." I'm still a little foggy. "But I-I can't go home like this."

My throat's scratchy and raw. He nods, not asking questions, and I'm so grateful for that small mercy. I don't have it in me to explain why. If I went home in this state, my brothers would demand to know what happened. Where I'd been. Who touched me. Who hurt me.

And if not them, then their wives would. They're like sisters now, just as protective, if not more intuitive. Less oppressive, maybe, but every bit as watchful.

I don't want to start another war. I don't want blood on my hands. I don't want to see anyone else punished.

This was one person. One predator. And he's already paid the ultimate price.

I stare at Seamus.

Who *is he*?

And what else is he capable of?

"I know, lass," he says, his brogue curling around the words. "I'll take you back to my flat. But only for a bit. Just a little while. You know it's dangerous," he adds with a sad smile. "And I don't want your brothers coming after me."

He winks, and that damn dimple appears again, sharp enough to cut through the haze in my head.

But there's something underneath his words that makes me hesitate.

"Are you sure?" I ask, unsure of everything, especially myself.

"I'm sure," he says, more resolute. "Come with me now, lass."

He leads me by the hand past the bleachers to the open night air, before he bends and lifts me. I stifle a gasp as his arms come around me and he cradles me to his chest.

I shake my head stubbornly. "I can walk," I sing out as we march forward quickly, trying to sound confident.

"That's enough now, Zoya." My belly melts when he says my name. "Come back with me. I'll get you something to eat. You make up an excuse about why you're not home. Who's back at your house now?"

Thankfully, tonight is one of the easier nights. My brothers are at some big event—something formal they go to. Every three months, like clockwork, they throw on suits, shake hands, donate obscene amounts of money, and buy themselves temporary amnesty from the local authorities. It's a system that works. A necessary evil.

I can't complain. Not really.

"Nobody's home tonight," I murmur.

"Then tell them you're staying with a friend," he says, his voice low, suggestive.

Maybe it's the lingering drugs or the adrenaline crash, but suddenly my skin feels too tight, my body too warm. I swallow hard, nod, and grab my phone.

I text Rodion first—the youngest of my older brothers. He's the most laid-back, the most forgiving. He's covered for me before.

He knows what it's like to get into trouble too.

> Hey, I'm staying at Mia's tonight. We're gonna watch some movies, have popcorn. Nothing wild.

He doesn't reply immediately, but I know he's seen it. I know how this works.

Mia and I have a system.

I always carry a tracking device on me. A small, sleek little thing clipped into my clothes. She has my backup stuffed animal—my old Teddy. All she has to do is bring it into her room and drop the tracker inside. My brothers won't ask questions. They never do because I never give them a reason to.

Until now.

Until I'm about to do something that would make them lose their minds.

I can already picture it—the vein popping in Rafail's forehead, throbbing like it might burst. Semyon's cold, disapproving glare, slicing right through me. Even Rodion, who'd usually take my side, would cross his arms and shake his head. Not angry. Worse, disappointed.

I'm not a child anymore. They can't ground me or take away my phone. But I'd still be in massive trouble.

I text Mia next.

> Hey, sorry, but I left early. I'm gonna be out the rest of the night. Can you cover for me?

She replies instantly.

Mia
Of course. Fill me in on the juicy details
later.

Guilt twists in my chest. I'm lying to my best friend.

Sorry to disappoint, there are no juicy
details. Not the kind you're thinking of.

I gulp. My heart is beating too fast.

Mia
Fair, fair. I get it. But if juicy things do
happen… you better tell me.

Will do.

I send it, even though we both know I won't.

What am I supposed to say?

*Hey, I almost got raped under the stadium bleachers. Then
the dangerous Irish guy who's definitely some kind of crimi-
nal, the one I've been quietly obsessing over, murdered my
attacker and took me back to his flat. NBD, hugs!*

Yeah. No.

Rodion's response finally comes in. It's brief, but it's
enough.

Rodion
Okay. Be safe.

That's all I need.

My alibi is set.

The night is mine.

CHAPTER 4

ZOYA

I GLANCE toward the place where the body had been. My attacker. The man who tried to hurt me.

I should feel sick. I should feel guilt curling in my belly... but I don't.

This isn't the first dead body I've seen.

And if I'd had a decent weapon? I would've killed him myself. And it wouldn't have been the first time.

I only remember flashes of the night my parents were murdered. I remember Semyon shoving us into a closet, Rafail yelling for us to stay put, Rodion trying to run—and Semyon threatening to hurt him if he did. I remember reaching for Rodion's hand. Holding it. Holding my breath as the unmistakable crack of gunfire echoed around us.

That's all I have. I don't remember their funeral or the days after.

Just small bits and pieces. Glimpses.

The rest of my life has been one long act of survival, raised by brothers and a sister who love me fiercely. Maybe *too* fiercely.

"Well then," I tell Seamus, my voice steadier now. "I'm set?"

"Alright," he says, reaching down to brush his fingers against mine. A gentle, grounding touch. "Let's go."

A few minutes later, I'm tucked into the passenger seat of a sturdy SUV. It smells like him, leather and spice and something clean and wild. Probably a rental. He's not from here.

He doesn't turn on any music. Just drives and talks.

He asks me how my night was. Who I was with.

I give vague answers, careful answers. I don't want to give him too much.

I wonder where his flat is. I wonder what it looks like.

Will it smell like him?

This moment with him, in the confines of his car... it feels stolen. Illicit. And yet I can't help the way my thoughts spin, racing with questions I shouldn't be asking.

What would it be like to go home with him... *without* having to hide?

To just *be* with him?

I can't even imagine. But oh, I want to.

God, I want to.

I'm a virgin.

And now I'm going home with the man I've been crushing on hardcore. Of course my mind leaps to sex.

Not that casual sex has ever appealed to me.

But this?

This wouldn't be casual.

Nothing with Seamus could ever be casual.

He pulls up to a high-rise building tucked into the city and drives all the way to the back entrance. Discreet and private. Makes sense.

"This it?" I ask.

"Aye," he says. "You think you can walk on your own, lass?"

I glance at him, playful. "You offering to carry me again?"

His eyes sparkle. "My god, yer so fuckin' cute," he says, shaking his head.

Then he's distracted for a second, talking to someone on the phone, low and clipped.

"Go within the hour," he says into the receiver. "Before the game's over. Don't ask me again, McGekrin. You heard my answer."

A pause.

"Right. Go. Call me."

He ends the call and slides his phone into his pocket. Then leans in close to me, his blue eyes piercing mine.

And that damn dimple again.

"You hungry, lass?"

I nod, the fog lifting. The drugs are wearing off, and I feel it now. I'm so damn hungry. Hollowed out.

"Yeah," I whisper. "Starving."

As we approach the building, he nods at an elderly neighbor with a cane, and the man smiles and greets him back as if Seamus isn't dangerous. As if he didn't just kill someone tonight.

And when we reach the entryway of the building, there's a woman trying to balance a baby on one hip and an armful of grocery bags on the other.

"Here, I've got it," he says softly, taking the door with one hand and the grocery bags with the other. And my heart melts.

He's exactly the kind of guy who would hit the news because of something terrible he did, and the neighbors would all say, "But he was the nicest man!"

He's strong. Dangerous. But still a gentleman. I love that about him. I love everything about this man. I know it's a schoolgirl crush, and I'm well aware of my foolish heart. I know I'm infatuated, maybe even delusional.

But right now? Right now, I enjoy it. My god, I *savor* it.

And our secret relationship? It feels so good to have something of my own. Something I don't have to share with my family. Something that's mine, just *mine*.

I wonder if he feels the same?

So I watch him help his neighbor inside with the groceries, and I take note.

If there are bodyguards nearby, they're damn good at discretion because I don't see any.

And if anyone in this building is afraid of him, they hide it well.

He seems liked. Trusted, even, which doesn't add up. But nothing about him ever really does.

Even if this persona of his is just a front or a cover, the interactions seem real. Genuine. And when he opens the door to his flat, I don't know what I was expecting—but it sure as hell wasn't this.

It's simple. Stoic.

Clean, but lived in. There's a stack of unopened mail on the counter, a single coffee cup abandoned in the sink. There's a kind of old-school charm to it all. On the coffee table, a scattered pile of books, worn and used. Beside them, a notepad and a laptop.

It's a studio apartment, compact and efficient.

His bed is tucked in the corner, across from the television. A dark-green comforter that's thick and sleek. One single nightstand with a clock and a half-full glass of water. Nothing extravagant. Nothing that screams *"Killer."*

And yet...

"How are you feeling?" he asks gently. "Let's get you some food."

All I want is to spend time with him. I want to know that I'm safe, that no one is coming after me. I want to live in this fragile little bubble we've created. Just us. Just for now.

Please, just for a little while.

"I'm definitely feeling better," I say, almost surprised by my own honesty.

"Aye," he replies with a smirk. "That boy was a novice then."

The way he says it—it's grim. Final.

And maybe I should feel something. Horror? Sadness? Guilt? But I don't.

"A novice?" I ask, my brows furrowed. I press for more. "What do you mean?"

But he doesn't answer. He only gestures toward the couch. "Sit down, Zoya," he says. "Let me take a look at you."

Then he crouches in front of me, his hands on either side of my hips. His hair curls slightly at the ends, brushing the tops of his ears. His eyes—god, those eyes—they're the brightest shade of blue I've ever seen.

His features are carved, symmetrical, and his cheeks are ruddy. There's pride in the way he holds himself. A fierce, quiet confidence. It makes me feel safe. Untouchable.

"Did I do the right thing? Texting you?" I ask, unsure, whispering my doubt out loud.

"I told you to call me if you needed me," he replies firmly. "Of course you did the right thing."

"I was just afraid that I—" My voice catches. He presses his finger gently to my lips, silencing the fear.

"I understand. If you'd called your brothers, you would've opened a whole new kettle of fish, wouldn't you?"

I nod. I've always liked the Irish turn of phrases.

"I did the right thing," I whisper.

He smiles. "Aye. You did."

His approval does something to me, something that feels a lot like longing.

Since I was a little girl, I always knew how this would end.

I'd be married off, arranged by Rafail, no doubt. He'd try to find someone suitable for me, someone proper. My brother isn't a monster, but the family comes first.

Love, though? Love has always been out of the question.

"Let's get you settled, hmm?" he says, standing back up.

Thank god. I could listen to him talk all night. His voice soothes something raw in me. I want to ask him to read to me. To tell me a story. Anything.

"I love your voice," I whisper, my cheeks pinkening with the honesty.

He glances at me and smiles, and I wonder... I wonder.

Maybe he's *not* as dangerous as I fear. Maybe I've been so conditioned to see trouble where there is none that I've made him out to be more dangerous than he really is.

Maybe we *could* have a future, just the two of us.

It's stupid, I know. I've barely even kissed this man. He's only kissed me once.

He's Mr. Thursday, not my fiancé. And yet... he saved me tonight.

He protected me.

I battle myself inside. My feelings. My logic.

"I'll get us some grub."

I smile. "Seamus," I say, trying it out.

His eyes darken, his lids heavy. He steps back toward me. His pale-blue shirt stretches tight across his chest, making his eyes glow even brighter. Low-slung jeans. Heavy boots. A casual masterpiece.

Mine.

"Say that again," he growls. "I love my name on your lips. Say it again, lass."

It's both a plea and a command. I'm powerless to disobey.

He crouches down again, both knees to the floor, and takes my hand gently in his.

"Say my name again, Zoya."

So I do. I cup his cheek, my thumb brushing under his eye.

"Seamus," I whisper.

He closes his eyes, then brings my palm to his lips, kissing it softly before folding my fingers and pressing them against his chest.

"Thank you." He exhales. "Nobody calls me that where I'm from."

Huh. Really? "What do they call you?"

He shakes his head, a sadness lingering in his eyes. "Not today, Zoya. We've already broken too many rules."

He wraps his arms around me and pulls me close. I rest my head on his shoulder and breathe him in. He smells so damn good. Feels even better.

I feel safe.

And yet... there's that voice in my head again, whispering warnings.

Reminding me that nothing this perfect lasts.

"The best thing after a night like this is rest. Food. Hydration. A warm bed. Come on, sweet angel," he murmurs, kissing my cheek. "Now, what can I get you for dinner?"

"I'm not really hungry anymore," I admit.

He shakes his head. "Eh, no. That's not an option, lass. I asked you what you want. I expect an answer." He quirks a brow, all command, and heat rushes through me. "Do you understand me?"

"Yes, sir."

It slips out before I can stop it. Something instinctual. And I love the flash of approval in his eyes.

"You can say *that* again too," he says with a crooked smirk.

I shrug. "My brothers raised me to be polite."

"Good girl," he praises. "Such a good girl."

I rest my hand on his shoulder, feeling the solid heat of him. His arms are steel, sculpted. I swallow.

"I don't know if we'll ever have a night like this again," I whisper. "Seamus... what do you want most?"

He groans, deep and primal. "My fucking god, Zoya. Don't tempt me. Can't you see I'm trying to do right by you?"

"Yes." I nod. "I know."

"Doesn't mean I don't want more," he mutters. "Doesn't mean I don't ache for you."

He runs a hand through his hair, frustrated. "Tonight, you called for me because you were in trouble. Tonight, I killed a man for you. Protected you." He sighs. "But who protects you from *me*, lass?"

He means it. He *means* it. He's not playing games, and he's not trying to impress me.

He cares.

I sigh. "I don't know. It just feels like... like we won't get another chance."

He groans again. "Aye, I know that. Don't I feckin' know it."

He straightens, his voice shifting into command.

"But right now, you have some basic needs. You'll eat. Then you'll get yer pretty arse into bed."

That makes me giggle. "My pretty arse?" I repeat, standing.

"Aye," he growls, his gaze heated as he grips "my pretty arse" in his big hand. "You do what you're told," he growls playfully. "Where I'm from, women obey their men. So— are you going to listen?"

He raises a brow, daring me.

My heart stutters.

And to my shock, he gives my ass a sharp smack.

I laugh, and my cheeks flame.

I nod. Because I'll do anything he asks.

And that might just be the problem.

"How about toast?" he asks. "Mam always said toast was good for a sour stomach."

"Mam?" I echo.

"Aye."

He says it with so much affection, I can't help but smile.

"What about your dad? Do you get along with him?"

"Aye. He's a good man," he says thoughtfully. "I mean, by my standards."

I frown. "What do you mean?"

He tilts his head. "Like your brothers. Would you say they're good men?"

I nod slowly. "Now that makes sense," I say softly.

And I exhale as he walks to the kitchen and puts bread into the toaster. I watch, perched on the edge of the couch, as he butters it, cuts it into triangles, and brings it to me.

I eat it hungrily, crumbs falling onto the little plate while he watches me. "That's a good girl," he says. Then he talks to me about the little shops at home and how he'd love taking me to D'Agostinos, the only Italian place nearby.

"They've got the best homemade bread with this seasoned olive oil," he says with a smile. When I finish the toast, he speaks gently.

"Alright, enough chatter. You need rest. You take the bed. I'll sleep on the couch."

Oh hell no. I did not wait six months to be alone with him so he could sleep on the couch.

"Why?" I ask, playing innocent.

As if I don't already know the reason.

He growls under his breath, his eyes flashing with something hot and intense. He shakes his head, like he's trying to cast off the thoughts racing through his mind. When he brushes his palm through his hair, it stands on end, shaggy and untamed, and I fucking *love* it. "Should find you something to wear."

I shake my head. "It's fine," I tell him." I've got little boyshorts undies and a tee. I'll sleep in those."

His eyes darken, and his jaw clenches.

"Tempt the fuck out of me, why don't you?" he growls.

I shrug, all innocence. But I want him to want me. I need to know I affect him the same way he affects me.

No one ever has, not like this. No man has ever looked at me the way he does.

Why not me? Why not now?

"You won't even notice," I say innocently, "if you leave a little space."

But I'm not innocent. Not even close.

Fucking hell.

He makes me feel things I didn't even know were possible. My heart doesn't just race—it slams, wild and unrelenting, before my pulse sinks low, sending heat between my legs. I didn't know a man's voice could make adrenaline burst through my limbs like wildfire. I didn't know a simple touch, or even the thought of one, could light me up from the inside.

I'm discovering a world I never knew I needed. A world of adrenaline and breath and heat. And I want to explore every inch of it with him.

So, I make a show of it.

I shimmy out of my clothes... slow, deliberate. My boy shorts cling to the soft curve of my ass, barely covering anything. He groans—deep and guttural—and I feel it slice through the silence.

I draw in a breath, then let it out, shaky and uneven.

Then I reach under my tee, unhooking my bra. My breasts are small and perky, the nipples peaked beneath the thin cotton.

"My fucking god, woman," he growls. "A man would have to have fucking nerves of steel not to be tempted by you."

Oh really? I think, fighting a smirk.

Just because no one's ever claimed me doesn't mean I'm not worth wanting. But rejection sinks in deep. I've gone to parties. Dances. I've smiled and flirted, tried. But my classmates knew who I was, and all it took was my brothers lurking in the background to make anyone vanish, like they already knew the price they'd be forced to pay. Like I cost *too much.*

And maybe it's normal to internalize that.

To start wondering if something's wrong with you.

No man has ever truly wanted me. Not once.

Mia used to say they looked sometimes. But boys back off when faced with real men. Boys don't step up. They don't defend you.

They don't murder the bastard who drugged your drink.

They don't protect you.

I'm *not* in the presence of a boy.

And I'm not a little girl anymore. I may be young, but I've lived through some shit. I'm not interested in childish games or small talk or endless flirting that goes nowhere.

I want something real.

With him.

Forbidden or not.

Because they're *all* forbidden except for the pathetic hangers-on my brothers approve of, the ones who are happy to lick their damn boots for access to the Kopolov throne.

So I turn toward his bed and let him look, really *look*. Let him take me in like I'm something rare and forbidden. His arousal strains against the fabric of his pants, and the sight does something to me. It makes me feel... radiant. Danger-ous. *Desired.*

He's undressing me with his eyes, and I can feel every slow, deliberate stroke of it across my skin.

I swallow hard, my heart hammering like a drumbeat in my chest.

I lie back on his bed, the pillows cool beneath me.

"Kiss me, Seamus," I whisper. I say his name softly, hoping the sound of it will break him. That maybe hearing it will be enough to make him touch me.

His responding growl is raw, desperate.

"Stop it, Zoya," he says, barely controlled. He's losing his grip. I can see it.

I shake my head slowly.

"I want you to touch me. Please."

He growls again, a warning this time.

"*No.*"

Fine. I know exactly what I'm doing now.

If he won't touch me... then I'll do it myself.

I spread my legs and slide a hand under my panties, between my thighs, slow and shameless, my breath coming faster as my fingers move through my slick folds. He watches, frozen, his chest heaving.

I let out a moan.

Then he curses and moves, prowling over. I circle my clit faster.

He stops me, catching my wrist in his hand. Then he slides onto the bed beside me, curling his strong body around mine. His fingers find me—his touch rough and reverent all at once.

I gasp, my hips jolting. Oh my *god*.

"*Seamus.*" I moan, immediately drowning in pleasure.

He strokes, slow and skilled, until I'm shaking... until I'm moaning his name into the dark.

His mouth meets mine. Our tongues touch. And when I come apart in his hands, it's not just release.

It's surrender.

CHAPTER 5

SEAMUS

SHE WALKS in like she doesn't have a fucking care in the world. Like I didn't just rescue her from a goddamn predator two nights ago, take her back to my forbidden flat, make her come, then watch her all fucking night as she slept between my sheets.

And still—I watch her.

My avenging, beautiful angel saunters in with grace that makes my throat tighten. She's wearing this low-cut white dress, the kind that clings to her like it was sewn directly on her. I honestly don't know how the hell she gets out of the house wearing that. She's got to have a decoy or something.

I stifle a growl, eager to smack her perfect arse again for walking around on display like this.

A halter top, V-neck, the cut dips low, deep enough to make my brain short-circuit. Perfect, soft cleavage peeking out, daring me to look and daring anyone else to try. I always feel her before I even see her. Zoya fucking Kopolova.

My enemy. My obsession.

She glides over to the table like she owns the room, her eyes locking on mine with that mischievous sparkle. She nods.

"Didn't know if you'd make it tonight," I say, shaking my head slightly, trying to maintain my cool.

"Why not?" she replies with a wicked little smile. "*You* are my Mr. Thursday."

Her Mr. Thursday. Jesus. If her brothers ever heard her say that, they'd lose their fucking minds. She's completely oblivious to the way men turn and look at her as she walks by—how their gazes linger.

But the moment they see she's heading to my table, their eyes dart away. Fast. Nobody wants to cross me.

Good. I like it that way.

I'm sitting in the same corner booth I always do. Just like back when she didn't even know my name. Back when this was still a game. I waited for her then, and I wait for her now.

She smiles at me, like she always does. And I don't smile back.

"What's the matter?" she asks, giving me that little pout of hers that should be illegal. It's too cute. Too perfect.

I lean forward, my voice low and dangerous. "Do you have any idea what wearing something like that costs me? I ought to spank your little arse red for that."

She swallows hard, her cheeks flushed.

"Would you really?" she asks, leaning toward me. "Tell me."

Are we really playing this game?

"I'd take you over my knee," I say, watching as her pupils dilate and her breathing hitches. "Lift that skirt up. Tug down your panties—"

"I'm not wearing any."

Jesus feckin' Christ on a cracker.

She giggles at my growl.

I'll remember that.

Sobering, that adorable little divot forms between her brows. "I'm sorry about the other night. I'll repay you. Somehow."

My mind goes straight to the gutter, my dick twitching in my pants. My little lass knows exactly what she's doing. Every button, she presses with precision. She always does.

"You shouldn't have been there the other night, Zoya. You should've known better. Your brothers would've skinned you alive if they knew."

She sighs, brushing a strand of hair behind her ear.

"If that was my sister, and she pulled what you did... I'd lose my goddamn mind," I mutter, shaking my head.

"You have a sister?" she asks, surprised.

"A couple," I snap. "Don't change the subject."

She exhales heavily, and her voice softens. "I know. I don't even know how it happened. We were just hanging out… I was drinking a fucking *soda*…"

"Language," I growl. "I don't like those words on those pretty lips."

She nods, a playful smirk forming. "All right, okay. Honestly, though—I didn't mean it all to happen. And thank you again. You're right. My brothers would absolutely kill me. But I'm thankful. Really."

"You think you're untouchable now?" I ask, my eyebrow raised.

"No," she says. "I know I'm not."

Her pout kills me. I want to wrap my arms around her, press my mouth to her temples, and kiss the bridge of her nose, all the way down to the curve of her lips. I want to hold her until she stops being reckless—and then flip her over my knee and punish her for being so damn careless.

"Where I'm from," I tell her sharply, "women know their place. They're submissive to their men. They know not to put themselves in danger."

"Is that right?" She pauses. "I think my brothers like to believe the same thing."

My fearless, reckless little lass.

She gives me a teasing smile, and I shake my head. Despite myself, I smile back.

Fuck.

"And if you were mine," I growl, "I mean it, you wouldn't sit for a week after pulling that stunt. Do you understand me? I'm not joking."

I picture it—pulling back my chair, draping her over my lap, spanking that perfect little arse of hers until her voice breaks from begging. *Please, Seamus, stop, Seamus!*

Her breath hitches. Her cheeks flush that irresistible shade of pink. She squirms in her seat and swallows hard.

"You said that. Lucky for me, I'm not yours," she whispers—but there's a crack in her voice. A sliver of sadness she can't quite hide.

"Not yet," I murmur. "Not *yet*."

She leans closer, and her tone is soft now. Vulnerable.

"Would you really punish me, Seamus?"

My body tenses. Fuck, I live for this game with my little Zoya.

"Would you?" she asks again, like she's innocent. But she isn't, not even close.

"I would." I lean closer, my fingers brushing the back of her neck. I squeeze, just enough to make her shiver.

"Tell me again what you'd do." She sighs, her eyelids fluttering shut.

My fucking god, she's into this.

"I told you, I'd put you over my knee," I whisper. "Where I'm from, the women are protected because they trust their men. And when they don't..." I lower my voice. "They pay the consequences."

"Is that right?" she asks, her breath shaky. She's trembling, and I *know* how badly she wants this. How badly she needs it.

"That's right."

"Tell me," she says, reaching for my drink. She takes a slow sip, staring at me over the rim. "At least you don't lie," she murmurs with a smile. "Most men do."

"What do you want to know?" I ask her.

"Tell me exactly what a punishment at your hands would look like."

She swallows hard, and I see the past in her eyes. Her brothers. The way she's had to harden herself, just to survive.

But this—this is different. She wants to feel my strength. Wants to know what it's like to surrender. To be safe and still tremble.

To submit to me.

"I'd take you back to my flat," I murmur. "Ease you onto my couch, slow and possessive. I'd hike up that little skirt, inch by inch, feel the tremble in your thighs. And then, love, I'd spank your perfect arse until you're gasping. Until you're shaking. Until you're sobbing my name and begging me to do it all over again."

I pause, letting the words sink in.

"And every time you went to sit that week, every single time you thought about defying me, putting yourself in danger again—you'd remember... *This isn't what Seamus wants. I do what Seamus says. Seamus takes care of me.*"

"Then why are you doing this?" she whispers, her voice cracking. "We meet here in a bar, week after week. You don't own me. You took me to your place once because there were no other options, then watched me leave."

I blow out a breath, exhaling the truth.

"Because I want you," I tell her.

"But you're my Mr. Thursday," she whispers, tears welling in her eyes. "Mr. Thursday only sees me on Thursdays. Why do you pretend like you want me? Why do you pretend like you want more?"

"It's not pretend," I snap. My voice turns hard. "Listen, lass. Now isn't the time. We can't. Not with who you are. Not with who I am."

Her eyes go wide, and she stares at me.

Does she know?

Does she fucking know?

I sigh, reach across the table, and take her hand.

"Come here," I whisper. "Please."

She stands and walks to me.

I slide her onto my lap and tuck her against my chest, breathing her in. I feel the way her racing heartbeat slows.

"Nobody ever sees us. Nobody ever notices. I have men at every door. Watching. Tracking. I've come here every goddamn week. Rearranged my life. Lied to my father. Made up stories just to be back in Russia. I don't belong here, Zoya. I shouldn't be here."

And yet—I am.

All for one little taste of Zoya Kopolova.

"I have to go," she says suddenly. "I wasn't even supposed to be here tonight. I've got a dinner thing I'm supposed to go to."

My heart sinks.

I nod. I knew she had somewhere to be, but I needed to see her.

"Go," I whisper. "Next week. I'll be waiting."

I watch her leave, disappearing like a ghost.

Like she was never here.

CHAPTER 6

ZOYA

I THINK about Seamus for the next week. I can't get him out of my mind, no matter how hard I try.

My brother Semyon throws a surprise party for his new wife Anya at her bakery. The place smells like sugar and warm butter, with trays of pirozhki, medovik, and sweet poppyseed rolls covering the counters. We laugh, we eat, we drink too much tea and vodka. It's this cozy, sort of chaos that I usually love.

All our friends come. The whole extended family shows up —wives, brothers, even the littlest nieces and nephews, sticky-fingered and wild. We're a big family now, with my brothers' wives and their children, and somehow there's still space for more.

"Zoya," Anya says from behind the bakery counter. She beams at all of us, happy to have us here. Anya's had a rough go of it and appreciates the found family she has with us now. "I made your favorite."

I have a lot of favorites of hers. I smile at her as I walk behind the counter. Anya's little brother, Stefan, comes at me with a running tackle, nearly knocking me down.

"Careful, Stefan," my older brother Semyon chides. "You'll knock her over."

"Oh, I'm alright," I tell him, even as Stefan rights himself and pats my shoulder to make sure I'm okay. "Look how much taller you are! Your whole head is higher than the counter!"

He grins bashfully as we go to see the treats Anya's made us.

I enjoy everyone's company. There's laughter, storytelling, shouting over music, and clinking glasses as the bakery's closed for the night, and we're reveling in each other's company.

But I'm not here, not really, because I can't stop thinking about *him*.

I *have* to stop thinking about him.

"You seem distracted, Zoya."

I look up to see Ember watching me, her gaze flashing with mischief, her coppery red hair twisted into a messy bun. "Someone's got your attention at school," she says, sly and teasing. Her eyes glint like she already knows that I'm obsessed with a certain man with a thick Irish brogue, heavy brows, and those shocking blue eyes that seem to look right through me.

As if I could have a crush on a boy from school. *Please.* I smile, barely, and shrug one shoulder, not really sure how to respond.

I definitely don't, no. I'm not crushing on a *boy*. I'm in love with a *man*. A man I barely know.

But I know enough, don't I? I know he's fiercely protective. I know he's the kind of man who listens, who doesn't flinch when things get ugly. He's gentle with me. Kind, even. Even when he's ice-cold with everyone else.

I know he loves his family. That he speaks well of his parents and younger siblings, talks with his hands when he tells me stories, a wistful glint in his eyes. It makes sense, I guess, that a girl like me, the youngest, would fall for a man who makes her feel seen.

And I want to go to him. Why did Anya have to have a birthday on a Thursday? Thursdays are usually the easiest day I can sneak away, and now it's all I can think of.

Finally, *finally*, Stefan yawns wide and Semyon ruffles his hair. "Time to pack this party up."

I help them clean, then pretend to head home.

It's harder than usual to get away—my brothers are home, making plans, watching everything. And it's late, much later than I mean for it to be, after the birthday party. I think he'll be gone by the time I get there. Maybe he'll think I ditched him.

I have it down to a science now as I sneak out through the hedges, my decoy in place... and head to the bar.

But when I walk in, he's still there, seated in the back corner, nursing a club soda like it's the only thing anchoring him to this earth.

I walk up to him slowly, my head bowed, biting my lip. "There you are," he murmurs. "Thought you wouldn't come. Almost didn't make it myself," he adds, shaking his head.

"Did you?" I ask. "Why?"

He shrugs. "Eh," he mutters. "Don't want to get into the details. Let's just say I was... detained for a bit. But I made it out."

Detained? Made it out? What the hell is he talking about? But I don't ask. I don't press.

I don't want to know.

Do I?

"I made it too," I say softly, somehow suspecting that my "making it out" without my brothers noticing my deception is a whole other level from his.

But then there's movement behind us. A tall, lanky guy with a tuft of blond hair and muscles and tats for days leans toward Seamus. Tension cuts through the room like a knife.

"Sir, you need to come here. We need to talk."

The tone is sharp, urgent. And suddenly I'm on edge. Last time a guy got in his face, I thought someone might lose a tongue. That's what would happen if they tried it with my brothers. I've seen it happen.

So this guy talking to Seamus now is risking everything. It must be important. Seamus's nostrils flare... *eek*. He scowls, glances at his phone, then groans under his breath.

"Tonight? For *fuck's* sake," he mutters, his voice low and venomous.

His brows draw tight together. His gaze lifts to the young man beside him, eyes glinting with something dark, more than irritation.

And I know, just from the way Seamus looks at him, this isn't a friend. This is someone he tolerates. Barely. Maybe even someone he'd rather destroy.

He leans toward me, lowering his voice. "Hold on a minute, Zoya. Just wait."

He turns and talks over his shoulder to the blond guy.

His phone is right there, screen facing up. I *know* I shouldn't look. It feels like spying. But when I see the word *Kopolov*... I can't look away.

The words hit me like a punch to the chest.

> Kopolovs at Wolf and Moon tonight.
> Everything in place. Destroy them.

Oh my god.

It takes a minute for my brain to catch up. This is... this is *a* kill order.

It's a fucking kill order to destroy my family.

On his phone. In front of me.

I've heard my family talk with fear about the man they call *The Undertaker*. I have a picture in my mind because I'm not new to the underground. I can already picture his wizened features and hard, cold eyes. The way he sits behind a desk, his fingers steepled, as he barks out orders to bring every family that rivals his own to their knees.

Men like him prey on the innocent and have no scruples.

Does he... does Seamus work for The Undertaker?

Panic surges through me. My pulse rings in my ears. I need to do something. I have to stop this. *Now.*

"Not tonight," Seamus hisses through gritted teeth.

The man standing near him doesn't flinch. "This... decision isn't yours, sir. It came from above."

I blink, half expecting murder in the next breath.

Seamus curses, then leans over the table and covers his phone with his hand.

But it's too late.

I've already seen it.

I know. I know they're coming for my family.

"You need to go home, Zoya," he says sharply. His voice is tight, almost panicked. "Go home. Now."

He clenches his jaw and swallows hard. Like there's more he wants to say—but he doesn't. He can't.

"What's going on?" I whisper. "Seamus... What is this?"

Who are you?

He doesn't answer. Just looks at me with that same tortured expression.

I want to believe he's protecting me. That he wants me safe because he cares.

Of *course* that's it. It has to be.

But I'm shaking. I don't know what to do next.

He reaches for my hand, warm and steady, even as his voice is cold as steel. "Stay in your house tonight. Do you understand me?"

His eyes lock with mine, full of something desperate and raw. "*Zoya,*" he says again when I don't answer.

I nod, swallowing the lump in my throat. It feels like a rock. "I understand," I whisper.

And when I stand, he does something unexpected. He grabs the back of my neck, pulls me in, and kisses me like it's the last time. Like he doesn't know if we'll survive this.

"Next Thursday," I whisper against his lips. But my voice trembles. "Right?"

"Yes," he replies. "Next Thursday." But he won't meet my eyes.

When I'm home, I make a call.

I dial Aria Romanova with shaking fingers. Polina's brother's wife.

She's good. I trust her. There aren't many I do.

It's early evening in America. I pray she answers. I've only spoken to her a few times, but after what happened with our families... we all know each other now.

"Hello?"

"Aria?" I whisper. "It's Zoya Kopolova." I swallow hard. "I need a favor," I say, my voice cracking.

"Zoya? Are you okay?" she asks gently.

"I... I don't know. I saw something I shouldn't have. And I need details." I take a breath. "It's about someone Irish. A message... It mentioned my family. It said they were going to be destroyed."

She's silent. Then her voice turns icy.

"And why come to me, Zoya? Why can't you tell your brothers?"

Heat flares in my chest. I'm feeling desperate.

"Because you know what they'll do. You know if they think they're under attack, they'll burn the whole world down. They don't have the resources right now." My voice breaks. I'm telling the truth. "They'd go to war... and lose."

I can tell she's warring with herself before she finally blows out a breath and answers.

"Okay," she says with a groan. "I'm on it. But I need *every-thing* you know."

"All I know is his name is Seamus. He's Irish. And I think... I think he's trying to protect me."

She goes still. Her breath catches. "Seamus," you say. "And he's Irish."

"Yes."

Sometimes you don't ask questions—because the truth is, you're not ready to hear the answers. Because the moment you do, everything becomes real. Tangible... and irreversible.

"And you were with him," she says.

"Yes." My voice shakes, just slightly. But enough. Enough to make it real.

"Okay. All right." Her tone is softer now. "I got you. Now... what did you see?"

"A text," I tell her. "A message sent to this... man named Seamus. I saw a message on his phone that my family is going to the Wolf and Moon. The text to him said... destroy them."

She goes silent for a beat. Then, "All right. I need a few minutes. I've got a mountain of hay and a thousand needles buried in it, okay? But tell me, what did this Irish guy you know say to *you*? What does he think you know?" she asks. She isn't speaking sharply anymore. She sounds knowing... wise.

"He told me to go home," I say quietly. "Said I'd be safe there."

I want to cry.

"I see."

Does she though? Fuck my life.

"I think you should probably do what he said and stay home. It sounds like the wisest choice, doesn't it?"

I swallow... hard. My throat is tight, feels like there's barbed wire wrapped around it.

"Yes," I manage.

Aria sighs. "Stay home, Zoya."

She whispers it like a secret she doesn't want the world to hear.

I pull out the tracking app, my fingers trembling. It's basic, but it works. We all have them, though Rafail's is leagues beyond. His is wired into something ten steps ahead of the rest of ours.

I look for every one of them.

Yana, my sister, is in her home in South Africa.

Rodion and Ember are at their place.

And it looks like Vadka and Ruthie are together.

I track the rest of them—Rafail, Polina, Semyon, Anya, Matvei, and Anissa.

Then, a few minutes later, my phone rings.

It's Aria.

My hands tremble, and my stomach bottoms out like I've just stepped off a cliff.

"Okay. All right," Aria says. Her voice is flat now, not emotionless but controlled. Brutally steady.

"This is where the shit hits the fan, Zoya. The Irish rivals have ordered a hit on your family."

The Irish rivals. The *Irish fucking rivals.*

I *knew* I shouldn't have been with Seamus.

I knew it. I *knew* it. But I still went. I still spoke to him, touched him, trusted him.

I still let myself *fall in love.*

And he never gave me a single reason to think *he* was my enemy. Not one.

But he got a message. A message that said he needed to destroy my family.

So what does that make him? My enemy? Or just another puppet in this godforsaken war?

Am I just lying to myself again?

I swallow, my belly plunging straight to the floor.

"Okay. All right. What are you telling me?" I ask her.

"This is what you need to do." She's all mission now. No hesitation. No apology.

"You're right. If your brothers know there's going to be an attack at the bar, they're going to show up, guns blazing. But I'm telling you, this is bigger than they know. Bigger than they *think.* And you cannot hold them back. Do you understand what I'm saying?"

My skin feels clammy, my pulse a desperate thud against my throat. I'm shaking.

"Yes," I whisper. "I think I know."

"You're going to lie to them, Zoya." Her voice is steel. No room for discussion.

I nod to myself, swallowing.

"Have you ever lied to your brothers before?"

Only every Thursday night, I think bitterly. But I don't say it.

"Yeah," I say truthfully. "Not... often."

"Then you're going to have to give it your very best shot. Best if you do it by phone. Or text. Don't let them see your face. Don't let them read your body language. You hear me?"

I nod again, even though she can't see me. "Yes."

"You're going to send them to the warehouse near Anya's bakery. It's empty. Vacant. But they won't know that. You're going to tell them that's where the danger is. You're going to make it real. *Undeniable*. You cannot suggest it. You cannot *hint* at it. You have to make them believe it's the *only* option. Do you understand?"

My stomach is acid. My throat feels like it's closing. But I whisper, "Yes. Yes, I do. Please tell me what to do."

"You're going to get them the hell out of their houses. All of them. Send them to the warehouse. It's far enough from the Wolf and Moon. Then you're going to stay. Let the Irish do whatever the fuck they're planning at that bar, but your family will be nowhere to be found. Got it?"

"Yes," I whisper. My nerves are threadbare.

"All right," she says. "I'm going to do what I can from here. And you, Zoya, you be *very* fucking careful. Do you under-stand?" she repeats.

"Yes. Okay. Thank you," I stammer. "What do I owe you?"

"Just stay safe," she says. Her voice softens and cracks just a little. "I know how bad these stakes are. I know what's at risk. Please, Zoya—stay safe."

And then she hangs up.

I'm staring at my phone.

I choke on a dry sob. My chest heaves, then I draw in a deep breath.

I call Rafail first.

Her words are still ringing in my head. *Make it compelling. Don't suggest. Don't hint. Make them know.*

I'm crying by the time he answers, which honestly helps.

"Rafail." My voice is broken. Ragged.

And I lie. Through my goddamn teeth, I lie.

I make up the best fucking story I can. The one that will get him out.

"They're gone," I whisper. "*Gone.* There was an attack on the warehouse. You have to go. *Please.* They're all gone. All of them, Rafail. Rodion. Semyon. Matvei. All of them."

I'm begging, whimpering... pathetic. But I have to make him believe me.

And he does.

He questions me, of course. He's not stupid. But eventually, he says he's going. He *promises* he's going.

Thank fuck.

Then I call Semyon.

Rodion.

Matvei.

Vadka.

And I lie to *every one of them.*

I make it believable. I make it sound real. And one by one, they say they're going.

My time is running out.

And I can only pray that it's enough. That the distraction will hold. That it'll *work.*

Because right now? Right now, all that matters is that they go.

I walk around the house. I feel like I've betrayed everyone. My brothers, my family—every single person who ever trusted me.

And worst of all? I've betrayed the only man I've ever loved.

I don't know what the hell to do with myself now. I walk around like a ghost, every step heavier than the last.

My first call is to Mia. My voice is broken when I whisper her name.

"Mia," I say, barely getting the words out. "I've never needed you to lie for me like this. Never. But I need it now. I need you to lie like your life depends on it. Please."

I tell her as little as possible—just enough to get her on my side. I don't want her to be in danger. I don't want anyone else dragged into the mess I created. But she gets it. She always does.

"Yes," she says. "Of course. You were here the whole night. What happened, Zoya? Are you okay? Are you safe?"

"I am now," I lie. Or maybe I don't. Am I? I'm not sure anymore. But I reassure her anyway. "I think I am."

The sob tears out of me before I can stop it. I've betrayed them all. Will Seamus find out? God. What happens if he does? Why is that what terrifies me more than even my own brothers finding out? Why is he the one I'm afraid of?

He had that message on his phone. Because he was hiding something big. He was in league with someone who wants to burn my family to the ground.

No wonder we rarely left the bar. No wonder everything's always on edge. He's been lying to me. Keeping things from me. Playing a game I didn't even know I was in.

Has he been seducing me this whole time? Was I just another part of the plan?

I sit in the quiet, waiting for the fallout. And it comes faster than I imagined.

CHAPTER 7

By some miracle or maybe divine intervention—the Kopolovs don't show up.

"Destroy them all." Orders straight from my boss.

But I don't destroy the Kopolovs. The Kopolovs never come.

It's my chance. My chance to enact what I've been plotting now since I first heard the rumors.

I know why my men followed me to Russia. To undermine me. I see every step they've taken to usurp the throne.

My throne.

But I'm the son of Keenan fucking McCarthy, and I'm not giving up a damn thing.

By the time I empty the Wolf and Moon of all its occupants with a fire alarm trigger, I know my time has come. Her brothers aren't here and aren't on the way, but my boss will think they are.

When I arrive, it's just me and the traitors.

Excellent.

But when I get there... *she's* there.

Zoya, my willful little lass, toe to toe with fucking Finnegan. The big fucker has the goddamn nerve to *touch* her.

"Get your fucking hands off her."

My voice cuts through the chaos. They freeze. She doesn't move, just turns, her eyes wild and a bit guilty, her lips parted like she can't believe what she's seeing.

I draw my gun and start with the fucking redhead who has the goddamn nerve to touch her.

No warning. No speech. One shot to the skull. He drops. Zoya stifles a scream she doesn't release.

The rest panic when they see him go down. Some reach for guns, others run, but it doesn't matter.

"Stay back," I growl to Zoya, making damn sure she's out of the line of fire while I send every last one of the mother-fuckers to hell where they belong.

"For betraying me." *Bang.*

"For your lies and theft." *Bang.*

"For laying fucking hands on her." I put a bullet through Finnegan's skull to finish him off.

That one I take slow. I make it hurt.

When the last one drops, the silence rings louder than the gunfire. She's shaking, pressed to the wall like her legs won't hold her. The blood on her face isn't hers. Her breath stutters.

My phone rings.

Boss.

I lift a finger toward her. *Wait. Don't speak.*

She nods, just once. Swallows.

"Yeah."

His voice is thunder on the line. "What the fuck happened?"

"Bad intel," I say, calm as the grave. "Handful of Russians. I tried to hold them off. Couldn't." I let a thread of grief weave through my tone. "They're dead. All our men."

His voice splinters. I hear it, the shock, the loss. It's real. "*Any* survivors?"

I know what he means.

Did anyone see what you did?

I look at her.

She looks back. Doesn't blink. Doesn't beg.

I crouch in front of her, thumb brushing a streak of blood from her cheek. Soft. Reverent.

I lift the phone to my mouth.

"No," I say, my voice broken. "None."

Then I hang up.

Every man who came to take down the Kopolovs died by my hand.

No, this was about loyalty. About betrayal. Those men crossed me. They tried to usurp me, to take what was mine. And the McCarthy clan, *my clan*, belongs to *me*. I made sure they would never forget that, even if they had to die to learn it.

I turn back to look at Zoya.

The fury I feel—nothing compared to the times I wanted to scold her for putting herself in danger. This is deeper.

She dared to come back here when I told her to stay away. She defied me.

But here she is. Wide blue eyes. Heart-shaped lips.

I'm shaking with the effort of holding myself back.

I don't trust myself not to hurt her this time.

"Go home, Zoya."

THURSDAY NIGHT. I made it.

By the skin of my fucking teeth.

And here she is. Walking in like she owns the place, like she's got every right to.

She slides into the seat across from me and says, "I want you to tell me everything."

"Excuse me?" I say, my voice like ice. She's trying to be all tough, but she has no fucking idea who she's talking to.

"I want to know why you were here that night. Why you told me to stay away and then sent me home."

She won't look at me, though, but looks away.

"I saw the message on your phone," she whispers. "I'm not saying anything else here. Not in public. I want to go to your place. I want to talk there."

She breaks a little. Cracks open. "Please," she says.

I'm already on fire. But that does it. That fucking *does it*.

I want her back at my apartment too—flat, bed, table, I don't care. I want her over my knee because I'm going to punish her. She doesn't get to risk herself like that and think there are no consequences.

"You don't disobey me when it's for your own goddamn safety. Do you understand me?" I growl, low and furious.

I want to grab her by those narrow shoulders and shake her until the truth rattles out of her mouth.

She just nods. Sniffs. Then nods again.

"Let's go," I say.

I stand. I take her hand, and I don't let go.

There's a car waiting outside. I've planned for this. Tonight is the night I tell her everything. Every ugly truth, every dirty secret. I tell her who I am, what I've done, and exactly why.

Tonight, I'll tell her I love her.

That I'm choosing her over everything. Over the Irish. Over the Russians. Over bloodlines and revenge and orders.

Tonight, I end the war.

Tonight, I stop the hunt on the Kopolovs.

Tonight, I take her back.

And before it's over, I'll make her feel every ounce of the fury, the need, the protectiveness that drives me. I'll make her understand.

Because tonight, Zoya Kopolova learns exactly who she belongs to.

And I look forward to teaching her how to be a good girl. *My* good girl.

But when we reach the car, my hand just brushing the door handle, something shifts. It's subtle. A glint in the corner of my eye. A shadow where there shouldn't be one.

I freeze.

Feckin' hell.

"Get in," I say to her, my voice low, controlled. Fuck it, I can't have her roped into this.

She frowns. "What—?"

"*Now.*"

I have to keep her safe no matter what.

She obeys, slipping inside. I shut the door behind her just as the street lights flare too bright. Just as the silence breaks.

Not with a shout. Not yet.

Just a presence. Too many of them. Wrong posture, not the sound of casual footsteps.

I straighten, my hands loose and calm, like I've got nothing to hide.

I shoot off a text to my driver.

Bring her home.

The car pulls away with her inside.

That's all I needed.

By the time I turn around, they're already here. I blow out a breath.

"Seamus McCarthy," a voice calls out behind me, loud and deliberate, no room for misinterpretation. Handcuffs slide over my wrists. "You are detained."

CHAPTER 8

ZOYA

HE SENT ME HOME?

I thought we were going to talk it out, that we'd finally get a chance to clear the air.

He warned me before. And I've felt that dominant energy of his before, heat rising off asphalt, quiet but scorching. But this? This is something else entirely. This is colder. Sharper. Like he's aiming all of that tightly coiled power directly at me. And I don't know what to make of it.

Is he angry with me? Is that why he sent me away?

He told me to go home. Told me to stay safe. But I didn't. I couldn't. I walked straight into the fire without flinching.

I warned my brothers, something he might already know—or maybe not. Then I did the one thing I told myself I wouldn't do. I showed up, right in the goddamn line of fire. And even I know I could have been killed.

I know that. I'm not fucking stupid, but I had to see for myself. I had to know he was okay. And now I don't know what I'm supposed to expect from him anymore.

And honestly? I'm a little scared. Not of him, exactly, but of how deep I've fallen. Of how much I want to trust him, even now.

Even after he sent me home. Forced the issue. Had his own fucking driver bring me.

The rejection cuts.

But deep down, I know he would have protected me. No matter what, he *would* have. I need answers now, and I want them straight from his mouth.

I look at the last message he sent me, the day before he sent me home: *Under no circumstances do you come to me. Is that clear?*

I told him yes. Sent the message back like I was playing it cool. *Yes, yes, I understand,* I replied. *Fine.*

I get it. I know why he's this way. I know men like him because I grew up with them. Men who bark and growl and throw up walls, but underneath? There's something more fragile. Something that's terrified of loss. Of weakness. Of watching someone they care about get hurt.

He gets angry. He blusters. But I swear to god, his real anger is because he doesn't want to see me broken.

At least, that's what I keep telling myself.

So, the next Thursday, I go to the bar. I know we're going to have it out—that talk he's been itching to have with me about what I did. Fair enough.

But I want my turn too. I want to look him in the eye and ask him who the fuck he really is. Also fair.

Only this time? When I get to the bar?

He's not waiting for me.

I was afraid that after he sent me home, this would happen. I feared it, day after day, when the texts I sent him were unanswered.

A strange, heavy silence settles in my gut.

But I wait.

And wait.

And wait.

I wait until the bar starts to empty out. Until the glances from the staff stretch a little too long. Until even the music sounds like it's playing for someone else. And still, I sit there like a fucking idiot, holding onto hope.

My brothers are already suspicious. They know I lied. They just don't know how deeply. And honestly? I can't blame them.

So what now?

I wait until I'm practically the only one left... until the lights dim and last call echoes hollow through the room. And only then do I finally face it.

He's not coming.

I pull out my phone and I text him. Again. And again. And again.

Where are you?

Where's my Mr. Thursday?

I'm sorry, okay?

I'm sorry.

Forgive me, Seamus.

Where did you go?

Aren't you coming?

But my messages go unanswered. Each one is like screaming into a black hole. No reply. No explanation. Nothing.

The following Thursday, I go back, even though I already know. Already *feel* it. And I sit there again, trying not to let the hope rot me from the inside out.

He doesn't come.

Nor the Thursday after that.

Nor the Thursday after that.

After five straight weeks of going, I finally, fully admit it to myself.

Seamus lied to me.

He betrayed me.

He used me.

He came here to Moscow and tried to destroy everything—*my* everything. My family. My people. My blood.

And when he couldn't? When he failed?

He walked away.

There's nothing left between Seamus and me.

It was all a sham. A performance. A ruse wrapped in charm and whispers and moments that felt too fucking real to be fake.

He used me.

And I will never—*never*—be the same again.

CHAPTER 9

ZOYA

Rafail stands in the shadowed doorway of the kitchen, silent for a moment before speaking. "I need to talk with you. Let's take a walk."

That's all he says. Just like that.

It's been a long time since my oldest brother asked me to take a walk. That used to be his thing—his way of handling things when words got too heavy for the kitchen table or when he didn't want the younger ones listening in. I don't blame him. He was only eighteen when he had to step into the impossible role of father figure. Thrust into it like a soldier thrown into battle without a choice, too damn young to be raising four wild kids who didn't know any better.

But he did it. He tried, and he did what he could.

When something came up—if we got into trouble at school, or if one of us hit a milestone we weren't ready to talk about —he'd say it then, the four words we all dreaded.

Let's take a walk.

And we would. Through the backyard, down the trail by the river, even in the dead of winter. Rafail was tough as nails, never wavered, never flinched. He was a stern disciplinarian, the kind who could make you shiver with just a look. No one got away with anything. But now that we're older, none of us blame him for that. Not anymore.

He held our family together when it could've shattered. And honestly? It's because of him that we're still standing, that we know how to have each other's backs, that we understand the value of loyalty and blood. It's Rafail who taught us how to protect what's ours, to defend what's precious.

But taking a walk always meant one thing: trouble. He'd caught on.

I'm surprised it took this long, really.

God. He knows about Seamus. He knows I've been sneaking away. My half-hearted excuses and careful lies have finally caught up with me. Bitten me hard. So I swallow and wipe my hands on the front of my apron, suddenly hyperaware of everything.

I shove that thought away, scrap it. No time for sentiment.

"Sure," I tell him, setting the stew to a low simmer and sneaking a glance at the rising bread on the counter. It still needs another thirty minutes before it's ready to bake. That gives me time. Not much, but maybe enough. Maybe.

He doesn't meet my eyes. A shadow drifts across his features, unreadable.

Well, this is new.

My heart drums against my ribcage. "What's wrong?" I ask, trying to keep my voice steady.

"Thirty minutes should be plenty," he says simply, then turns and walks out the door.

I check my phone, nerves twitching beneath my skin. No messages. Nothing from Aria, Mia, or anyone else who might have known what's happened.

I don't know how much I trust Aria, anyway. Did she rat me out? What would I do if she did?

But somehow, miraculously, Rafail doesn't ask. He doesn't push. Doesn't press. Not yet.

Instead, he heads down the gravel path that winds through the rose bushes, his steps slow and deliberate. It's late spring just outside of Moscow.

The air still holds a chill, the scent of thawed earth and everything, giving me hope. The streetlamp casts golden halos through the mist following rain.

The pussy willows droop slightly, casting long shadows that slither across the path. It smells like the sun's coming, like life waking up again after too long in sleep. I've always loved this time of year. The green buds on the trees, the slow retreat of winter, the way summer promises longer days and fewer obligations. It always made me feel free.

But I don't feel that anymore. I haven't in a while.

Not since Seamus left.

Still, I shove the thought out of my mind the second we fall into step, side by side. Even thinking of him feels dangerous. Feels like invoking something I'm not ready to face.

Rafail exhales sharply. His breath fogs in the evening air. He's got a little gray at his temples now, something he didn't have when he first became head of the family. The years have marked him, but they've also hardened him. Refined him. We're more powerful now. Financially stable. Feared, respected. His name carries weight across every organized crime ring from Europe to beyond.

But it wasn't always that way. We've survived betrayal, infighting, chaos.

"I knew we'd have to have this conversation eventually," he says, scratching the back of his neck. For a moment, he looks almost boyish.

"What conversation, Rafail?" My voice is wary, tight.

"You knew, didn't you, Zoya? That eventually I'd have to marry you off."

Oh god. *That's* why he's here?

I nod. The lump in my chest rises, thick and sharp. Six months ago, I would've broken down. I would've cried, screamed. Raged. Because back then, I still believed I might get to choose. Still hoped I might get married for love.

But now? Now it just feels like the next inevitable season of my life.

God, I only hope he doesn't marry me off to some fat, ugly relic with hairy ears and sausage fingers.

I'm only twenty.

"Yes," I say. My voice cracks. I try to hide it. "I know."

I blink hard, swipe at my eyes before he sees. The tears aren't because I'm afraid of marriage. It's because I know deep down it won't be to the man I want.

"We did the best we could," Rafail says quietly, shoving his hands in his pockets. "But Morozov's brother Pavel... he'll be a good match for you."

I steel myself. "What can you tell me about him?"

"He's Bratva, like us," Rafail says. "His family's got businesses that'll blend well with ours. Strategic. Profitable. He's... a little older, widowed."

"Pavel?" I repeat, eyes narrowing. "I thought you hated him."

He shakes his head. "I don't hate him." But the way he says it—the shrug, the tension in his shoulders—tells me all I need to know.

There's something about this arrangement he's not telling me.

They've all been watching me lately, and not in the usual way. Not with suspicion, not with curiosity. With concern.

I've lost weight, I know it. My clothes hang differently, looser around my waist and collarbone. My appetite's disappeared, like someone snatched it away in the night and replaced it with this constant, hollow ache in my chest. I don't sleep. I can't. The nights blur into mornings, and no one dares ask me why.

How do you explain the kind of grief that can't be named?

That's what happens when you fall in love with someone you were never meant to have. Someone you can't keep.

Seamus.

Just thinking his name is enough to send my chest spiraling into a tight knot. Mourning something that was never mine in the first place feels even more impossible. But I've done it. I'm doing it.

Because I have no choice. This is the only way.

"We tried to make dinner plans, tried to put it off," Rafail says, shaking his head, a hint of regret in his voice. "But it didn't work. He wants you now, Zoya. We barely talked him into the end of the month."

I nod, trying to absorb it, but it feels like I'm underwater, his words distorted and muffled, reality pressing in around my ears. The kind of cognitive dissonance that settles into your bones when you hear life-altering news and your mind refuses to fully register it. Like it's protecting you. Like it knows if it sinks in all at once, it'll shatter you.

Still, I nod. Go along with it and ask the only question that matters. "Will this help our family?"

That guilt, always simmering in the background, flares up, hot and nauseating. Every secret I've kept, every stolen night with Seamus, every lie I told, every cover I spun—it all boils to the surface.

I hate lying to them, I whisper inside my own head. *But I'd do anything for them.*

"Yes, Zoya," Rafail says, meeting my eyes, his tone serious. "More than I can even tell you." He pauses, shakes his head as if the weight of it all is too much.

I nod again, slower this time, absorbing his words like they're some kind of absolution. Like if I just believe them hard enough, the rest will be easier.

"What happens if I *don't* marry him?" I ask quietly.

He exhales, his shoulders slumping just a little. "Then I find you someone else. Someone who still brings benefit. But if it's not him... then I'm afraid it might be someone older. Maybe meaner. Maybe not so understanding. And I don't want that for you."

He sighs. "You deserve someone who's going to take care of you."

"That's what this is?" I ask, forcing myself to stay steady despite the storm swirling in my chest—curious, suspicious.

"Yeah. Pavel was just a kid before. Young and full of himself. Pompous, too full of his own goddamn hubris." Rafail sighs, blowing out a breath, his eyes flicking up like he's asking the heavens for patience. "But he's grown up. That was a couple years ago. He's had a hard life, Zoya. He's ready to settle down now."

I arch a brow. "Is that your opinion, or do you actually believe that? So I'm engaged to a player?"

There's a smirk tugging at my lips. I can't help it. It's the only armor I have left.

Rafail groans, clearly exasperated. "For fuck's sake, Zoya. No. Not a player. He was... wild. Known for it. But that's not who he is anymore. He'll be loyal. He'll be good to you."

"And exceptionally wealthy," I mutter dryly, rolling my eyes. "As if I care about that."

He glances sideways at me, something unreadable behind his eyes. "I expected you to be more emotional about this."

I shrug. "I expected me to be more emotional too. But why? I knew it was going to happen eventually."

What I don't say out loud is that if I can't have the one man I want, what good is there in hoping for anything else?

I swallow the lump in my throat and look away.

"You said he'll be good to me," I murmur. "He'll take care of me?"

"Yes. He will."

"When do I meet him?"

"Tomorrow," Rafail says. "I've invited him for dinner."

I sigh, trying to brace myself. "Great. If that's what you want, Rafail."

After all the lies I've told, after all the ways I've betrayed them, this is the one thing I can do. The one thing I can give back. A shred of loyalty to pay for all the secrets I've buried.

Seamus isn't coming back.

And I don't want another man.

"It's more than just what I want," Rafail says, his voice turning heavier. "If you're with him, Zoya, we gain protection. Power. Our family's standing with the Morozovs solidifies. No one questions us. No one moves against us." He shakes his head and runs his fingers through his hair. "It's mutually beneficial on every level. Financial, political, strategic. Every one of us has made sacrifices."

I nod, resolute. "All right. I'll do what you say. I'll come up with something good to cook."

Rafail leans in, presses a kiss to my cheek, and wraps me in a rare hug—tight, grounding. "No, I'll have it catered this time. You are so good to our family," he whispers. "So loyal. So brave."

Am I? I think. *Am I really?*

I sigh and nod. "I try."

"I was afraid you'd fight me on this," he admits. "Afraid I'd have to make you."

"Make me?" I ask, lifting a brow.

He shrugs. "I'm just... relieved. It's best you make a good appearance," he adds. "Do you want to go, I don't know... shopping? Haircut? New dress?"

I shrug. "Does it really matter?"

Can you cover up the face of heartbreak?

He gives me a sheepish look and shrugs again. "Honestly? Yeah. It does. We want to make a good impression."

I nod. Because that's what this is. A performance. A sacrifice. A war disguised as a wedding.

And *I'm* the weapon.

"You think this will be a good match?" I say, unable to hide the snideness threading through my words. There's no point pretending anymore, not with him. I don't know if anyone else has figured it out, but he should know. This is how it works. He knows.

"I do," he says.

The weight of his voice makes me pause. "All right." I nod, trying to stay composed. "If this will help you, I'll do it," I agree, swallowing my pride. *I'll sign everything away*, I think silently. My hopes. My dreams. Any lingering fantasy of marrying someone who might actually love me.

Maybe it won't be as bad as I fear. Maybe we'll learn to coexist, even find common ground. That's all I can really hope for now. Love? I've let that go. I've let *him* go. But I won't run. Not again. *Never* again. This is a new chapter.

No, a whole new *volume*.

CHAPTER 10

SEAMUS

I STARE at the fucking walls of this prison, wishing I were anywhere but here. And at the worst moments, when they drag me out to brutalize me, when they hurt me, when they torture me for information, I think of Zoya.

Sweet, perfect Zoya, with her trusting eyes and her soft voice, and that innocence I'd die a hundred times over to protect. My sweet little angel.

I know she's not perfect. But she's perfect for me.

I imagine her going to the Wolf and Moon week after week. Picture her walking in, maybe looking around like she's expecting to see me. Like she's still waiting. I know I can't come. I know I can't reach out. I can't send her a message.

If I try to contact her now, it's over. Too risky. Anyone could intercept it. And if that happens, it's not just my life or everything I've built over the years that's in danger, but hers too. And I won't risk that. I can't. Not even if she betrayed me.

Some part of me knows that, logically, I don't blame her for what she did. Hell, I would've done the same. The message was right there, sitting on the fucking table.

She knew I was ordered to kill her brothers. What else does she know?

Footsteps sound, coming my way. That fucking asshole prison guard lives to torment me. Gets off on it. Loves to watch me bleed.

We'll see how he likes it when I get the fuck out of here. And I will. My lawyers are already working on it.

Yeah, I've done enough in Russia to be locked up for three lifetimes. Most of us have. But I will not give up when there's someone out there I need to protect. Someone I still need to love.

My father, he's as loyal as they come. A good man. Good to me, to my mother, my siblings, and to every last soul in his clan. But even he would lose his goddamn mind if he knew the truth. If anyone knew.

I think back to that night at the Wolf and Moon. The way I took out the men who plotted against me and my father.

That plan? I still can't tell my father about it. Not now. Not with this war against the Russians heating up.

I stand and move toward the exit. I get one phone call a week in this fucking place. One. I take it.

"Yeah?" I say.

The guy on the other end hesitates. "Sir," he says, his voice tight. "I've got news."

I clench the phone tighter. "Spit it out. I've got thirty fucking seconds before I'm thrown back into hell."

He swallows hard. I can hear it. His silence is a weight. "If you have something to confess," I growl, "just know I won't be able to punish you for a long time."

"No, sir," he stammers. "It's not that. It's... I'm afraid of what you'll do when I tell you."

"Spit. It. The fuck. Out. Or I will reach through this phone and tear your goddamn throat out."

"Yes, sir. Sorry, sir," he says, rushing now. "Zoya Kopolova is engaged. To be married."

And my world just—stops.

Of *course* she is. Of *course* she's fucking engaged. Of course *Rafail* Kopolov would do this—arrange her future for her like he always planned. She has no reason to say no. She can't.

This is the next move. This is how it plays out. I'm such a goddamn fool.

I exhale, sharp and bitter. "When?"

"End of the month, sir," he says.

A week. One goddamn week.

"Jesus Christ," I mutter under my breath.

"I knew you'd want to know," he adds. "And I know you want to stop it, don't you, sir?"

How much does he know?

"What is it?" I growl. "What are you trying to tell me?"

"You've got one person behind those bars who can help you. You know that, don't you? One favor left to cash in."

I nod slowly, though he can't see it. "Now's the fucking time," I agree.

Zoya. Married to another man.

Over.

My.

Dead.

Body.

CHAPTER 11

ZOYA

My eyes drift to the beautiful white wedding gown hanging from the back of my bedroom door. It glows, almost ethereal in the soft evening light, mocking me with its purity. I've been primped and preened within an inch of my existence. Waxed, plucked, exfoliated, scrubbed raw and moisturized back to glowing perfection. There's not an unwanted hair on my body, not a single one out of place on my head.

My complexion? Spotless. But my eyes betray me. There's a sunken, hollow look in them I can't quite hide. Since Seamus left, food has been tasteless. My appetite died the day he walked away—no, the day I learned he wasn't who I thought he was.

I've always been slim, but now I border on fragile. Gaunt. A whisper of who I was.

I sit at my vanity, a small white one from my childhood, painted in fading pastels. I used to sit here and pretend I was a princess. Pretend Prince Charming would rescue me from this world and that I'd wear glass slippers and command a court of talking mice. I knew, even back then, it was just pretend. Because I was already a princess. A Bratva princess. And there are no Prince Charmings in our world.

I've seen too much to believe in fairy tales.

Once in a while, you see a family that genuinely loves each other. A couple that thrives on real affection. But that only works if they live by a code entirely their own.

That's not my fate. I've already met the one man who could've loved me like that... or so I thought.

And now? I've seen my future fiancé twice. The first time, he arrived with an entourage—wealthy, slick, polished. He looked more like a model on the cover of a finance magazine than a man about to be married.

He's rich, no doubt about that. I'll have everything I could possibly want—except, of course, the only thing I really need.

He came with sleek, black SUVs, the kind that scream power and protection. But I didn't show how impressed I was. And that pissed him off. He scowled at me, clearly expecting me to swoon.

Not happening. That's not who I am.

The second visit, he took me to a restaurant so exclusive he rented out the entire first floor. Some people might've been flattered. I wasn't. He treated the servers like dirt.

Sent his steak back three times. Complained about the air quality.

Who does that?

And my brothers are marrying me off to him.

He's not hideous. He's actually pretty attractive. Strong, tall, fit, I guess. But he barely looks at me. His voice is nasally, and he never shuts up about finance and politics. It's exhausting.

Tomorrow should be a celebration, but instead, it feels like I'm being led to the executioner's block. I stare at the dress as if it's a pair of handcuffs.

Sigh. I'm being dramatic. He's not... *that* bad.

But he isn't Seamus either.

I hear a soft sound at the window.

I freeze. One tap. Then another.

My stomach plummets. I see the flash of a hand.

My room is on the second floor. Who the hell...?

Whoever it is had to get past cameras, then scale the side of the damn *house*.

Heart pounding, I walk to the window. I open it just a crack. The smart thing would be to call my brothers, but something stops me.

"That's my girl."

My chest constricts, and my body heats. Anger flares, but it's tangled with something else—something dangerous. Something like... hope.

Seamus?

"What are you doing here?" I hiss. "They'll fucking kill you."

"Language," he whispers.

No. We can't fall back into old rhythms. I can't let him drag me back into his orbit.

And then—he's there. I help tug him through my window and into my room.

Seamus. All six feet of hard, masculine beauty. Blue eyes even brighter than I remember. That messy hair, dimpled cheek. That jaw.

Those lips, god, those lips I've wanted on every inch of my body. The ink on his arms. The Irish lilt in his voice that still unravels me.

The room isn't big enough for the two of us.

I slam the window shut behind him. Thank god, we have no cameras in the bedrooms.

"You can't be here."

"I am," he says simply, but his smile is wrong. Distant. Guarded.

Is he angry? At me?

"Why are you here, Seamus?" I snap, tossing my head. "You left me."

"Left you?" he growls, prowling closer. "Zoya. Jesus, baby. I was arrested."

His voice is a hush, and I hear footsteps in the hall. I press my ear to the door—then silence.

We're safe... for now.

My heart beats so fast I'm dizzy.

He was... arrested?

"I was in jail," he says, and now that he's closer to me, I can see the scabs on his neck and shoulders, the haunted look in his eyes. Russian prisons are notorious for their brutality. My stomach plummets.

He was in... he was in prison?

"I'm getting married tomorrow," I whisper, shaking my head, trying to push him out of my mind. "Whatever we had—it was never real. You orchestrated all of it."

But I'm only whispering what I've feared. I want him to prove me wrong.

"Me?" He steps closer, his eyes dark. "You betrayed *me.*"

"What?" I throw my hands up. "What the hell are you talking about, you idiot?"

He growls, and suddenly I'm on fire.

I thought I was over him. I thought I was free. But he's here, warm and real, and my heart aches.

"I know you're getting married. Do you have any fucking idea how hard it is to break out of prison?"

He broke out of prison. For me?

Oh my *god.* That's why he disappeared. Why he didn't

answer. Why he vanished week after week, month after month.

"Why?" I ask, even though I know it's pointless. He could've done anything, just like my brothers.

"Doesn't matter," he growls. "I never left you. I tried to come back. I couldn't." He's standing too close, his hand wrapped around the back of my neck in that possessive way that makes me melt. "And now you're marrying someone else."

"Do you think I want this?" I snap. "Do you think I *want* to marry this pompous asshole?"

"Language," he bites again, hand on my jaw now. I step closer, jab my finger into his chest.

He doesn't flinch. "Fine. You were arrested. But you still left me," I say, hating the way my voice breaks. "I told you to come back—and now what? You got out because you found out I was getting married? You couldn't send me a single message?"

Footsteps again. We freeze. A soft knock.

"Zoya? You okay?" It's Polina. Sweet, gentle Polina. Rafail's wife.

"I'm fine," I call. "Just on the phone. Sorry."

Lying. Again. Ugh.

"Okay," she says gently. "Let me know if you need anything. I know how hard this night can be."

She doesn't know. She couldn't.

"Thank you. I'm just going to sleep now."

They all feel guilty. They know I'm marrying someone I don't love.

I wait until her footsteps fully retreat before I lower my voice. "Why are you really here, Seamus?" I ask. "You went to prison. Probably deserved it. I'm getting married." I swallow hard. "Maybe I deserve that too."

"It was too risky," he whispers. "Too risky to reach you. I couldn't."

"Everything we had…" My eyes are stinging. "What was it, really? Secret meetings in the back of a pub?"

He narrows his gaze. "You think that's all it was?"

"I know who you are now," I say. "You work for The Undertaker."

And the flicker across his face confirms it. I was right.

"He owns all of Dublin. Maybe more. He's done terrible things, hasn't he?"

And Seamus *works* for him.

"I *know* who The Undertaker is," I tell him, my voice trembling despite everything in me willing it to stay steady. "I've heard the stories, Seamus. I know what he does. And you— you *work* for that man. You work for the most ruthless, cold-hearted bastard in all of Ireland. I know you do. I heard you on the phone with him. Right after you killed all those men. You slaughtered them, just hosed them down like they were nothing." My voice breaks. "And it was supposed to be my family."

He opens his mouth like he's going to say something, but I shake my head.

"*No.*" The word slips from me in a whispered rasp, harsh and cutting, because I can't risk raising my voice. Not when Polina's right down the hall. Not when my family's teetering on the edge, prepared for my collapse.

They fear me, fear the moment I break, because no one wants to see Zoya Kopolova shatter. If I fall apart, it was all for nothing. Every sacrifice, every calculated move... meaningless.

If I fall apart, then none of them will be able to stand tall either because I'm the youngest. I'm the one they all think is made of iron and spite. And if I can't hold strong in the face of this, then who will?

"I know who you work for, Seamus," I repeat. "And you know just as well as I do, there can never be anything between us. Not now. Not ever."

I try to step away, but his grip is too tight.

"Why did you think I didn't mean it?" he asks, his eyes narrowing like he's trying to understand something that won't quite fit in his head. "Why did you think I came week after week and risked everything for you?"

"Risked everything?" I hiss, shaking my head, my voice bitter and sharp-edged.

I blink, and hot, fat tears slip down my cheeks. "You won't even risk being seen with me. You won't even let anyone know we were together."

"Will *you*?" he asks.

And I look away—because we both already know the answer.

No. Of course I won't.

"You thought I left you?" he asks again, and the way he looks at me, like his heart is breaking right there in his chest, hurts. "You thought I'd do all that, come week after week, and just abandon you?"

"What else was I supposed to think?" I say, and I blink again. More tears, hot and fast, streaming down my face in thick, silent rivulets.

"What was I supposed to think, Seamus, after everything you said, everything you promised, and then you didn't show? You couldn't send a message? You couldn't get word to me? Nothing? All this time?" I shake my head.

"I showed up for you," I whisper, and I can't bear to look at him. I don't want to see the pity in his eyes. I don't want him to see how weak I really am.

"I showed up. Week after week after week. I sat in the same corner, drank the same drink. I came looking for my Mr. Thursday. I risked everything just to *sit* there and wait for you. But you..." My voice breaks. "You never came back."

"I couldn't, love," he says softly.

"Don't call me that." I shake my head, turning away again. "Don't. And now you say I betrayed you? How dare you?"

His gaze sharpens. "Zoya, you looked at information that wasn't yours."

"You were going to kill my family because The Undertaker told you to!"

My voice comes out too loud. I clamp it down and whisper instead.

"You work for a man who wants to wipe out my family, Seamus."

There's no room left for negotiation. "There can't be an 'us' anymore," I say bitterly. "Leave. Let me marry this stuck-up." I stifle a sob. "Go away. Go back to Ireland. Go serve your *Undertaker*."

And I can't even pretend to hide the bitterness bleeding through every word.

"Zoya," he growls, but before he can finish, there's another knock on the door.

"Zoya, it's me, Yana. I just have something to show you."

He lets me go, and my hand flies over my mouth. How can I hide him?

The doorknob turns, and *my god*, there she is. I gasp, expecting shock on her face, expecting her to draw a gun and shoot him between the eyes. But she doesn't even blink. Not even a hint of surprise.

I swallow hard and risk a glance over my shoulder.

The window's wide open. Curtains billow in the breeze like ghosts.

He's gone.

Seamus is gone.

My Seamus. The man I hate.

The man I still long for.

He came back into my life at the worst possible time, right

when I needed him the *least*. And now, he's disappeared again.

"Are you all right?" Yana asks, her face drawn and pale. "You look like you've seen a ghost."

Have I?

A ghost would've been easier to handle.

I sigh and offer her a watery smile.

"I'm fine."

It's the biggest, boldest lie I've ever told. Bigger than the night I sent my brothers to that warehouse. Bigger than the wild goose chase I sent them on. This lie is darker. Deeper.

"I'm fine," I whisper again, hoping that maybe if I say it enough, it'll start to feel true. Hoping it'll stitch the bleeding pieces of my heart back together.

I CRY myself to sleep the night before my wedding.

I try not to because who wants photos with swollen eyes and blotchy cheeks?

But I don't know how to stop. I don't know what else to do.

I don't know what else to think, or how to stop the aching inside me. It feels a lot like the hollow grief I felt when my parents died.

Raw. Scraped out. Gutting.

Only then, I was just a kid. Too young to fully understand.

Now, the pain cuts from a different place. Because now, I know too much.

And that knowing is a different kind of wound.

I wake early and stare out the open window. I half wish, half beg for him to be there. To see him again, just once more, even though I know it will kill me, and it won't soothe the aching in my heart. If anything, it'll make it worse.

I can imagine him there.

Perched on the windowsill, blue eyes steady on me, cheeks flushed with emotion, that maddening dimple in the corner of his mouth.

I saw how it hit him like a two-by-four when I said the word *Undertaker*.

He doesn't know that I know who it really is. But now I've said it out loud. Now I've exposed him for what he is.

And because of that... he'll never come back again.

He can't. After today, there will be a ring on my finger, and I will be Zoya Morozova.

Oh god. It could be worse, I remind myself. It could've been someone cruel.

That's something, I guess. I swallow hard, swipe at my eyes, furious with myself for crying. And when I catch my reflection in the mirror, they're not as puffy as I feared. Not great, but not ruined either.

I dress for my wedding. Alone.

What if Pavel *is* cruel? I've heard horror stories. We all have. It's why none of my family will make eye contact with me anymore.

There's a soft knock at the door. "Yes," I say, resigned. And Polina slips in.

Polina, with that blonde hair so long it brushes the top of her butt. With those soft, understanding eyes and that gentle spirit that makes everything feel a little less sharp. "How are you doing?" she asks tenderly, like if she's careful enough, she might make this bearable.

I only sigh.

"Oh, honey," she says, settling on the edge of the bed and taking my hand. "You've been crying. I'm so sorry."

Her voice wobbles. "When I tell you that Rafail *agonized* over this decision... When I tell you..." She trails off and shakes her head. "You had suitors, you know. Plenty. Men who wanted you. But he went through every single one of them."

She's not being dramatic. "He vetted them. We talked, just the two of us. We spoke to their families. We asked the right questions. It was like... they were applying for a job or something." She lets out a dry laugh, the kind that doesn't reach her eyes. As if that absurd detail is supposed to make me feel better.

It doesn't.

"He just wanted someone who'd take care of you," she says softly. "This guy? He will."

I nod stiffly. "Worked out well for you, didn't it?" Her marriage to my brother.

She brushes the hair from my eyes, leans in, and kisses my temple. The gesture is small but sincere. "Yes, sweetheart. It did. It *can* work out, you know," she continues, coaxing. "Especially when someone's married to the likes of you."

"I've seen it not work out," I counter, needing to argue. To push back, just a little. To remind her that this isn't all hearts and flowers.

Because yes, I've been crying. And maybe, just maybe, she's right about why. She wouldn't be that far off.

But she can't know the real reason. No one can.

"All right," she says gently, shifting back to business. "Your brother said it's time to get this over with."

So it's an early wedding. He didn't want me to have to sit with it or dwell. "Let's get you cleaned up, okay? I have these little eye masks you can wear to bring down the puffiness."

She offers me a soft smile. "All those sleepless nights with babies, I swear by these."

We stand as she helps me to my feet, our fingers linking briefly. I do look pretty, I'll admit that much.

And I'm glad. I don't want to walk in there looking like a forgotten orphan.

"Look at you," she says with a smile that feels like sunshine. "So beautiful. My god, this dress."

It *is* beautiful, sleek and elegant in its simplicity.

She shakes her head slowly, a grin tugging at the corners of her mouth. "I absolutely love it. All right, show me your shoes."

I lift my skirt just enough to reveal the rounded toe of my pearly slippers.

"Oh, they're so pretty. Everything's beautiful, Zoya. You're a gorgeous bride."

"Thank you," I whisper.

"All right," she says. "I'm going downstairs to appease your brother. He's pacing a hole into the rug. I'll tell him you're getting ready and that you'll be down soon. Do you want anything to eat? Drink?"

"I'm good."

She smiles again. "All right. Twenty minutes, okay?" I nod.

"Okay. Thank you," I say, looking away. There's a lump in my throat that won't go down. I stare at my vacant window.

She's right. Maybe, just maybe, there'll be something there to like. Something waiting for me.

I'm told he has a beautiful home. I haven't seen it yet. And honestly? I don't want to.

My gaze spins toward the window, irrationally hoping Seamus might materialize there like a phantom. He left last night. So why do I think he might come back?

He said I betrayed him. And I did—I read those texts, and I accused him of conspiring with a murderer.

What would I even do if he showed up? He didn't come for me.

I'm here, alone.

Polina comes back, a tray in her hands with ice water and some small snacks. "Try to eat something," she says, setting the tray down gently, her eyes full of concern.

She sits across from me.

"Can I ask you a question, Polina? Or... if I do, do you have to report *everything* back to Rafail?"

Her expression softens, lips curving in a knowing way. "Girls can have some secrets," she says, lifting her chin and meeting my gaze. "What's your question?"

Can I trust her?

I swallow hard, nerves prickling my skin. "What do you know about The Undertaker? The Irish—"

"Oh, I know who you're talking about." Her whole face changes. She bites her lip, turns away from me, troubled. "Why do you ask that?" she says quietly.

"Because I overheard you all that night. In the kitchen. After the bar."

"Of course I remember," she says. "Now why are you asking about The Undertaker?" She gently adjusts a pin in my hair.

I watch her in the mirror as she smooths one curl and straightens out the other, methodical, careful. Her fingers work fast, and she pins them in place like she's done it a thousand times before.

"I've heard a lot of people talk about him," I go on, a little too calmly. "But I want to know what he's really like. Will you tell me? Please?"

She exhales slowly, like she's been holding something in for a while. "I can only tell you what I know, darling," she says gently. "And I know that one of the reasons Rafail is marrying you is because The Undertaker told Semyon he was coming for his sister."

Her voice drops to a hush. "And we assumed," she says, "that the sister he meant was you."

I blink. Of course.

Yana is already married. There are no other sisters. Who else could he have meant?

"He said he was coming for me? Why didn't anyone ever mention that? That's... strange."

What does Seamus think about *that*?

"Right," she says with a sigh. "And Rafail didn't want to risk that happening. The Undertaker... the things they've said about him. He... he can disappear in a crowd, but you *feel* him. They say he once made a man confess his sins just by folding his coat in front of him."

Oh wow.

"He doesn't always carry a weapon, they say, because he *is* one. Never raises his voice, yet even the most hardened criminals fear and obey him."

I swallow. And Seamus works for him?

"No one's ever seen him bleed. He doesn't threaten either—everything he says is a promise, they say."

My heart thunders.

She blows out a breath. "They call him The Undertaker because no one has ever survived crossing him, and anyone who tried was buried. His code is older than dirt, and he doesn't break it, not for anything."

"Oh," I murmur, quiet and shaken. "Well. Isn't he married?" I ask. "I mean... men like him usually are. Older. Settled. Right?"

She laughs, a light sound that doesn't match the weight in my chest. Shakes her head. "He's not *old*," she says. "And no, he's definitely not married."

"Oh."

A chill creeps down my spine, trailing like icy fingers. I sit up straighter and try to swallow—but something hard and dry is lodged in my throat.

I reach for my water glass and sip. Just a little. Just enough to wet my mouth.

"He's... he's not?" I manage.

"No. Not The *Undertaker*. He's quite young considering his reputation and rank, actually." She tilts her head, considering. "Older than you by about ten, twelve years. About Rafail's age."

"About Rafail's age?" I echo. "What else do you know about him?" I ask, trying to sound offhanded.

"He's the oldest son of Keenan McCarthy," she tells me. "The head of the McCarthy clan."

I blink at her. "The McCarthys?"

"They're powerful," she says. "In Ireland. Old blood. They live in this little place called Ballyhock."

The words drop like stones in my stomach.

"Ballyhock," I repeat, the name catching in my throat. My voice sounds hollow. "That... coastal village. Just outside Dublin."

The one Seamus has told me about over and over and over again, so vividly I feel like I've been there.

Oh my god.

Nooooo.

"Oh my god," I whisper. "Holy shit. Okay."

I try to play it off, casual. "Do you happen to know his real name?" I ask. "The Undertaker's?"

I feel so stupid. Idiotic. How could I have not seen this? How could I have believed something else, *anything* else? But I know. I know the truth before she says it.

My body knows. My bones know. Every nerve ending is screaming.

She looks me straight in the eye. "I think his name is Seamus," she says.

The lights flicker.

Downstairs, someone screams. It's like someone flipped a switch—sunlight replaced with shadow. The bedroom is swallowed in darkness.

"That's strange," Polina whispers, rising to her feet. "Zoya, I need to see what's going on. Stay here," she says quickly. "Do you have a weapon?"

"Of course I do," I reply, steadying myself.

What is *happening*? Is it just my hopeless romantic brain wanting to believe he's coming for me—that he meant it when he said he would? *No*. He came last night. We exchanged words, fired off every emotion like bullets. And now... even if he wanted to claim me, he can't.

I'm engaged to another man.

Then why do I feel like I'm about to cry?

I square my shoulders as calm settles over the house again. I've made up ghost stories in my head as if there's something to fear. No. I need to get this wedding over with. Now.

Polina returns. "All good. I'm not sure what happened there."

Interesting. I swallow hard when she smiles at me. "You ready?"

I turn to my makeup. If they're going to take pictures, if I'm going to be a bride... I will be the most beautiful damn bride they've ever seen.

Concealer, thick and perfect under my eyes. Foundation. Powder. A touch of highlighter, not too much. Mascara, eyeliner, lipstick. I never go this far. Never. But today... today feels like it calls for it.

Still, it all feels like a dream.

"I'm ready."

I walk down the stairs as if facing my execution. My steps echo on the floor, but I don't shake. I won't.

Strings of music play. Everyone looks gorgeous, all dressed in formal wear. The house has been decorated in whites and ivory, gold ribbons and bouquets of white flowers.

Rafail smiles at me. I give him a half smile back.

One day, maybe I'll forgive him.

I look to the altar, but don't see my groom.

That's a little odd.

Rafail looks where I do and frowns.

"Open the doors," he orders.

A gasp rips through the room.

Because it's not Pavel Morozov standing there.

Rafail's gun is drawn, and Semyon is already moving.

"Stand down," Rafail orders, his voice hard.

Seamus holds my gaze across the crowded room.

I can't *breathe*. Because even now, even knowing who he is, what he's done, my heart betrays me.

Another gasp echoes, but Seamus's voice cuts through the tension like a bullet.

"Quiet," he says with authority. "Everyone, stay still. This entire place is rigged."

My breath catches. The air is suddenly thinner.

"Kopolov," he says, his eyes locked cold on Rafail. "Before you even think about pulling that trigger, know this. I was under orders to take your family that night at the Wolf and Moon. You remember that? The night your little sister betrayed you?"

Rafail nods. Frozen.

My heart pounds, loud and erratic.

"My testament," Seamus continues, eerily calm. "That night, I ended the lives of the men who betrayed me. My boss believed it was you. They'll know the truth soon enough. I told them they'd pay for their betrayal, and I *always* keep my word."

He looks at Semyon, who's now ghost-pale. Rodion's hands curl into tight fists. Rafail refuses to look away.

"I promised you one thing," Seamus says, eyes on Rafail. "Didn't I?"

And then, *oh my god*, he turns to me. "I told you I would come for your sister. I remember it vividly. I bet Semyon does, too. And I never, ever back down on my word."

He gestures, his hand steady, his voice quiet. "Come here, Zoya."

My body refuses to move at first.

"Go," Rafail whispers in my ear. "You have to do what he says now. I can't stop him."

The room is rigged.

Seamus's voice rolls through the room. "I have forty plants

stationed on this estate. Every exit. Standing right beside you."

My head snaps up. The guards, uniformed, still, all armed, are *everywhere.*

We're surrounded.

Holy shit.

He snuck them all in.

For me.

A promise. A vendetta. A reckoning.

"What did you do with Morozov?" Rafail asks flatly.

Seamus's eyes ice over. "You know exactly what I did."

Oh my god.

"Did you start a war, Seamus?" I whisper.

Rafail's gaze on me hardens. No one calls him Seamus. I shouldn't know his name.

"It's hard to start a war that's already begun," Seamus replies, his tone glacial.

Then he turns to me again.

And even now, my traitorous heart expects a flicker of warmth. A softened look. *Something.*

But his gaze is frozen.

"I said come here, Zoya."

My legs are made of jelly. But I walk.

"Zoya, come," he says, gentler. "I won't hurt you, little lass. I promise. You have my word. Please, just come to me now."

Polina's hand is on her mouth. Yana's watching us both with narrowed eyes. Anya's pale, her eyes wide.

Everyone watches. Everyone heard him.

So I go. I walk down the aisle. Past my family. Past everything I've ever known. Still clutching my flowers to my chest.

Into the arms of Seamus McCarthy.

Knowing what I've done. Knowing what this will cost them. Knowing they will never forgive me. That the blowback will be brutal. Unforgiving. Total.

I go to him.

He takes my hand.

Then he turns to the priest and nods once.

"Vows, Father," he says. "Make it quick."

Rafail makes a move to come to us.

"Don't, Kopolov," Seamus growls, and I see something in him I've never seen before, a dark glint in his eyes, the hardened set of his jaw. He's ready to kill. All of them.

And then he'll take me away anyway, no matter what it costs.

"Over my dead body," Rafail growls. "So kill me. But you won't take my sister. You won't."

"No!" I scream. "Enough!"

I wrench myself away from Seamus, slap at his hands when he reaches for me. And to my shock, he actually stops. He stares at me like he's never seen me before… and takes a step back.

My brothers freeze, and the whole room goes still.

Everyone, every single person in the goddamn room, is staring at me.

"I will *not* let you war over *me*," I say, my voice rising.

"No. Enough. Too many people have died already." My words rip through the silence. "Too many! I won't risk it. Stop. All of you. Just—*stop*."

Silence falls, the kind that weighs heavy, thick, and unbreathable. I feel like I might throw up as I look at my brothers, trembling but resolute.

"Rafail, I'm going to marry Seamus."

I swallow hard.

"I'm going to marry him… because I love him."

A startled gasp breaks the quiet. Rafail's eyes narrow on me, disbelief hardening his face. "Zoya, don't you—"

"No!" I scream again, and I think it might be the first time I've ever raised my voice to him.

"Stop talking," I snap, then turn to Seamus, pointing straight at him. "Listen. I didn't know who he was," I say, pushing through the weight of grief. "And it breaks my heart to know what he's done. But I want you to know something."

I look at Rafail, and my voice cracks.

"Next to you, there's no one I trust more."

The look of betrayal on his face shreds me. Cuts me straight down the center.

"Zoya," Rafail whispers, confused. Hurt. So damn hurt.

"He's given everything to come for me," I say, my tears flowing freely now. I know my mascara's running, my makeup smeared—but I don't care. I can't care. Not now. "I have to stop this war."

"What are you talking about?" Rafail asks, barely audible. "What do you mean?"

"You heard her, Kopolov," Seamus says, steady and clear.

"I said I love him." I lift my chin.

Or I used to, anyway, before he broke my heart.

I glance at Seamus out of the corner of my eye. "He'll have to prove he's worthy of my love. He'll have to prove he didn't lie to me. He'll have to prove a hell of a lot." I let out a shaky breath.

"And I will too," I whisper. "God, I will too."

Turning to the priest, I echo Seamus's words.

"The vows, Father."

I sniff, wipe my face with the back of my hand, and whisper to myself like a mantra.

I dreamt of Seamus rescuing me. But the fantasy was a lie. It was nothing like this.

In my dreams, he was noble. Kind. In my dreams, he didn't kill Morozov to get to me.

My *god*, does the man even have a conscience? I fell in love with Mr. Thursday.

With Seamus.

Is The Undertaker someone I can love too?

CHAPTER 12

SEAMUS

STILL FEELS LIKE A DREAM.

She's here.

She's really fucking here.

Zoya, in white. My sweet little lass, wrapped in silk and silence, standing beside me like she's about to be executed.

She says something, but I don't hear it. My ears are ringing. All I can focus on is her face. The way she looks like she's somewhere else. Like she's already mourning herself.

I warned them. I fucking warned them.

And they had the goddamn nerve to arrange a marriage to a *Morozov*.

When *she's mine*.

And now *I'm* here.

The world may collapse behind us. Her brothers may never forgive her. She might never forgive herself.

But I've got her.

This woman may be the literal death of me.

We take our vows.

It wasn't how I wanted it to go.

Hell, I hadn't imagined anything at all. I just knew I'd promised to come for Zoya.

But nothing prepared me for this.

I knew I wanted her. I knew I needed her. And I know... she may never forgive me for the way I did it.

Still, I have no choice. I'm the head of the McCarthy clan. I can't grow soft—not for anyone. Not even for love.

Her family watches as we take our vows. Her hand trembles when I slide the ring onto her finger.

Then I snap my fingers. A signal to my men.

From here, I can see the dead body of the man I killed to make it to this altar.

That's the Kopolov's problem now.

The distant hum of tires draws every eye to the windows.

"Do you have a bag packed for your honeymoon?" I whisper in her ear, my blood still heating at the thought of her alone with another man, even though he's lifeless, not ten yards behind her. "Yes," she whispers, guarded. "It's in the front hallway."

"Take it with you, but I'll buy replacements." I want to choose what she wears. "You'll come with me as you are. My bride. Zoya McCarthy."

It sounds wrong in my mouth. Strange. Twisted.

Zoya, the Russian princess. McCarthy, the Irish stronghold.

Zoya McCarthy. She's mine now.

She is mine.

My beautiful lass who hates me and once loved me.

I've sworn the men with me to silence. They will obey. No one breathes a word outside of the McCarthy clan.

I'll tell my father on my own terms when I've laid the groundwork.

"You can leave," Rafail says. "We will come for her."

"And if you do," I say with an iron voice, "you know exactly what the fuck will happen."

"Oh, will you two shut *up*," Zoya snaps. "Didn't you hear a word I said?"

A ripple goes through the crowd. I killed a man planning to marry her, and they're shocked she told me and Kopolov to shut up.

This girl. This woman. She's going to end up over my knee before the sun goes down.

I've told her before, and I'll say it again: McCarthy women submit to their husbands. She'll learn her place.

Yes, she will.

She turns to them, her eyes fierce and her voice breaking.

"Don't chase us. Don't come after me." She shakes her head. "I told you, I love him."

She's only saying that because she doesn't want more bloodshed. Still, something in me yearns for her words to ring *true*. Some day. *Some day*.

I take her by the elbow. Her skin is soft, warm, electric against mine.

I want to carry her, hold her, kiss her.

God help me, I will.

So I do. I carry her over the threshold of her home, and I'll do the same over mine. I lift her into my arms.

She gasps in wonder, wide-eyed, and meets my gaze. I kiss her in front of everyone—her brothers, my men. Let them watch. Let them come after me.

I know exactly what I've done. I know what I've started, even with the weight of my reputation and the reach of my power.

I've murdered my men. I've stolen the Russian princess. I'll have to answer for it, and I've taken steps that even my father will never forgive.

If Kopolov is half the man I believe he is, there will be hell to pay.

But I've made my decision.

And if everything goes as planned...

The vows are said. She's wearing my ring. I will mark her as mine. *Only mine.*

I walk her to the car, open the door, then buckle her in like she's fragile glass. She looks shell-shocked, her eyes wide.

"What did you do to Pavel?" she asks tensely.

Pavel. My god, this was too close. She called him by his goddamn first name.

I shake my head and exhale hard. I don't answer right away. Instead, I shut her door, climb in, and give the driver a clipped command. "Take us straight to the airport."

We're going home. Back to Dublin.

"Seamus?" she whispers.

"Quiet," I tell her. We're not safe yet. I don't want my men to hear her call me by name.

She's the only one who ever does.

It's sacred to me when she says it.

She stares, stunned. Her mouth drops open.

"Are you telling me I went from one commanding boss to another?"

"I don't give a fuck who you came from," I bite out. "What I'm telling you is—you're mine now. Do you know who *I* am, Zoya?"

She swallows, her eyes glossy with fear.

"You're The Undertaker," she whispers.

I laugh, leaning down to press a gentle kiss to her forehead.

"And now I'm the head of your house."

CHAPTER 13

ZOYA

My heart aches.

I dreamed of this, fantasized about this, but now that he's *actually* taken me...

Oh god.

My *family*.

I love them so much. They don't want to see me taken away by someone they believe will hurt me. They can't stand the idea of me being victimized. But once again, it's me, little Zoya.

Always me.

The youngest one in the family, the one expected to stop the bloodshed. The one expected to keep the peace.

I didn't expect him to storm the castle the way he did... like he had a death wish. Like he knew the rules and burned them anyway.

Will my brothers retaliate? Will they forgive me?

I confessed. Told them I was in love with him.

"*In love*," I said. Even though now, I don't know if that's the truth. How could it be?

I was in love with him. Once. I think?

But I confessed my betrayal right alongside his.

Does anyone trust me anymore?

And here I am, facing my absolute worst fear of all: being powerless. Being used.

Being complicit in cruelty.

Betraying my family.

My whole life, since I was a small child, I've given everything I could to my family. I've poured out my heart and soul in loving them, being faithful and loyal, and now... now they must hate me.

All I ever tried to do was the right thing. And now I sit across from him, from Seamus McCarthy, the man who calls himself my husband.

Am I in shock?

My husband.

He's coldly efficient, commanding, and brutal with his authority. There was a time I maybe even loved that about him.

Now? I'm afraid.

He keeps saying he's the head of the house.

What will he do to me?

"Are you tired, love?" he asks, after we've settled on the plane.

I nod. "I'm exhausted," I murmur. "I want to close my eyes and sleep forever."

And when I wake, I want to believe it's all a dream. That I did nothing wrong. That my family is safe. That I'm married to someone who loves me.

The weight of it all is crushing. Absolutely crushing.

"I'm a little hungry," I say, my voice soft, almost unsure. "Are we going back to Ballyhock now?"

"Aye," he says, pride sliding into his tone. "But not back to my family. Not yet. We go to our home first."

Our home.

He doesn't meet my eyes when he finishes. "My family doesn't know what I've done yet, but they will soon. It's... complicated."

Oh god.

"Will you be in trouble for what you did?"

He laughs. It's dark. Joyless.

"Let me see," he says, holding out his hand and counting off his sins. "First, I escaped a Russian jail. Second, I murdered the man you were betrothed to, which won't just bring your family's vengeance, but his as well. Third, I threw the gauntlet at your entire house. So now I'm wanted in a Russian prison, and I've likely started at least two wars that will end in bloodshed."

He nods slowly, deliberately.

"Aye. You could say I'm in trouble."

I swallow hard. Do I care that he's in trouble?

"But there's one thing you're going to learn about me, lass— something I don't think you've quite grasped in those last six months of our little rendezvous."

My cheeks flush.

I stare at him, silent, waiting.

He reaches out, brushes a lock of hair from my eyes and tucks it behind my ear.

"I don't care about being in trouble," he says. "I care about winning. I care that my commands are obeyed. I care about my family's lineage. Their safety. I care about *you*, sweet lass." He leans closer.

"When we get back to Dublin, I'm taking you to my personal home. Not a safe house. It's a beach house. Private. Quiet. There, I want to spend time with you," he murmurs, his voice suddenly warm. Dangerous. "I want to show you how a husband treats his wife."

Oh *god*.

He knows. He knows he's the only man I've ever even kissed.

"I'm going to show you what I expect of you as a McCarthy woman," he says, a wicked glint in his eyes.

A McCarthy woman. I'm nauseous. Literally, sick to my stomach.

"And once the word's out about what I've done, I'll need to come up with a strategy." He sighs and looks away, his eyes wistful. "This started back at the Wolf and Moon, didn't it? And if I'm honest? It started well before that."

"What do you mean, Seamus?" I ask softly. Now that we're alone, I say his name, and he allows it.

Did he bait and switch me? Pretend to love me, pretend to care, only to reveal the monster underneath?

What have I done? What has he done?

I think back to Morozov's body. To the blood. To the ruin he left behind.

He killed a man just for standing between us.

Now what?

"Come here, darling," he says, softer than I've heard in what feels like forever.

And my heart aches. Maybe, just maybe, beneath that cold, unyielding exterior, he does care for me.

Maybe this wasn't just a political move, like I'd always feared. But he said those words. I heard him.

I told you I was coming for your sister.

Even Polina said it, that he told everyone he was coming for me.

This has been in motion since the beginning. But I don't say any of that.

No. I keep it to myself.

I don't trust him. Not now. Not ever.

He says I betrayed him, but just look, look at how this has all played out. I swallow hard as he reaches for me, pulling me gently onto his lap like I belong there.

"The next few months are going to be very difficult," he says quietly, almost like he regrets it. "I have many things to sort out before we're at peace."

What will that mean for my family?

"Do you understand me?" he asks, still gentle, still careful with me.

I nod, because honestly, what choice do I have? "Yes?" I answer, barely holding steady.

"So this is what you're going to do, my love," he continues, and though his tone is tender, it's wrapped in steel. "Are you listening, lass?"

I nod again, swallow hard. "Yes," I whisper.

He cups the side of my face, forcing my gaze up to meet his. "When I ask you to obey me, I expect you to say it like this, little Zoya." His voice dips low, his finger under my chin. My gaze is locked on his. "*Yes, sir.*"

I stare at him, my throat tight and heart pounding. I want to feel what it does to me when I say it.

"*Yes, sir,*" I whisper back.

Why does a tiny thrill spark down my spine at that?

Why do his eyes go dark and heated with approval and lust?

"That's a good girl," he says, his words brushing over me like velvet. "I want you to know, I've already forgiven your betrayal. Because I know why you did it."

My betrayal... telling my family a lie. Agreeing to marry a Morozov.

I swallow hard.

"You're loyal, Zoya. But now, there's something else. Something I need you to understand."

He pinches my chin between his thumb and forefinger, keeping me locked in place. "Do you hear me, sweet girl?"

I nod, swallowing again.

"Yes."

"You tried to save your brothers from my hand. And I understand that. But you must never, ever do that again."

A sharp sting of fear pricks the back of my neck. I don't trust my voice, not at first, but after swallowing a few more times and wetting my lips, I manage to say, "Yes... sir." I tack on the *sir* like an afterthought, but it still earns me a small smile.

"That's a good lass," he says approvingly, brushing his thumb over my cheekbone. Then he leans in and kisses me, softly, tenderly, like he's trying to make a point with his mouth. And I melt, just a little more.

"You've heard of the ways of the McCarthy clan, haven't you?" he asks once he finally pulls away.

I nod. "Rumors," I whisper. "I know Matvei's wife, Anissa, used to work for you."

"Aye, she did. For a time. In exchange for our protection. And what did she tell you, lass?"

I laugh, a nervous sound. "Um... she said you guys were old-fashioned. Dominant. That you expect your women to be... submissive." My cheeks heat. "And that she'd never be cowed under the thumb of one of you."

"She wouldn't," he says with a little chuckle. "Which is why she's now married to a Kopolov man." He chuckles, low and amused. "But it's different for my family, lass."

He straightens a little.

"I'm the head of the house. And I'm the head of the Clan as well. Do you understand that?"

I nod.

"And you understand, it's not just in the bedroom, aye?"

I nod again, even though I'm not sure how I feel about that. Right now, the only thing that feels safe is to play along. To give him what he wants. That's how you survive.

"But I promise you, little Zoya, my sweet little lass," he says, both hands now cupping my face. "You'll want for nothing. My protection. My care."

I want to ask him, what about love? Do you love me?

I already made a fool of myself once, blurting out that I loved him in front of everyone. I did it to stop a war.

But do I?

Can I?

I don't know. I honestly don't know.

What if he gives me a command that turns me against my family? What if I've already betrayed everyone who's ever mattered to me?

He pauses. "I'll be the one to choose your things. What you wear. What you don't. Understand?"

"My clothes?" I ask, caught off guard. "All right... if that matters to you."

"It does," he says quickly. "And you're not to leave without permission. And you'll be guarded at all times. Do you understand that?"

"Yes," I murmur.

"And whatever I tell you, you'll obey or suffer the consequences. Do you understand me?"

Wait a minute. "What will the consequences be?" I ask hesitantly.

His eyes darken.

"Whatever I decide, lass."

Of course.

"Okay," I say, trying to look away. But he holds my face so tightly I can't move. I nod. "Alright."

His face softens. I've agreed to his terms.

I blow out a breath. I'm tired. I'm so, so tired.

"What happens next?" I ask quietly.

"It's time to gather my men. To assess the damage. To see if your family will retaliate."

My family? Wait.

"What did you do to my family?" My mind spirals, imagining all kinds of bloodshed. Did he hurt someone? Did I marry a man who actually hurt my family? Did he do something behind my back that I didn't know about?

But he doesn't answer. He only looks at me.

Then he leans down and presses a kiss to my temple.

"My sweet," he says gently. "I took their most prized possession."

CHAPTER 14

ZOYA

Back in my seat, I close my eyes and look away because I need a minute. This is hard. I still haven't gotten used to the emotions he stirs in me, how sharp and sudden they are, how they demand space I don't have to give.

Is this about me or his need to win?

He dared come to my home, my private, sacred space, and took me from my family. Took me from the people I love more than anything in this world... without any communication with me.

And yeah, I know he was in jail and that it was impossible for him to reach out. I get it. It makes sense. It was too risky. But knowing that doesn't erase the ache. It doesn't soften the sharp edge of being left behind.

I can't help but feel like he abandoned me when I needed him most. After everything I'd survived... he vanished. Just disappeared. My heart hasn't caught up. The impressions he left behind, they've been wearing on me for a while now. And now he's sitting here, giving me this speech about being the head of the house and his rules and the way it's going to be. It's not exactly strange, not completely out of the ordinary, and it's not unacceptable.

But still. It stings.

He finally meets my gaze, and I turn my face, shielding my chest with my arm like I'm trying to keep something vital from spilling out.

"Do you think giving me everything I want will make me fall for you? Make me melt?" I ask in a sharp whisper.

"I'm not just going to Ireland. I'm being taken there. After all this time. After everything." I exhale hard. "And I did it because... because you say I'm yours."

I pause, searching for the words. "You say that, and yet..." I shake my head, pulling back into myself like I'm retreating into a bunker.

We are on a plane that is taking us to his home in Ireland.

And a whole new life.

What about the holidays? What about seeing them again? My birthday?

I swipe angrily at the tears gathering in my eyes, hating how they betray me.

"You can't hold onto your feelings like this and not tell me anything," he says, gentle but firm. "I can't help if I don't know."

And I don't want him to know. Not really. Not all of it. So I stay stubborn, resolute. Like if I pretend hard enough, he won't see through me. But he does.

"It had to be this way," he says, quiet again.

"You're The Undertaker, Seamus," I whisper, barely audible.

His brows pinch together. "Why is that a problem?"

"Don't you know what you've done?" I look away. "Do I even really want to know?"

I've heard the rumors. I've seen shadows of the truth. I've witnessed things with my own eyes, my own hands.

But do I really know what my brothers have done?

That's different, I reason stubbornly. That's my family. I never had control over them.

But this? Did I ever have control over this?

"We've got a long flight ahead of us, love," he says gently. "What can I get you to eat?"

"I'm not hungry anymore," I say, and even I hear the petulance in my tone.

"You need to eat something, darling," he says softly, almost like he's speaking to a wounded thing. And it guts me. How can this man be the same one wrapped up in all those rumors?

"What else are you hiding, Seamus?" I ask, almost pleading. "Tell me the truth. Please. Now that we're married." My voice catches on the word. "Now that we're married, I want to know everything."

"Aye," he says. "Now that we are, there's nothing I'll keep from you. Not a single thing, lass. Do you understand?"

"What, nothing?" I ask, a little shaken. There are things even Rafail wouldn't tell me.

"Nothing," he repeats. "Ask me anything."

"All right... You told me you have four brothers and sisters. Is that true?"

"Aye," he answers without hesitation.

I blink. Nod. Of course. That tracks. Families like his, like mine, tend to be big. There's strength in numbers. Stability. Legacy.

"And you're the oldest?"

"Aye," he says, nodding.

"Who else is in your family?"

"Well," he says, "me da, Keenan... You'll meet him, eventually." He says that casually, not pressing. "Not right away," he adds, almost apologetic. "Because I shouldn't be bringing you home."

"Okay," I say softly, trying not to let the sting show. "Is he not going to want to meet me?"

"No, no, not at all." He shakes his head, quick to reassure. "Just... not yet."

How lovely. I nod, swallowing the lump in my throat. My lips press together, and I lift my hand to my mouth, an old habit.

He watches me with a softer expression, eyes lighting up as he switches gears. "And my ma. Her name is Caitlin. You'll love her. Everybody does."

"Oh?" I manage a small smile. "What can you tell me about her?"

"She lived a wild sort of life before she ever married me da," he says, thoughtfully stroking his chin. "She was a lighthouse keeper's daughter. Dad kept her away from the rest of the world, bit of a recluse, that one."

There's something magnetic about Seamus when he speaks like this. Now that we're near each other again, even under such strange, high-stakes, damn near impossible circumstances, I just want to listen. Let him ramble. Let him fill the space between us with words and warmth.

I love the way his eyes dance when he's lost in memory. The way his hands move with the story. That Irish lilt, gentle, rhythmic, so full of emotion, especially when he talks about his family.

"But Seamus..." I say quietly, looking at him. "You know I... I love mine too."

"I know, little lass." He reaches for me then, his voice thick with understanding. "I know ye do."

"And I promise," he continues, "it won't always be like this, yeah? It's just... for now, it's what's safest. You understand?"

I nod, turning to the window again, not trusting myself to speak.

"Who else?" I ask after a moment.

"Me da's cousin Megan, she's married to a lad named Carson," he says, ticking names off in his head. "Then there's me da's older brother, Cormac. Bit tough around the edges, but heart of gold. And me uncle Nolan, married to a lass called Shana."

He pauses. "Then there are others, men in the clan. Some older, some young and rough, some seasoned. All types. We've got a much bigger, more established clan than yours, y'know."

"I gathered that," I reply, raising an eyebrow. Is he teasing my family?

"We've been around a long time," he says, not unkindly. "When me da, Keenan McCarthy, took over, he was second in line. First in line was Seamus McCarthy. I was named after him, you see."

"I see," I murmur. "So your ties run deep. Real alliances. Real enemies."

We talk for a while, and soon, the plane is landing. A car rolls to a slow crawl outside, and he glances at it.

"Let's get you home," he says, but the words fall flat. They sound hollow in my ears.

He can take me back to Dublin. He can take me to that house we're meant to share. But that doesn't make it home. No. That place isn't home.

It won't ever be home.

CHAPTER 15

SEAMUS

Jesus feckin' Christ, I'll regret this.

But if I had it to do over again, I wouldn't change a goddamn thing, not one, even though the consequences will be severe.

I had to. I *had* to.

Zoya McCarthy is mine.

"This is your home?" she asks, her voice soft and uncertain. Gentle and sweet as anything.

I don't deserve a woman like her.

I always imagined I'd be wed to someone my father hand-picked. That's the Irish way. Hell, it's the way for most of us raised in power and expectation.

But I broke every damn rule to get her into my bed. And I'd break them all again.

I nod. "Aye. Bought it years back. No one comes here unless I let them."

She swallows, and her eyes go wide. She's starting to see, it's not just a house. It's a sanctuary. A choice.

I park the car and catch her trying to open the door.

"Ah-ah," I warn gently. She freezes. Smart girl, obedient without being meek.

I get out, walk around, and open her door myself. Then I hold out my hand, and she places hers in mine. It's small, delicate, chilled from the night air.

I bend down a little. "Why didn't you tell me you were cold, lass?" I ask, taking both her hands in mine, rubbing warmth into her skin.

Once I feel the cold leaving her, I kiss her fingers before letting go. She stares up at me, wide-eyed.

"It's chilly here," she whispers, giving a little shiver.

"Aye, it is," I say. "Ballyhock nights are damp and seep into your bones, even this time of year. I'll get a fire going."

"You have a fireplace?" she asks, smiling just a bit, her eyes still wide with wonder.

I shrug. "One of those electric jobs, not the real thing, but no mess either. We've a fire pit out back, but..." I trail off, looking at her. "I want you inside till I say otherwise."

She nods, swallowing hard. Doesn't push back. I don't press her either. Not tonight.

"Come on," I tell her gently. "This is my home, for now. We'll be here a little while."

She doesn't ask how long.

I may not have married the woman my father chose, but I married right.

Zoya is gentle as a doe, but there's steel in her spine. She knows the ways of men like me.

She moves quietly through the house, careful, taking everything in with those wide eyes.

Stone floors catch her attention. She asks about them. I nod, get the fire going, and put the kettle on.

I'd open the windows so she could hear the sea, but I don't want her getting cold again.

I like her here with me. I imagined her here with me.

This is the one place in the world where I don't wear a mask.

My cousin Colm shows up just before dark. He's loyal, brutal, and knows his place.

I step outside and speak to him quickly. He doesn't ask questions. He knows better.

I cut him off when he pries, and out of the corner of my eye, I catch Zoya watching us through the window. Her eyes are wide, curious and wary, and I can't help but wonder what she sees when she looks at me. The cutthroat commander? The man who gives orders like gospel?

But when I step inside, I soften. I give her the gentlest voice I've got. Like a skittish fawn, she'll bolt if I raise it. I reach for her arm and brush my fingers over it, light as air.

"You hungry, love?"

She blinks once, then nods.

"All right, darling. Let's get you snuggled up here. I'll cook something."

"You cook?" she asks, a tiny tilt to her lips. It's the first hint of anything playful since we got in the car. Back then, I could see it clear as day—she was bracing herself against me, building walls. I wasn't sure if she'd ever forgive me for taking her from her family.

And I know what I did. Christ, I know. I shattered whatever future her brothers imagined. Burned their bridges to ash. There'll be retaliation, eventually. But I've got to move first.

Right now, though, in the quiet shelter of my home, it feels like maybe, just maybe, we're starting to patch things up. Starting to find our way back to something that once felt like hope.

Does she remember how she felt about me before I left? Because I remember every feckin' second I spent thinkin' of her in that fuckin' cell.

I shrug. "I try to cook. Know a little bit." I scratch my head. "A bit shite at it, but you've had a long day. It's all right. Sit down and I'll fetch us some grub."

"Seamus," she says gently. "I've cooked for my entire family for years. I like doing it. I'm good at it. Just show me the kitchen."

I shake my head, sharp, but not unkind.

"What did I say on the plane, Zoya?" I remind her, calm but firm.

She sighs and drops back onto the couch. Lips pursed, but she doesn't fight me on it. I grunt under my breath and march into the kitchen.

And promptly make a goddamn mess. Haven't done any shopping in a bit, so the choices are scant.

Burnt eggs. Dry toast. I even manage to butcher half the berries, tryin' to slice them for the side. "Goddamn it," I mutter. Should've just ordered food like a sane man.

She laughs. Finally. And Christ, it hits me square in the chest like a hammer. That sound. I love her laugh. And more than that, it means something. She's relaxing. Letting her guard down.

Why does that matter so much to me?

"Seamus," she says, getting up. The fire's going, and she's shrugged off the coat, still in her wedding dress. "Please, let me do this."

She nudges me aside, and I let her. *I let her.* I don't let anyone push me around. Haven't since I was a lad, and only then 'cause mam had the final say.

I watch her, amused, as she puts on the kettle. Her movements are confident. Easy. Like she belongs.

The eggs come out perfect. The toast is golden and buttered. She works some kind of kitchen magic with the odds and ends in the fridge, turns the meal into a work of art.

"Here," she says softly. "Let's eat."

She settles into one of the little chairs I pull out for her, and I sit across from her. The food's brilliant, but I barely touch it because I'm too busy watching her. I feel as if I blink too hard or fall asleep, I'll wake to find she's vanished, that I only imagined her here with me.

"Something the matter?" she asks.

Is something the matter? Christ. The whole feckin' world's the matter. But none of that means anything right now. Now that she's here with me.

I reach for her hand and brush my thumb over her knuckles.

"No, I just…" I look away, my throat tight. "I've made some terrible decisions. But this, you, this isn't one of them." My voice cracks.

"Be careful, Seamus," she says, and her voice breaks too.

I tilt my head. "Why, lass?"

"Because you're making it very difficult to stay angry with you," she whispers.

And then she blinks, and a single tear slides down her cheek.

"Zoya, why're you crying, love?" I ask gently.

"Because I hate that you've made me choose between you and everyone I love."

She swallows hard, then looks away. I nod, but don't speak. Just clear the dishes.

"Here, I'll—"

"No," I say firmly. "We've got a rule. Actually, we'll have many rules. But this one starts now—one cooks, the other cleans." I glance back at her. "I watched my mam work her fingers raw. My da was old-school, you know? Not a tyrant, nothing like the bastard I'm named after, but he didn't lift a finger in the kitchen. Didn't want to. Ma didn't want him to either."

I shake my head. "That's not how it's gonna be with us, Zoya. I might be the one in charge, but I can wash a feckin' dish. Period."

She lets out a soft laugh. "All right."

"Why don't you change out of that dress and take a shower? You'll feel better, won't you?"

She nods. "I think so."

I show her to the bathroom, and she looks around with wide eyes.

"This house is beautiful, Seamus. Nothing like I expected from you."

I don't ask what she did expect. Just nod and shrug. Her words make me feel... bashful. *Christ.* No one ever makes me feel bashful.

Around Zoya, I almost forget who I am. I almost forget who she is too. And that's dangerous.

While she showers, I leave some clothes on the little table outside the door. Mine, of course. Way too big on her, but fuck, I can't wait to see her in them. I looked forward to this more than I did seeing her in that wedding dress.

When she comes out, her hair's still wet, skin flushed from the heat. She walks to the fireplace and sinks down without saying a word. I join her.

We sit in silence for a long while.

"So," she says eventually, "you bought this house with… I don't know. What do you call it? Blood money?"

I don't flinch. Just shrug.

"Aye. First job that ever mattered."

She stares at the fire. "I believe you." Her voice isn't accusing, it's accepting, soft like an exhale.

It's nothing less than what her brothers have done, really. I've heard stories. "Your brother became the guardian of all of you when he was still just a lad, eh?" I say gently. "I don't envy him that."

"Right," she murmurs. "It was rough, you know. I was only a child."

She trails off, her eyes dim. "I only remember bits and pieces."

"Do you remember the night your parents died?" I ask, quiet as a breath.

"Yes," she replies, even quieter. A whisper. "One of those memories I sometimes wish I could forget."

"Do you want to tell me about it?" I ask her, and to my surprise, I want to hear it. Every brutal, blood-soaked detail. Not for the gore, god no, but because I want to know her. All of her. Even the parts that hurt to hold.

"Why?" she asks, almost to herself.

"What happened?" I press, gently now. "I want to know."

She draws a breath. "We found out years later that my mother was having an affair," she says, her eyes distant. "And the man she was seeing… he came to kill my father. She wouldn't leave my father for him, so he killed them both. He was disturbed. Madly in love or whatever."

She stumbles over the words, like they're stones underfoot. Her gaze goes somewhere far away.

"I don't remember much," she admits. "I remember someone shoving me into a closet, probably Rafail. And Semyon barking at us to stay put. He was young, too, but he had that voice. That tone. Like there'd be hell to pay if we didn't listen, so we did."

"Rafail was eighteen, Semyon about sixteen. I was only six." She pauses. "To me, they were giants. Legends. I did whatever they said."

She gives a soft laugh, the kind that doesn't quite reach her eyes. "Rodion. He's the youngest, yeah? He tried to help my brothers, but they weren't having it. Semyon yelled at him to stay put, threatened to hurt him if he didn't." She takes a deep breath.

"They didn't know better and did what they knew. Violence was language in our house. Old-fashioned, maybe. Brutal, definitely."

She swallows hard.

"We all sat there in the dark, and we heard everything. The screams. The gunshots." Her voice falters. "All I could think about was my mother. I just wanted to see her face. Wanted to know she was still there."

Her hands tremble slightly. "I wish I had more memories of her."

She speaks so quietly, I barely catch it.

Zoya nods, thoughtful. "My brothers are... protective. Rodion lets me think I'm free. Rafail doesn't."

And there we are, our families at war, a moment of stolen peace.

She leans against me, barely a shift in weight.

"This won't last," she whispers.

"I know."

But mother of god, I wish it would.

For a moment, the war is distant. For a moment, we're not enemies. We're just two lost souls putting together the pieces.

I notice her eyes flick to the bedroom and back again. A quick little move, as if she doesn't even know she's doing it.

She's afraid of me. Of what I'll do to her when we're alone.

And I can't blame her.

I took her from her home, her family. And my reputation? She's heard every fucking word, I'm sure.

She probably thinks I'll hurt her.

But I won't.

Never.

I'll treat her like she's breakable, like glass.

And I won't fuck her tonight. No, not yet. She's been through too much. God knows, I want her. I ache for her.

But not tonight.

Tonight, I'll ease her into this mess I've made, before my family turns on me, before my father finds out what I've done.

"Tell me more about your family," she says, hopeful, her eyes searching mine.

And so I do.

I tell her about my sister, Kyla. And the youngest, Bronwyn. "Kyla's only a few years younger than me, but you'd never guess it from the way she carries herself. She got our grandmother's red hair, but not her softness. Kyla's like iron, burns hot, never bends. Put our parents through hell. Still does. Then there's Bronwyn." My voice softens when I speak of her. "You'll like her," I say. "Not sure you'll like Kyla."

"She sounds like someone you have to warm up to," she says with a little smile and a wink. "I know the type. Did you forget who my brother is?"

"Tell me about them again," I say. "I only know them as my enemies."

She flinches, but barely. She quickly rights herself and swallows hard.

"There's Rafail, you know him. He's about your age, I think," she says quietly, glancing at her hands.

There's a gap in our years, but I like it. I like knowing she's younger, a little more untouched by the world. Some would call me a bastard for what I plan to do to her, but they don't know the half of it. I've done worse. Much worse.

And I'll take good care of my little Zoya.

"Rafail is... hmm." She thinks for a second. "Probably the most loyal person you'll ever meet."

Great. That bodes brilliantly for me.

"He's good to his wife, his kids. His family. Gave up his whole life to raise us after... well, after everything. Against some heavy odds too."

I don't want to admire the bastard, but I do. Reluctantly.

"Eighteen years old, your whole life ahead of you, and you become a father figure overnight? No thanks." I shake my head.

"And then there's Semyon," she says, her brows knitting. "He's... harder to explain. With Rafail, what you see is what you get. But Semyon, he's different. Doesn't show emotions like the rest of us. Some say he doesn't feel them at all."

She pauses, her voice going soft. "But that's not true. It's not."

There's something about the way she says it, like she's trying to convince herself too.

"He married his childhood crush. Her name's Anya. She's the one who owns the bakery. And she has a little brother, Stefan. They became his guardians, the pair of them." I nod. I know all this on paper, sure I do, but it hits different, hearing it from her own lips.

"Then there's Rodion," she says with a smile, her voice warming. "He was always kind of our class clown, you know? Always, and I mean *always*, in trouble with Rafail." She shakes her head with a soft laugh.

"There's nothing any of Rafail's kids can throw at him that he hasn't already seen or had to handle, thanks to Rodion."

I smirk. Yeah, I understand that well enough.

"The youngest probably thinks he's bulletproof, eh?" I say, and she nods with that knowing little grin. But then, just for a moment, her expression falters. She looks a bit sad.

She misses them. I can tell. They're practically all she's ever known. Her whole world.

"And Rodion's married too, yeah?" I ask, softening my tone.

"Yes," she says with a nod. "He married a girl named Ember. She's the one who got me into romance books."

"Romance books?" My brow quirks. "You like to read romance?"

"Like?" She laughs. "I read two hundred fifty books last year."

"Jesus, Mary, and Joseph. I don't think I've read two hundred fifty books in me whole life," I admit.

She laughs again, and it's bloody adorable. She covers her mouth like she's trying to stifle it, her shoulders lifting a little. It's bashful, sweet. I want to pull her into me, tuck her under my chin, and kiss that little temple of hers.

"What do you like about romance novels?" I ask, genuinely curious.

"Oh gosh... everything," she says, and there's a dreamy look in her eyes. "I've always been a hopeless romantic."

Good to know. My little lass likes the sweet things. And here I am, the devil who dragged her out of her homeland and across the sea.

"And then I came along and swept you out of your home and your country," I say with a wry smile. "But I don't regret it. No. I'd do it a thousand times over." She gives me a sad smile. I reach for her hand. "Is there anything romantic in that?" I ask her, searching her eyes.

She pauses, thoughtful. Her gaze drops for a second. "It depends on why you did it," she says quietly, her voice shaking just a little.

"If you did it because of pride, or to prove something, or just to get one over on my brothers... then no. I wouldn't think that's romantic at all."

And I know her. I know her enough to hear the hope in her voice, that it wasn't that. After all those nights in a dimly lit pub, all the conversations... I know her.

I'll tell her the truth.

Christ, I'll tell her the truth.

I lean back on the big sofa, legs spread, and pat my right thigh with my palm. "Come here, Zoya."

It's soft, but it's still a command. One I know she'll obey.

She rises slowly, wearing nothing but my oversized T-shirt. Her hair's a chaotic mess, half-damp, half-dry. Her face is bare, slightly pink, beautiful. Her eyes, wide and wondering.

She walks toward me, hesitant.

"Right here," I say, and she perches lightly on the edge of my lap.

That won't do.

I wrap my arms around her and haul her fully into me, until she's nestled properly where she belongs. She smells bloody divine. Feels even better. I close my eyes and breathe her in.

I'll go to hell for what I did. And if me da has his way, it'll be sooner rather than later.

But I don't regret one fuckin' second.

"Look at me, little lass," I whisper into her ear.

She turns to face me. I frame her face with both hands, gentle but firm, and I make sure she doesn't look away.

"My sweet, beautiful girl," I say, barely above a whisper. "I was in jail when I found out you were engaged."

Her eyes go wide, lips parting.

"I broke out, Zoya. Broke out to find you. Because the thought of you belongin' to another man, of him even thinkin' he had a claim on you, made me lose my fuckin' mind."

She swallows. Her eyes shine.

"There were plenty of things I could've done to stick it to your brothers. Believe me, I thought of all of 'em. But takin' you wasn't about them."

I shake my head slowly. "I took you because you were mine. Always were. Always will be. I took you because the idea of you being touched by anyone else made me want to put a bullet in my own skull."

She swallows hard, and her voice is a whisper. "I'm afraid, Seamus."

She trembles under my hands as I hold her by the shoulders. I could hurt her easily. Too easily.

But I won't. Never.

A man like me... we learn our strength early. I was just a lad when I hurt one of my sisters by accident, and me da made sure I never did it again.

I just didn't know my strength then.

I do now.

And most of the time, I use it. I bend it to my will. I use it to protect, to intimidate when I have to. But around her... I restrain myself. She's delicate, in all the best ways.

That challenge was part of what drew me in. She made me question everything. Made me feel things I didn't know I could feel.

I didn't think I had feelings. Not like that. And definitely not for someone Russian.

We were raised to hate each other. And I followed that rule, like all the rest, for the good of the family. Always for the family.

Until her.

"I'll make this better," I promise. "I'll make this right."

She blinks up at me.

I grit my teeth.

"I want you to promise me something, Zoya. And I want it now."

She nods, solemn. We don't lie to each other. Not anymore.

"You're my wife now. I'm your husband. If I ask you something, I want the truth. And if you ask me, I'll give it to you. Will you promise me that?"

She nods. "I'm an honest person, Seamus."

Then she looks away. "Until you," she adds softly. "You're the first person I've ever lied over."

I tilt her chin up with my finger and make her meet my eyes.

"Why'd you do it, love?" I ask softly.

"I felt... trapped sometimes," she says. "At least, I thought I did. Like a caged bird. I just wanted to breathe outside the family, just for a moment."

She pauses. "I saw my brothers getting married, traveling, living. And I imagined myself always stuck there, little Zoya in the kitchen, with only a few friends, not much beyond my family."

She blinks rapidly, tears slipping down her cheeks. "But I do love them, Seamus."

"I know," I say, pulling her in. I kiss her forehead, then her damp lashes, tasting her tears.

"I know you're honest. And I know sometimes pressure makes people do desperate things. Things they're not proud of. But that doesn't define you."

Maybe I'm saying it for both of us.

"Will you give me that promise, love? Please?"

She nods. "And I promise too. You ask, I'll answer. Truth for truth."

I nod.

"So let me ask you something, then." I lower my voice. "What are you afraid of?"

"You," she whispers.

And I know, in that moment, she's telling the truth.

"When I was with you... before I knew who you really were... I thought you *worked* for The Undertaker, and that was bad enough. God, I was such an idiot."

I growl low and shake my head. "Ah-ah. You don't say a word against yerself like that again, hear?"

Swallowing hard, she nods and continues. "I never imagined... not in a million years... that you *were* the man. The one everyone fears."

Now the tears fall freely. Her voice breaks as she says it, raw and real.

"And I thought I loved you," she says. "But I don't know how I could love someone who's done those terrible things."

It's the truth. And it cuts deeper than I care to admit. But we've only just begun, haven't we? There's still time. I'll show her, no, I'll prove it. Right then and there, I make her a promise.

"I'll make a vow to you, lass. I will earn your love for me," I tell her.

"What we had back in Russia, that wasn't the full story. That was heat, tension, chemistry, but it was filtered. We weren't truly ourselves, were we? Everything I knew about you was through one lens," I say. "And everything you learned about me... well, it came from another."

"Yes," she whispers, barely audible.

"Then give me a chance," I say again. "Let me show you how deep my love for you goes. If I wanted to marry just any old woman, I would've. Could've, easily."

I don't need to tell her I could've had any woman I wanted. Wealth and power make for easy hunting. But that was never the point.

"I wanted you," I say simply. "But you didn't give me the whole truth just now, did you? You're afraid. Afraid of me, of what I've done. But, lass, you were raised around some of the most dangerous Russians alive."

And I know she knows how to love even the darkest of men.

"I never thought about my brothers as wicked," she says softly.

Maybe one day she won't think of me that way either.

"There are men," I continue, "who chase power for the sake of breaking others. They want money, status, worship. That's not what this is. Everything I've done, every bloody thing, was for the same reason your brothers did what they've done. Loyalty. Protection. Family."

She goes quiet for a moment, then says it, so gently, like she's afraid even her own voice will shatter something fragile between us.

"That's the other reason I'm afraid, Seamus."

"Yes?"

"I'm afraid you'll make me choose. Between you and them."

She draws in a breath, lets it out in a whisper.

"Please don't make me do that. I took my vows to you, but I meant every word. I don't go back on what I say."

I cup her face, my heart tight.

"My fierce little lass," I whisper. "I know."

And I won't lie to her.

"I can't promise that choice will never come. I won't do that to you. But I swear to you, I'll do everything in my power to make sure it never comes from me."

She looks up at me.

"How much power do you have?"

"That," I say with a small smile, "remains to be seen."

"Yes," she says again, barely audible.

"Is that all, Zoya? Is that all you're afraid of?"

Her gaze flickers back to the bedroom. Her cheeks flush a deep, burning red.

"You know..." she whispers. "I'm a virgin. That one time with you... well, it was the only time."

She pauses. Swallows. Then does the most adorable thing I've ever seen, buries her face against my chest like she can't stand to look me in the eye.

I wrap my arms around her gently. I don't force her to meet my gaze.

"And you're afraid," I say softly, "of what happens between a husband and wife?"

I run a hand down her small, fragile, perfect little back. She's so damn tiny, it undoes me.

"Yes," she whispers. "I don't know how to do anything. What if I disappoint you? What if I... What if it hurts?"

My chest swells at her honesty. Christ, I've never wanted to protect someone so fiercely.

"Those are all fair fears, love," I tell her. "But I'll teach you. I will. One step at a time. There's no rush."

I shake my head and sigh, but inside, I feel a rare, quiet peace.

CHAPTER 16

I FEEL like I'm betraying my family just for enjoying even a second of this. But I am. God, I am.

The way Seamus holds me, it makes me feel protected in a way I never felt, even at home. Yes, my brothers would've killed anyone who dared touch me, but this… this is different.

This is my husband.

I've taken his name. Have I taken a new identity too?

I look up into his deep blue eyes. If I didn't know who he was, if I hadn't heard the whispers and the warnings, I might've said he looks almost boyish, just now anyway. Almost. But the rugged scruff along his jaw, the way his lips press in that tight, serious line, remind me who he really is.

"It's been a long day," he murmurs. "Let's get you to bed, lass."

I like it when he calls me that. Lass. Love. All those little endearments, dipped in that Irish accent. I'll give myself a moment to grieve everything I've left behind, but maybe, just maybe, I can still make something out of this.

"Let's get you to bed," he says again.

The rest blurs after that because all I can think is—what if he touches me? What if things go further?

I remember his apartment. The way he held me. The way he kissed me like I was already his. It felt... right. And now? After everything?

He doesn't push. He just lifts me as if I weigh nothing. Carries me like I'm precious.

"To bed with you," he says once more.

Gentle. Quiet. Protective.

And for the first time, I start to wonder... maybe this is who he really is. Maybe the Seamus McCarthy the world fears isn't all there is.

Maybe... this is the man I've married.

This man, this man is the one who says he loves me.

Does he though? He says he does. Swears it, even. Says he'll prove it.

And here I am, standing in the middle of it all, dressed in his huge T-shirt. Not a stitch of makeup on. Hair a complete disaster.

And still, he looks right at me and says I'm beautiful. Says I'm his.

I wasn't prepared for the house. For the bedroom. For how it would all feel.

It's nothing like I imagined. Nothing like the man who's brought me here. The outside is all old stone and ivy, with coastal views that hit you like something out of a dream. This place feels like it's been carved into the edge of the world, tucked between sea and forest. Ancient. Safe. Hidden.

Seamus's.

Inside, it's clean and sharp. Everything intentional. He told me he doesn't come here often. That catches me. Where else does he go then, if not here? That thought clings.

His bedroom is a study in contradiction. Spartan and expensive. Cold in the way it looks, but not in how it feels. Like him, it doesn't invite you in; it dares you to stay.

One whole side of the room is glass. Towering windows that stretch up, looking straight out over misty cliffs and the wide-open sea. I can't wait to crack them open, to breathe in the salt and brine. He's talked about the ocean so vividly, and now, I see why.

Heavy blackout curtains hang off to the side. Thick enough to blot out the world, but they're open now, as if he likes to see into the night. To be ready. To know what's coming.

The bed's massive, of course it is. King-sized, dark wood, low frame, no headboard. Iron fixtures. Stark. Utilitarian. Masculine. Him.

The sheets are charcoal gray. There's only a handful of pillows, nothing decorative, nothing soft or fussy. No clutter. Just the essentials. There's an electric fireplace humming quietly, and beside it, a single leather chair, scuffed and broken in. It looks like it's lived a life or two. Maybe it belonged to someone else once. Maybe it was gifted. Either way, that chair has a story, and I can already picture him in it, watching the fire flicker in the hearth.

The hearth is old stone, rough and warm to the touch. Across from the bed, there's a dark oak armoire. Everything else fades into quiet. Dark floorboards. Unassuming light fixtures. The faint scent of leather lingering in the air.

There's nothing personal here, no photographs, no knickknacks. Except...

One thing on the nightstand catches my eye. It stops me.

My pink hair tie?

He looks almost sheepish when he sees me staring at it. "Aye," he says. "You left it at the pub once. I wore it around my wrist for a bit when no one was looking. Kept it in my pocket after that. Like a little good luck charm."

"You kept my hair tie?"

"Aye. That a problem?"

And then that glint in his eye, that challenge in his voice. "Darling, when are you going to get it through your pretty head? I escaped jail for you, Zoya. And you're surprised I kept your hair tie?"

I wonder if he thought of it behind bars. If he wished he could have his little talisman.

I had let myself get angry with him. I gave in to that sharp, pulsing heat that flared inside me when he didn't show up.

That tightness in my chest, that sting behind my eyes, I felt it all.

It felt like my greatest fear came true.

He had used me. Just used me. Like I was nothing more than a pawn on his board. Like I was just a means to an end. That he never wanted me at all. Not really. Not Zoya Kopolova, the girl, not the woman, not the heart beating behind the name.

And while my family has never made me feel that way *intentionally*, that kind of fear still lived in the corners. Maybe it comes with the territory. The youngest. The smallest. The one they kept on the sidelines, out of the blood and bone and tragedy that make up our legacy.

My brothers and sister have always known things before I did. Always protected me in their own way. In that cold, unyielding Bratva way that still feels like love, even when it cuts.

So when Seamus disappeared, after the supposed attack on my family, and I kept coming back, week after week, praying for a sign of him... I knew. I knew the truth that gutted me. He was done with me. I was a game piece he'd moved off the board.

But now... now I'm in his home.

"Let's get to bed, love," he says, thick and husky, like smoke and velvet.

Morning will come soon. And I know, it settles deep in my chest, that our time together is limited. That something's going to break. I can feel it hovering just out of reach.

He looks away, his brows furrowing, like he's trying to stop himself from saying what we both know. That this, us, is going to go fast. Too fast.

I nod, biting back everything I want to scream.

"Bed," he says again. Firmer now.

But doesn't he want to come too? Isn't this the part where there are rules?

I stand there frozen, unsure, and he comes to me. Moves like a shadow over moonlight. He bends, brushes a strand of hair behind my ear, and his voice is a quiet growl that curls down my spine.

"My love," he murmurs. "I thought I explained my expectations to you. When I tell you to do something, I expect obedience." He pauses. "Is there a problem?"

My lips tug downward into a frown even as my pulse hammers. I swallow hard, the words caught in my throat.

"Another rule," he whispers, so soft it's almost cruel. "When I ask you a question, I expect an answer. Doesn't have to be your life story. Doesn't have to be much. But one answer, love. Or there will be consequences."

He kisses my cheek. Gentle. His mouth is to my ear. "It's our first week together. I'll let this one slide. But don't make me repeat myself again."

I nod, then swallow. Barely a whisper escapes. "Yes, sir."

His eyes flash, dark and knowing. He likes that. I can feel it.

My cheeks go up in flames. My belly swoops and tightens, and I swallow again.

"I'm going to take it easy on you tonight," he says, stepping back just a bit. "I won't punish you. Not on our wedding night. But I did ask a question."

He tilts his head, watching me closely. "So let me ask again. You seem like you don't want to go to sleep. What's the problem, love?"

I can barely get the words out. "It's our... our wedding night."

Doesn't he want me? Shouldn't we...? I fidget, flushed and nervous. "Aren't there... rules?" My voice breaks on the last word.

He chuckles, low and dark. Clearly amused.

"Ah, angel," he says, and kisses my cheek again. "Aren't you a sight."

Then he nods, just once. "Yes. There are rules. We're expected to consummate the marriage. Both the Irish and the Russians will expect it to be official."

"I... I know," I whisper. He laughs then, really laughs, and god, my heart can hardly stand it. It's so rare to see his face light up like that.

"You're wondering why I haven't taken you to bed," he says, his words thick with something unnamable. "Because I saw the way you looked. I saw the fear in your eyes."

He pauses. That shadow returns. "And I don't want you to fear me."

A beat.

"Unless you disobey me. Then? It's appropriate."

The heat that swells inside me is terrifying in its own way. It's not just fear.

It's something deeper. Darker. Something I've never felt before.

"Don't you want me?" I whisper.

He doesn't hesitate. Turns me to face him, sits on the edge of the bed, spreads his knees, and pulls me into the space between them.

"My sweet," he says, so gently it shatters me.

And that's when I feel it. The strain of his arousal pressing against his trousers. The hard, undeniable truth of what I do to him.

He's big. God, so big. And I can see now, see it in his restraint, in the tightness of his jaw, that he's holding himself back.

"Don't you understand?" he says. "It's because of the way I feel about you that I'm exercising self-control. You're the only woman who's ever made me feel like I might lose all of it, all my control. Every damn thread of it. Understand?"

I nod. Swallow. "Yes."

"Good," he says. "I don't want our first night to be anything but perfect. And by my logic, we've got at least a day before anyone comes looking. I've got surveillance on every entrance. No one's getting in."

He cups the back of my head, presses his mouth to my cheek.

"So tonight, we sleep. I get to fall asleep with you beside me. And when I wake, you'll still be here."

He kisses me, warm and tender.

"Tomorrow, we'll consummate our marriage."

I nod. "All right."

And suddenly, all the tension leaks out of me. I'm so tired I can barely stand.

But I've never felt safer.

My eyes feel heavy. My limbs feel heavy. I can barely move.

"Now lie down in bed," he says gently before he turns me around and lands a smack to my ass, not soft, not playful. It's affectionate, yes, but it still stings in that possessive way only he can manage. The heat rises in my cheeks, crawling up my neck. I swallow hard. Because I know there's more where that came from. More heat. More claim. More Seamus.

"Get up in bed. I want you next to me," he murmurs. "I want to feel you when I roll over in the middle of the night."

His voice is almost a growl now, like he's been starving for this, starving for me. His eyes darken, clouded with that storm I know lives in him, that pain he's always carried.

"I've dreamt of this," he admits.

And there's weight behind those words. Heavy, thick weight. Pain and longing twisted together. "Every time I wanted to escape that prison," he says. "Every time they tortured me... hurt me... I thought of this. I thought of you. Knowing you were out here. Knowing I was going to come for you. That no matter what they did to me, after everything settled, you were mine."

His. He says it like a vow, like a possession, like a prayer.

"Now, love, I want you to rest. Close your eyes." He cups my cheek, his thumb brushing along my skin like he's memorizing it. "I'm going to tell you a story, see?"

I nod.

He's going to tell me a story. *Seamus. My* Seamus. Telling stories in the dark like this? Is this... cute? Does Seamus even do cute? I have a feeling I'm the only one who'll ever witness this side of him. And I like it. I love it, actually.

"Okay," I say. "But give me a kiss first."

He chuckles softly, low in his chest. "Love," he murmurs, "always a goodnight kiss, aye?"

I tilt my face toward him, and he looks at me like I'm the most sacred thing he's ever held. His thumb sweeps over my cheekbone again, so slow, so reverent, and then he leans in and brushes his lips against mine, a soft, sweet, easy kiss that still manages to steal my breath.

It's our wedding night. And we're not making love. I'm tired. He's tired. And it's okay. It's more than okay.

I rest my head against his chest, and he starts.

"Once upon a time in a land far, far away... there was a man who was a prince."

I close my eyes. Let myself fall into his voice.

"He was in line for the throne," Seamus says, "but while he waited, his father's most trusted advisor betrayed him. Did terrible, wicked things in the name of power. All while pretending to serve the crown. The king trusted him, blindly. The prince tried to warn his father, but he wouldn't listen because he was younger, less experienced, and the king valued his advisor's word. But the prince knew," he continues.

"He knew that the advisor was plotting to steal the throne. And worse, that he wasn't working alone. There were others. Men who wanted the crown. Men who were willing to bleed the kingdom dry to have it. So the prince," Seamus says, "lured his men to a place where the advisor believed their enemies were. And the prince did what had to be done. Killed them all."

My heart stutters.

"His boss, his king, called. Asked if there were survivors. The prince knew that if he told the truth, if he said there was one left, the woman he loved would be hunted down. So he lied. Told his boss everyone was dead. But she lived," he says softly.

"The woman the prince loved, she lived. He kept his distance. Let her believe he didn't love her. Took the fall, went to prison. He deserved it. He wasn't innocent. But while behind bars, he found out she was engaged. That she was moving on."

He exhales.

"So he escaped. Came for her. But it was all to keep her. All to make her his. And he had a plan," he whispers. "To take the throne. To rule, with her by his side. And once he had it... he'd make peace with the Russians. He'd do right by her family. And put an end to war. And they did end the war," he finishes.

"Because he kept his vow. Loved her like she was a queen. And in the end, they ruled together. She was light to his dark. Kind and just, where he was brutal. And the king and queen lived happily ever after."

I fall asleep to those words. A fairy tale of blood and crowns. Thrones. Betrayal. Power.

I WAKE the next morning strangely refreshed, even though I dreamed all night, vivid, violent dreams of king-doms and broken loyalties, of bloodied hands and golden crowns.

I roll over.

Seamus isn't in bed.

I glance around the room, instinct prickling... and then I see him.

Outside.

Oh. My. God.

I saw him last night, of course. But I was too shy, too drained to really see him. Now though?

Holy hell.

He's drenched in sweat, shirtless, gleaming under the early sun, wearing nothing but a pair of black sports shorts and trainers. His body is carved, every muscle pulled taut, every inch of him straining with energy. He moves like a predator who's just been uncaged.

I watch him run. Then I see him stop, grab a pull-up bar I hadn't even noticed yesterday, and lift himself, body flexing, muscles bulging. Again. And again. Arms trembling, veins taut, chest heaving. It's mesmerizing.

This is my husband. This living, breathing, sweating god of a man is *mine*.

My breasts feel full. My thighs ache. I can feel that pulse low in my belly, needy and warm and desperate. I swallow again and just watch him, helpless against it.

He lets go of the bar and drops to the ground, crunches, elbow to knee, elbow to knee. Controlled. Brutal. Perfect. He's back up, doing tricep dips against a thick bench, over and over, pushing behind him like it's nothing. Then he's off, sprinting around the property in hard, fast laps.

Some men hit the gym.

Seamus? He builds his kingdom with his bare hands under open skies.

The earth is hard-packed beneath him, a mix of sun-scorched gravel and patches of grass. There's a homemade training setup near the edge of the property, ropes hanging from a tree, kettlebells, and tires flipped on their sides. He doesn't need machines. He *is* the machine. This man was forged for war, for survival.

I don't know if he sees me watching from the window, but my god, I see him.

And I can't look away.

I should pull myself away, make breakfast, explore the kitchen, do something useful. There has to be more food in this house, and I want to feed him. But... I can't move.

Because this man is a paragon of masculine perfection.

My king.

My monster.

My husband.

I think of the story he told me of the prince, the usurpers, the woman, and her family.

The war. The peace. He made peace.

Can I trust him?

God, I want to. I want to so badly, my heart aches with it. My soul reaches for him like a magnet pulled to its twin.

But I don't know if I can. Not yet.

And then he's off again, running like the wind, muscle and sweat and fire. Untouchable. Untamed.

There's something wild and tender all at once about the way he trains. It's not just strength, but survival. And as I watch, my whole body responds.

I'm watching a man become mine. And with every movement, every flex, every breath, my body burns hotter.

And hotter.

So aroused. So deep in this. My nipples are tight, beaded like pebbles, and my mouth is desert dry. I can't stand the suspense another second.

I remember the way he touched me that first time, how careful he was, how gentle, and I remind myself that this is who he can be with me. Who cares what he's like with everyone else?

I was raised by brutal men. Vicious, wild, unrelenting. But to me? To me, they've always been tender. That contradiction is carved into my bones. I watch him now, my breath catching in my throat.

Heat unfurls low in my belly, blooming, spreading, consuming me like wildfire. I'm burning from the inside out.

I've never felt anything like this. It's not just lust, it's something electric, something sharp and sweet. Every nerve ending is singing. My mouth is dry, but my thoughts spiral into want, into need, into a depth I've never tasted before.

Am I afraid? Maybe. Or maybe fear's just something I'm used to, something I've always mistook for anticipation. But this... he was gentle with me. He listened.

When I trembled, he didn't mock me. He steadied me. His hands, iron-strong but unyielding in their care, held me steady while his eyes, god, those eyes, looked through me. Past the fear. Past the front. He saw me.

And now? Now I'm aching. I want to be claimed by Seamus McCarthy. I need to be.

I pull myself away from the window, still raw and vibrating from watching him.

I pick up my phone. It's been off all night, charging on the side table. I hesitated turning it on, terrified of what messages might wait for me. Ember. Anissa. Ruthie, Vadka's wife. People I loved, people I left behind. People who saw.

Ruthie had been soft with me, like a sister. She had her own story, her own pain. And now she's pregnant. Of course she'd reach out. They all saw me get taken, but I told them, I told them I loved him. Would they even believe me?

My hands shake as I turn on my phone. I brace for a flood, but it's only four.

One is from Rafail.

> **Rafail**
> Even though you're married to Seamus McCarthy, I will protect you, Zoya. I'm one phone call away. I know you said what you did to prevent bloodshed. But if he still lets you keep your phone, if you're still in contact with me, I need you to use it. Please. Text me. I should've reached out sooner.

My heart stutters. He thinks Seamus took my phone. Why would he think that? Would Seamus do something like that? Or is that what Rafail would do?

Another text.

> **Rodion**
> Hey, sweetheart. Just tell me if you're okay. If he hurts you, if he even lays a finger on you, Zoya, I swear to god, I will drop everything and come.

Then Semyon. Always different. Always distant. His mind works in straight lines and sharp turns, and his texts sound like they were drafted for a military debrief.

> **Semyon**
> Zoya. Are you alright? Do you need
> assistance? Is there anything I can do?

And then, finally, Ruthie.

> **Ruthie**
> Sweetie, your brothers are losing it. I don't
> think I've ever seen Rafail cry. But he did.
> He's terrified that you're only there because
> you had to be. That you told us you loved
> Seamus to stop the bloodshed. Are you
> okay? I don't think you made it up.
> Did you?

My hands are shaking now as I answer.

To Ruthie:

> I didn't make it up. I do love him. I'm sorry.
> Please forgive me.

To Rodion:

> I love you so much. I'll tell you if anything
> happens, but trust me, he takes care of me.

To Semyon:

> I'm here of my own will. Please believe that.

To Rafail:

> I'm so sorry. I feel like I betrayed all of you.
> But it's true. I do love him.

I put the phone down and step back like it's burned me. More texts start to come in, pings and buzzes vibrating on the counter, but I can't bring myself to look. Not now. I need space from the guilt, the love, the war between loyalty to my family and my vows to him.

Seamus is my husband now. That has to mean something. Doesn't it?

I need to cool down. I need to stop thinking about the window and the way my body reacted to seeing him shirt-less, the way my chest still burns from the heat of it. I step into the hallway. It's oddly narrow for a house this size. The floor creaks beneath my bare feet as I pass by closed doors.

And then I pause.

One door is different. Not just shut, but locked. Solid. Old. The kind of old that knows things.

My curiosity flares. Why this door? Why locked? Why does it feel... sacred? Or secret?

I try the handle—no give. Firm and locked tight.

What's in there?

A private office? Something personal? Secure documents?

Or something darker?

Maybe I've watched too many true crime documentaries, but a chill crawls up my spine. Could be bodies. Could be secrets. Could be a red room of pain.

God.

I shake it off and head toward the kitchen. I need to ground myself. I need to do something.

Feed him. That's what I do. I take care of the people I love.

In the kitchen, I find more eggs. Oatmeal. Bread but nothing else to bake with. No matter, I can make something.

There are two wide windows above the sink. The view is breathtaking, the Irish coastline bathed in morning light. It looks like something from a dream. Nothing Seamus ever described to me did it justice.

And then, movement.

My eyes catch on him outside. Running shirtless, sweat gleaming on his skin. He's just finished lifting, probably, and now he's sprinting toward the house like he's chasing something.

Like he's chasing me.

God, he's beautiful. He always is, but when he runs, when he's wild and free and open like this, it's almost unbearable to watch. My heart thunders. My pulse flutters.

For a moment, I let myself believe.

Maybe this is real. Maybe this is my husband.

And then he's inside, windblown and flushed, his chest heaving as he brushes the sweat from his brow. His longish dark hair is damp and messy.

"Good morning, beautiful," he says, his voice low, roughened by exertion.

I'm already walking toward him, tea in hand. Ready to serve him. Ready to love him. Ready to fight every part of me that still doesn't know if she belongs here.

But maybe... maybe I do.

"You told me you like cream in your tea, no sugar, right?"

"Aye," he says. "Thank you, lass." He takes the tea, lifts it to his mouth, and takes a long sip. Exhales like the weight of the whole world is leaving his lungs.

His breathing begins to slow.

"You don't know what it's like to wake up and not be alone here anymore," he says quietly. There's something so raw in the way he says it, like he's afraid to name it, like saying it out loud will make it too real.

I don't say anything. Just reach for his hand.

It's maybe the first time I've initiated touching him, at least since we came here. My fingers curl gently around his, and I feel him still under my touch. Time feels suspended, hung in the air like dust in sunlight.

Two heartbeats.

"Any word from your family?" I ask softly as we sit on the stone steps outside.

The waves crash on the distant shore, and the scent of salt clings thick in the air. It's all wind and sea and salt air.

"Aye," he says, but doesn't offer any details. Just that one word, like it's enough. "And yours?"

"Yes." I nod. "They just want to make sure I'm okay. That I'm not here against my will."

He sets his cup down beside him, turns to me, and reaches for my hand again.

"And are you, Zoya?"

I let out a breath, long and shaky, like I'm about to hand him a piece of me I've kept tucked away.

"You're the only man I've ever wanted, Seamus. Things haven't gone the way I would've chosen... but maybe I can hope a little anyway."

Because it's true. All of it.

"I'm here because I want to be," I tell him. "With you."

He doesn't hesitate. His hand tightens around mine.

"And I will have you fall in love with me, Zoya."

I rest my head on his shoulder. His arm curls around my waist, drawing me into him like a secret he wants to keep close.

"You know, I used to want a bakery," I say, curled into his warmth. One foot is tucked under me, the other brushing against his leg like it's accidental. It's not.

He looks at me like he's waiting for the punchline.

"You? A bakery?"

I nod, smiling. "I liked the smell of baked things. Bread. Cinnamon. Sugar. Things that prove something soft can survive heat."

His eyes sharpen. There's something about that that gets to him.

"Aye. You can have that, if you want."

"Do you have one here, in Ballyhock?"

"No."

He starts listing the places they do have. His voice goes soft with familiarity; he knows every corner, every person behind every counter. It draws something from me.

"Aye, well, there's a place called the Ice Cream Shoppe," he starts. "Self-explanatory. And there's coffee… let's see. Let me tell you about Ballyhock."

Time halts again, a little.

"I'm eager to get to the actual city," I tell him.

"So we have a place called the Cottage Brew, right? Cozy coffee. Soda bread. Then there's The Blimey Pub, which kinda speaks for itself. Do you like Guinness?" he asks.

"I'm not sure. I've never had one."

"Wait, *what*? You've never had a fucking Guinness?" he says, utterly baffled, like I've just confessed a mortal sin.

I laugh softly.

"We'll fix that, love, we will."

"My brothers didn't really like me drinking," I confess.

He laughs, shakes his head like he can't believe it. "They practically wean us on Guinness in our bottles."

I laugh as he continues.

"There's ice cream there now. Gelato. We're getting fancy, thanks to the Italians. D'Agostino owns the Italian shop. And there's this place called The Cheeky Mackerel Coastal Eatery. But no bakery. Not yet." He pauses.

"Do you want to open one?" he asks. "Like Anya."

The mention of her hits strange… two worlds colliding.

I think about Anya's bakery, the one that's nearly caused war between rival factions, because location is everything.

"Do you want to open a bakery?" he repeats.

I hesitate. "I don't know. Give me time, please."

Because it feels like betrayal. Leaving my family. Marrying Seamus. Starting over with flour-dusted dreams and a storefront window.

I don't say all that, just keep it tucked inside.

"You want me to open a bakery in the middle of a feud?"

He shrugs. It's slow and deliberate.

"I've seen stranger things." Then he leans back.

The light catches his jaw, the faint stubble there. He's not smiling, not exactly, but his face is softer than I've ever seen. If I reached out, I think he'd welcome it.

"Did you ever want anything silly?" I ask.

He looks away, and his jaw tightens.

"Yeah," he says. "Peace."

That silences me. Not because it's dramatic, but because it's real.

So real.

"Let's say we had children," I continue, turning my gaze to the window. "Do you like kids, Seamus?"

"I'd like *mine*."

There's honesty there again, the kind you don't argue with.

"You planning something, love?"

"I am." But I don't tell him what.

"If I had children, it'd be a union of two families, wouldn't it?" I tease, rolling my eyes toward him. "It's hypothetical. Humor me. What would you name a boy?"

"Oh, I don't know. Never really thought about it. But I know a girl's name."

"Yeah?"

"Caitlin. After mam. Once you meet her, you'll understand."

"That's beautiful." I breathe the name. "Caitlin. You love her?"

"Of course I do. Anyone who meets her does."

I look away then, suddenly nervous, like I'm breaking open in front of him.

"What's the matter, Zoya?"

I don't answer, not until he squeezes my knees, and not gently.

"Remember the rules," he says softly. "Tell me the truth. What are you thinking, love?"

So I do. I tell him.

"What if your family doesn't love me? What if they don't like me? What if I don't fit in? I'm different, you know."

He turns to face me fully. His eyes hold mine, unwavering.

"Anybody who doesn't love you," he says, "is a goddamn fool."

And I believe him.

Because it's Seamus. Because he says it like it's the most obvious truth in the world.

A long silence falls between us. It's not awkward, but comfortable. Natural.

"I like this," I whisper when he brushes his thumb across the top of my hand. His eyes flick to mine, then tilt toward the sea. He cants his head. "What's 'this'?" he murmurs. "The quiet? The talking? The solitude?"

I don't answer. I just look out at the sea with him.

It's endless and constant.

"I like this too," he says, his voice quieter now. Thoughtful.

"I don't want to be negative, darlin', but I have to tell you. This quiet, it's the calm before the storm." His jaw tightens, and his breath catches like he already knows it too.

I nod.

"You know, I've got fears of my own," he says after a long pause.

"Tell me." The tea's grown cold in my mug, and my belly growls with hunger.

"I want to keep you."

He looks away. Then looks back.

"I know," I tell him with a shrug. "But what's wrong with that?"

"I don't know how to keep something safe unless I'm holding it so tight it might suffocate."

I reach out and touch his hand.

"You don't have to hold me so tight," I whisper. "Choose me, Seamus, if you have to. Then let me choose you back."

His fingers wrap tighter around mine, not a prison. And for the first time, he doesn't try to answer with words. He just holds me.

"I need a shower," he says finally. "Join me?"

CHAPTER 17

SEAMUS

I ᴋɴᴏᴡ my time alone with Zoya is ending. Today could be the last day I have her before my family comes for me. We're on borrowed time.

There's been a whole bleeding clan of bastards trying to shove me off the throne. But I've still got a few loyals. Real ones. And I didn't even bother to hide her. Could've, if I wanted. Hell, part of me still wants to.

But I want to claim my wife. I *need* to.

I want Zoya in a way I've never wanted anyone. It's time.

She follows me to the bedroom. She's barely dressed, just a T-shirt and a thin pair of panties, and the way she peels them off without hesitation tells me everything I need to know.

I can't believe she's *mine*.

Her eyes are dark, heavy-lidded, watching me from the doorway like she's already waiting to be devoured.

"Come here," I say, crooking a finger at her.

She walks toward me slowly, lashes lowered. The perfect goddamn submissive. She's everything I never knew I needed. When she gets to me, I lift her, and her legs wrap around my waist like we've done this a thousand times.

"I have so many things I want to ask you, Seamus," she whispers, her voice hitching in her throat.

"Ask me anything, doll."

I kiss her forehead. Her temple. Her cheek. Her jaw. Her shoulder. "I told you, I'll answer anything you want. What is it, love?" I murmur.

"So, those texts from my family."

I go still.

"Are you going to intercept my texts?"

"Not a feckin' chance," I growl, kissing her hard, right on the mouth. "I came here. I took you with me because you belong with me, Zoya. You know that as well as I do, don't you?"

She stares at me, like she's waiting for the catch. There is no catch.

"You were set to marry some gobshite who wouldn't know yer worth if it kicked him square in the stones. There's no way in hell my family and yours would've agreed to it. So I made it happen."

"Quite a visual..." she mutters, her eyes twinkling at me.

I lower my voice. "I made that happen because that's what I bloody do, Zoya. Some people hate that about me. I fucking thrive on it."

I lean in, pressing my lips to hers again.

"I wanted you. So I took you. And now that I have you, I swear I'll take the best care of you. Take your phone? No. But other things, love…"

I kiss her mouth again, my tongue teasing hers, just for a fraction of a second before I pull away.

"You may not get the privacy you want. Because I won't be letting you out of me bloody sight."

She laughs. "Why not?"

I shake my head, walking her into the bathroom with me. My body aches, my muscles are sore, and sweat is soaking my skin. But none of that matters. Not when I want her like this.

I turn on the shower, spin her around, and give a sharp slap to her perfect, perky little arse.

"You're fair beggin' for a proper putting in your place, aren't you now?" I ask.

"Put me in my place," she whispers back, and her eyes flutter half-lidded with anticipation. She likes this. Loves it. "Yes."

My sweet, dark little girl.

I guide her under the water, letting it soak into her hair, and begin washing her slowly. Reverently.

I lather her hair, watching the suds run down her neck, her breasts. Her perfect, upturned breasts. I rinse them off, then bring her nipple to my mouth and scrape each one with my teeth. She moans, head tilting. I take the opportunity to kiss the trail of sudsy water down her neck.

"Let me wash you too? Please," she says, her hands already on me, possessive and eager.

"Tell me," she murmurs, fingers trailing over my chest, "how you're not going to let me out of your sight, Seamus."

"You won't have a bodyguard, Zoya," I tell her. "I'm your shadow, your bloody shield, your man for every damn thing."

"And what, you'll be with me all the time?" she teases.

"It's feasible now," I say, my voice dark with promise.

My hands roam over the curve of her arse, and all I can think about is how fucking deserving she is of a proper spanking. I want to show her what it is to unravel for me, piece by bloody piece. She's been raised hard. Firm. She knows the Bratva's world.

She's about to know mine.

"What about when you work?" she asks.

"I'll take you with me."

"And when you travel?"

"I'll take you with me."

She grins. "What about when I need to pee in peace?"

"Now you're just looking for trouble," I say, gripping her arse and hauling her leg up onto mine. Her hands, those wicked, beautiful hands, are gripping my shoulders, my chest, my biceps like she's trying to memorize them.

She grabs my arse. I groan.

I want to take her right here, right now. But I'm not going to claim her virginity in the bloody shower. No. This is just the prelude. The foreplay. I want to make this last.

So I cup her lovely tits in my hands.

"Quiet now, love. Remember what I said about obeying me? There'll be time for questions later."

She moans as I roll her nipples between my fingers.

"What do you say, Zoya?" I murmur, a threat and a promise wrapped in velvet.

"Yes, sir," she breathes out. "Yes, sir."

She melts against me like honey.

"Tip your head back," I say.

She obeys. I finish washing her hair, then rinse. She does the same for me while my hands explore her all over again.

And this is just the beginning.

She's slick between her thighs, so fucking tight I can barely breathe. I slide three fingers inside her, slowly, working them in and out as her hips jerk and shudder. A soft, desperate moan spills from her lips, and I press a thumb gently, reverently, against her clit. She cries out again, a sound that's more than just pleasure; it's surrender.

I'm going to make her body sing for me. I'm going to train her to crave my cock, my mouth, my teeth, every dark and dangerous part of me.

"This is what you want, Seamus? Me?" she asks, trembling. "Are you sure?"

I've never been surer of anything in my fucking life. I shut off the shower, come out dripping, steam curling off our skin, and towel us both off. I wrap her in a thick towel, then lift her into my arms and carry her straight to my bed, where she fucking belongs.

We're both clean now. Naked. Exposed. Vulnerable.

I take a moment to hold her, then lay her down on my bed like she's the most precious thing in the world. "Hands above your head," I say.

"Keep them there until I tell you to move. Aye?"

"Yes, sir," she whispers, her eyes locked on mine like she trusts me with everything she is. She's still damp, water droplets clinging to the tips of her lashes like dew on petals. I dry her again, careful, gentle.

I kiss each droplet, one by one. I watch her lashes flutter closed under my touch. She looks like she's dreaming, and I want her to *feel* exactly that. Like this is the best dream, the kind you beg not to wake up from.

I'll protect her with everything I have, even when things get brutal. Even when the world outside these walls comes crashing in and tries to take her from me. I'll keep her safe.

"Part your legs, wife," I growl into her ear. That one word, *wife*, grounds me. Feeds something primal inside me.

"I want to taste you. I've been fucking dying to taste you. But hear me now, if you come before I give you permission, I will take you over my knee and punish you."

She lets out a shaky breath. Her hands stay put, but she arches just slightly. Just enough to test me.

"If your hands move, I'll edge you until you're screaming for release. Understand me?"

Her reply is a whisper, teasing, defiant. "Tell me how you're going to punish me."

I slam my palm against her arse, hard enough to make her gasp, but soft enough to make her wet. "Hush now, love, or I'll have to gag that pretty mouth of yours."

Her eyes go wide, but a sly little smile tugs at her lips. She's my sassy little girl. Always pushing. Always testing. I click my tongue and shake my head because she knows what she's doing to me.

She wants this.

I reach across, grab the pillow and rip the pillowcase off, twisting it into a makeshift gag. I tie it around her head. "Bite that if you need to scream," I murmur, brushing my mouth over her cheek, then down to her throat. "Permission granted," I whisper.

Her eyes widen, and I swear she moans.

Then I take my time. I kiss down her body, tasting every inch. From the soft curve of her shoulder to the swell of her breasts, to the sweet dip beneath. Her skin is silk beneath my tongue. I press kisses down her stomach, trace the indent of her belly button with my tongue, slide lower, until I'm between her thighs again.

I spread her open and breathe her in like she's the only air I want in my lungs.

She smells like sin and salvation, like sex and innocence, both wrapped in one perfect fucking contradiction. I groan when I slide my tongue between her folds, slow and deep, and taste her. *Fuck.* She's everything.

I tease her, circle her clit with my tongue, then suck gently. Her hips jerk up, but she can't make a sound with the gag in place. She's squirming, trembling.

I brace her with my hands on either side of her hips and start to lap at her again. I'm addicted. My cock is leaking, aching, and dripping with pre-cum.

She screams into the gag as I bring her to the edge. And when she starts to come, I don't stop. I ride her through every wave, licking her gently through the aftershocks, kissing her thighs.

She tries to push me away, as if she's too sensitive, and it's too much. But I'm not done. I'm nowhere near fucking done.

She'll come again.

So I worship her... over and over, until she's writhing again. Until she's begging without words and comes a second time on my tongue.

Finally, I pull away just enough to remove the gag.

She gasps, her breathing ragged. "Oh my god, Seamus... Oh

dear god…" She moans it like a prayer, like she's finally seen heaven.

I cradle her face and kiss her gently. "I want you to remember this," I whisper. "I need you to remember this. I meant to take my time. I meant to make you come again, but now… now I feckin' *need* you."

My cock is so hard it hurts. I'm shaking with how much I want her.

"May I touch you?" she whispers. Her voice is soft, unsure, and so sweet it tears me apart.

"Say it again," I murmur, trembling. "Say my name, *mo chroí*. No one else gets to. Just you."

"Please, Seamus," she says. "I want you inside me. I want you to complete me. I've been dreaming about this."

"Dreaming about this," I echo, my heart in my throat. She's my sweet, perfect angel. God help me, I don't want to hurt her. She's tight. She's untouched. And she's mine.

I'll burn down the whole fucking world before I ever let her go.

I want to claim her.

I want to pound into her. I want to erase the existence of anything but me from her mind. I want to mark every single thought, every nerve ending, with the weight of me. I want to brand her from the inside out.

But I can't… I won't. She needs time and patience.

So I take my time. She's so wet, open, and waiting for me. My self-control is hanging by a goddamn thread.

I can see the arousal in her eyes, feel it dripping down the curve of her ass. Beautiful, beautiful girl. "I love you, Zoya," I whisper.

As I glide the head of my cock to her entrance, emotion chokes me. "I love you so damn much." I can't breathe. I've never cried in my entire life, not once, but now? I feel that pressure building, coiled behind my eyes. I don't let it fall. I can't. Not yet.

I clear my throat and push in just the tip, sliding gently, so gently, into her slick heat. It's fucking killing me to hold back, to not bury myself all the way. My restraint feels like punishment.

Gently, I glide into her, back and forth, teasing us both. "Oh, darling girl," I whisper, as I slowly push my cock deeper into her. "Oh, my sweet angel..."

"Oh god, *Seamus*. Please..." she moans, her voice trembling, breaking. Her legs wrap tightly around me like she can't bear a single inch of space between us.

"Yes... yes," she whispers. Her arms come around my neck, and her soft lips meet mine. I kiss her, deep, consuming, while I move inside her.

Slow. Rhythmic. I thrust into her with pure, focused precision. It feels so fucking right. Like the way it was always meant to be.

I thrust in gently, shaking with the effort of holding myself back. "Does it hurt, love?" I ask, brushing her hair back. "Tell me if I'm hurting you."

I say it again, quieter. "I need you to tell me. The last thing I ever want to do is hurt my angel."

"Just a little," she says, biting her lip. "It's just tight... but I'm wet and..." She pauses. "Seamus?"

"Yes, love?" I still, waiting for her.

"I don't care if it hurts," she whispers, her eyes wide and unwavering. "You're the only one I want to feel this with. Please, take me. Take me with everything."

My shoulders are trembling from holding back, from not slamming into her the way my body's begging to. But I glide in again, slow and smooth. Her tight, hot, perfect pussy grips my cock like she was made for me.

In and out. In and out. I move in rhythm, matching her moans with every pulse. I continue pushing into her, losing myself.

"Oh, yes, please," she pants out. "Yes, that feels so good."

I thrust in and out, faster, deeper. I feel like a goddamn boy. I can't hold back much longer. I'm gonna come, and I can't stop it.

I have no control. She *owns* me. She's everything I ever fucking wanted.

I'm shaking when I ease into her again, and again.

Over and over. I've conquered cities, torn through empires, claimed my entire clan, and yet here, with her? I can't even hold myself together. I'm unraveling.

I've always prided myself on self-control. But now? Now it's slipping. It's taking everything in me not to pound into her like an animal.

"More, Seamus," she whispers. "I can take it."

"Love..." I breathe, then push all the way in. She gasps, sharp, breathless.

I reach up, caressing her breasts, holding her with reverence. My large hands curve over her shoulders, anchoring her to me as I begin to build a deeper rhythm.

In and out. In and out. Her body trembling under mine, giving herself fully.

She lets out a soft, hoarse breath. "I'm going to come again, I think."

"You said it, love. Just let go. It's all yours now, every last bit of it."

This is hers now.

I feel her climax around me, tight, clenched, then softening as she moans and her eyes flutter shut.

I can't help it anymore. I spill into her. Claiming her. My hot seed lashes against her walls as I groan, my body bucking with the force of release. Even now, I'm holding back. Still gentle, still careful.

Slowly, I thrust into her again, easing out, then in. Soft. Rhythmic. Ecstasy floods me as she holds me.

I'm boneless, paralyzed, spent.

My forehead touches hers. I'm breathless. "Oh god, Zoya... That was perfect," I whisper.

My body's still damp, a sheen of sweat clinging to me, but I don't care. She kisses my shoulder and whispers back, "Perfect."

Then she murmurs, "Hold me, Seamus."

Still inside her, I fold my arms around her body and hold her close. That's when I notice the tears streaking down her cheeks.

"Zoya?" My voice drops. "Oh my god. I'm a fucking asshole. What happened? Are you okay? I hurt you."

She shakes her head. "No... no..." she chokes out. Her eyes are wet, and when she blinks, fresh tears fall. "I don't know why I'm crying. But it's not because it hurt, I promise."

She clutches me tighter. "I'd do that a hundred times over. It's just..."

She sniffs.

"When you left... When you didn't come back, Seamus..."

She's crying freely now, burying her head in the crook of my arm. My own throat tightens, and my nose starts to tingle. I fight to stay composed.

My sweet, sweet girl.

"When you left... I thought you were using me. I thought you were just... just trying to get to my family. I thought I was a pawn. That you didn't really want me."

I stay silent, even though I want to beg her forgiveness. But she needs to speak. She needs this, and I owe her every word.

Of course she felt that. Of course she doubted.

"Even on my wedding day... when I agreed to the arrangement," she goes on, "I told myself I'd only fallen in love with an image of you. That it wasn't real. That I was just some foolish girl..."

Oh, Zoya. She's twisting that knife, and she doesn't even know it.

I nod slowly and hold her tighter to me. "Yes, angel. Go on."

"You came to me that night," she continues. "The night before my wedding. And I... I still thought it was a game. That you were playing me. That you were clearing the board for your family."

She swallows hard. "And then you took me. And married me."

She looks up at me, her voice a whisper, her face shattered. "Even then, Seamus... even then, I wasn't sure. I still had doubts. I still wondered..."

Her words fall from her lips like a confession, raw, ragged, and aching.

Her heartbeat slows beneath my palm. My hand is perfectly cupped right between her breasts, where I can feel it. My thumb and forefinger curve around her side, instinctive, protective. I want to hear that steady, comforting beat under my touch.

"Now there's not a doubt in my mind," she says, with no hesitation. "Not a doubt that you loved me. Not a doubt that you ever wanted me. I know now. I know you wanted me. That you waited for me. That you broke out of a damn prison for me." She sniffs. "And I know, Seamus." She says it soft. Steady. "I know that you love me as much as I love you."

I want to burn this moment into my memory. Me, with her. Holding her. Tucking her against my chest like she belongs there.

This... this feels like the edge of heaven.

But I can feel the tug, the fear of losing her. Of losing *this*. Raw vulnerability.

Certainty.

Something's going to drag me under, any second.

"I love you, Seamus."

But before I can respond, before I can breathe, a sharp sound slices through the air.

CHAPTER 18

ZOYA

I SHOULD MOVE, I want to move, but my limbs are limp. Jelly. I'm locked in place by the echo of that sound.

Then he moves, fast, out of bed in a blur. One finger pointed at me like a warning shot. His eyes burn.

"You stay right there, Zoya. You hear me? I'm not fucking around."

His voice isn't the lover's voice I know, the one that rasps into my skin, the one that begs and whispers and curses when he's inside me.

No, this is the commander.

This is the man people fear. The man they whisper about when they think he isn't listening. But I don't fear him. I never have. Because I know exactly what he is. What he'll do to protect me.

I swallow hard and nod. My throat is dry, but my voice is steady.

"I know how to use a gun," I say.

"You fucking heard me," he barks. "Stay *there*!"

He's never raised his voice at me, not like this. I stare, wide-eyed. I've never seen him like this.

Controlled. Fierce. Terrifying in his love.

"Yes, sir," I whisper.

And then he pulls on boxers like it's nothing. I don't even know how he moves so fast.

A beat later, he's yanking open the drawer beside the bed, pulling out the biggest fucking gun I've ever seen, and I know guns. Thanks to my brothers, thanks to Rafail Kopolov, I've seen an arsenal.

A semi-automatic. Sleek. Merciless. He loads it, cocks it, then cradles it like an extension of his own arm. Then he's out, moving fast, and locks the door behind him. One click, two clicks, three. Then I hear it, a mechanical hum. Bars slam down over the windows.

He's locked me behind a goddamn fortress.

And now I'm wide awake. I sit straight up in bed. My heart is racing, every nerve screaming. The adrenaline surges so fast I feel like I might throw up.

I pull the blankets up to cover my body, like I can hide from whatever's coming. Who's out there? Has my family come to claim me? Has his? Or worse, an enemy?

Then I hear him. His voice, sharp as a blade.

"Who the fuck's there?"

The front door groans open.

Another loud noise.

A voice, rough, distant.

Then silence. Nothing else.

It's killing me. Is he okay?

I glance around the room and see the drawer. I need something. I need to be ready.

There.

He left me a weapon, a gesture that says everything without saying it. Trust. Preparation. Protection.

I reach for it and check it. It's loaded, and the safety's off.

This one isn't for warnings; this is meant to kill.

I know what it does. I've seen what these bullets do to a man. They tear through flesh and twist organs into pulp. I hold it steady. My hands might be small, but thanks to Rafail, I know exactly what the fuck I'm doing.

I wait. Minutes crawl by. More voices. Another minute. Still, nothing.

His cum is still leaking from me, slick between my thighs and soaking the sheets beneath me. My breasts are red, marked by him. Every touch still lingers. The way he took me, there was no doubt. No question.

He does love me. He proved it. Every inch of him. Every kiss. Every growl and every gentle press.

I have to trust him now.

My sweet, wild man.

My beautiful, broken monster.

He *has* to be okay.

I clutch the gun tighter. He told me to stay. To wait. And I want to. God, I want to. But what if... what if he's hurt? What if that... *no.* I can't go there. But what if someone has him, and I'm just sitting here with a weapon in hand, doing nothing?

I run to the window. Sunlight slices through the bars. There's nothing but trees, nothing I can see.

I'm not sure I could get out, even if I wanted to.

And I start to think about disobeying him. I don't really fear punishment, but god, I don't want him upset with me.

But I don't know what he'd do if I did disobey him. And honestly? I don't want to know. I like pleasing him. I need to please him. That furrow between his brows when he's worried, it fucking wrecks me. I'd do anything to smooth it away.

I want him. I *need* him.

But if someone's got him...

And then, I hear it. Voices again.

One of them is his.

My breath whooshes out, and relief slams through me so hard I nearly drop the gun. I press my forehead against the cool wall and let myself feel it.

He's okay. He's alive.

I throw on one of his shirts and a pair of panties, just in time. Footsteps echo outside the door.

He opens the door.

Then he sees me by the window, dressed, with a gun gripped in both hands.

He holds up a palm..

"Easy, lass. Lower the gun. There's no threat. Not now. Put it down, Zoya."

I nod and gently lay the gun on his armoire.

"All right, now, lass." I walk over to him, tentative, trying to peer over his shoulder, but he's too damn big.

"I was scared for you," I whisper, tears pricking at my eyes.

He takes up the entire doorway, a broad wall of protection, so I can't see anybody behind him.

"It's all right," he says, though his voice doesn't match the words. There's something in his eyes, clouded and troubled, like a storm barely held back. "It's all right. For now," he amends. "Jesus, Mary, and Joseph. It's my mate."

He walks toward me, his muscles tense, voice edged in warning as he growls over his shoulder, "Stay back. My wife's not dressed. You'll not see her like this." Then louder, harsher, "Stay the fuck back, or I'll blow your fucking bollocks to bits."

"Easy, McCarthy. Jesus," comes another voice. It's rough, a little higher pitched than Seamus's.

"Let's get you dressed," Seamus says, like it's a casual thing, but I can hear it in his tone—if he could wrap me up from head to toe, hide every inch of me, he would.

Funny thing is, he's hardly dressed himself. I shoot him a glance. "You're walking around in boxers," I tell him.

"Zoya," he says, his words thick with warning, like he's dragging my name across coals.

And even now... even with all that tension humming through the air, it makes my heartbeat race. I like it when he gets like that with me, stern, possessive. Makes me feel small. Protected. Desired.

I grab a pair of leggings and slide into them. I glance at him. He's watching me, eyes narrowing like he's trying to figure out if I'm wearing a bra.

My breasts are too small for that to matter. "Nobody's going to see me," I mutter, grabbing my sweatshirt.

"Take my sweatshirt," he says firmly, as he pulls on a pair of jeans.

I open my mouth to sass him, maybe say something snarky about him walking around half naked, too, but I shut it just as fast. Probably not the time.

"Good girl," he murmurs, and damn, I like the way he rolls the Rs. "Come meet my best mate."

I follow him into the living room. Seated at the table is a large man with light-brown hair that curls at the ends, his brown eyes dancing with something unreadable. He's built like Seamus, broad and imposing. He wears a faded tank top and worn jeans. Muscular arms, tattooed sleeves.

Tough, but there's something warm in the way he looks at me.

"My cousin, Colm," Seamus says. "Colm." He lifts his chin a bit when he says it, pride in the word.

"My wife, Zoya."

"Very pleased to meet you, Zoya," Colm says, giving me a respectful nod.

"Pleased to meet you too," I reply softly. "I was just about to make Seamus some breakfast. Are you hungry?" I ask, still standing.

"Zoya. Sit." Seamus barks the order, and I sit without thinking, hands folded in my lap. Colm's eyes sparkle, like he knows exactly who Seamus is and what I'm learning about him too.

Apparently, he knows Seamus's ways well.

Seamus rests his larger hand atop mine. "I know, beautiful. And I promise, I'll give you another chance. But for now, I want you to sit." His voice is low, protective, not patronizing. He's not treating me like a child. He's shielding me. There's a difference.

"Now, angel," Seamus says, "Colm's come to tell me what's going on."

"I think if it weren't for you, ma'am, your father would've stormed the damn castle already," Colm adds, half-joking, half-serious.

Seamus lets out a breath, then turns to me. "Me mom has a way of gentling me dad like no one else could. At least a little."

"I think your dad suspects something's up," Colm says. "But you've got a lot of explaining to do, don't you?"

"No," Seamus says, quiet but final. "I've got very little explaining to do to anybody. What I have a lot of is work."

He turns to me, his steady gaze locking on mine. "I won't apologize for taking Zoya. She's mine. She belongs to me. There is none other."

Colm smiles and nods once. "Okay."

That's so very him. So very Seamus.

"My plan is to stay here with my wife as long as I can," Seamus says, with calm determination. "And when it's time... when it's time for me to go, I will. I reckon we've got at least one more night."

Colm winces. "I think your mom probably talked your dad into that, eh? Branson's gone for now."

"Fuck Branson," Seamus growls.

God. I remember the story he told me about the king and his trusted advisor, the one who tried to usurp the throne.

I know exactly who Branson is.

Colm holds Seamus's gaze without flinching. "It's time," he says.

Seamus doesn't blink, but something inside him gives, something quiet and worn thin. That weight, the fatigue of it, slides into his features.

"I figured," he answers. There's no fight in it, but there's no surrender either. Just inevitability. Colm's eyes flick to me again, sharp and cold, but not unkind. He's measuring me, calculating, adding up the cost of who I am and what I've already changed.

"They know," Colm says. "Or they will. You made it clear when you took her."

"Aye," Seamus replies. No apology in it. Just fact.

"Then get ahead of it, Seamus. Show your face before they start knocking down doors. You know how this works."

His voice shifts, deeper now, more serious, like the gravity just increased in the room. "You know your father. And you'll lose whatever grace you've got left if you don't move now."

Seamus doesn't speak right away. His jaw locks tight, that familiar twitch in his cheek giving him away. He stares at Colm like he's not sure whether to thank him or break something.

Then, finally, he gives a single nod. "Tomorrow, we'll go."

My heart stutters. Tomorrow. It's not just a looming possibility anymore, but a promise. A plan.

We're leaving this little pocket of stolen peace. Walking straight into the fire, into the center of all the fury and judgment waiting for us. What we'll find on the other side, I can't even guess.

Separation, maybe. Or worse.

Colm exhales, and there's something gentler in him now. He turns to me with a nod. "Pleased to meet you, love," he says, and there's a softness in it I didn't expect. Then he's gone, turning on his heel and slipping out the door without another word.

The lock clicks behind him, and Seamus is already moving, bolting it. He presses his forehead to the frame, his breath shaky and low.

"Fuck," he mutters.

I wait... letting the silence bloom around us.

When he finally turns back to me, that same weariness clouds his eyes, but they're still alive. Still burning for me, even when everything else in him looks like it's cracking.

"Come here, angel," he murmurs tenderly.

So I go. I step into his arms like I've always belonged there. He wraps them around me, and I press my face to his chest. I fit perfectly. Like we were carved for this, made for each other in a world that wants us apart.

"Listen, Seamus," I whisper. "We're going to survive this, aren't we?"

"Of course we are," he says immediately, like the idea of failure isn't even a possibility. That fire I've come to trust flares in his voice.

"Then let's get it over with. We know what we need to do."

He pulls back just enough to see me. His gaze digs in, searching, wanting more than just agreement; he's looking for belief. He lifts his hand and brushes a knuckle under my chin, so soft it aches.

"Tell me," he says. "Tell me what you think we should do."

There's something raw in him now, unguarded. As if this moment, this invitation to be his equal, costs more than blood. Like letting me carry even a fraction of his burden is the most intimate thing he's ever done.

And I feel it. God, I feel it.

I swallow, my eyes locked to his. "We need to have a baby."

His eyes widen like I just set a star in his hands. Shock cracks through him but not fear. No, it's something gentler. Hope, maybe. Wonder.

"We do, don't we?" he says, his voice barely above a breath.

I nod. "Even your father... even my brother. They won't be able to argue with that. If we join our families—"

"Right," he cuts in, the spark catching hold. "I know it. A baby," he repeats, like he's still trying the word on. "I never thought I'd want one. Never been one for babies... But with you, darlin'..."

He trails off, shaking his head like he can't believe where his own heart has led him.

"Yes," I say quietly. "A baby. I know it won't fix everything. I know what we're about to face. It's going to be dangerous. Brutal."

I run my thumb along the line of his jaw, feeling the coarse heat of his stubble, the warmth of him. He catches my hand, presses a kiss to my thumb, and then sets both hands on my hips, grounding himself in me.

"We do," he agrees. "My family's wrath. Branson. And whatever your brother decides."

"My family," I say. "I'm stalling. As long as they think I'm safe... they won't strike. Not yet."

He nods slowly. "I know you believe that."

"But you don't."

"I can't."

And I get that. He's not wired for faith, not when all he's ever known is betrayal and survival. Hope isn't a luxury he trusts.

Thunder crashes above us, so loud and sudden, it jerks me back into my body. I flinch.

He chuckles deeply and pulls me tighter. "Just thunder, baby," he murmurs into my hair.

"I know," I say, but even as the words leave my mouth, lightning splits the sky again, so close it feels like it might tear the roof off. "It just seems... close."

"It is close," he murmurs, his gaze sweeping the windowpane. Outside, the sky has darkened, thick storm clouds blotting out the light. Then comes the rain, sharp, sudden, relentless. It lashes against the glass like it's trying to claw its way in.

"Good," he says, more to himself than to me, as if he's pleased. "We might lose power. But it'll buy us time."

Then he turns, his eyes catching the soft lamplight, and there's that glint again. That crooked, wicked gleam that lives in his smile like a secret only I know. The devil incarnate, grinning just for me. "My father's men don't like the rain."

"Good," I echo, mirroring his grin with one of my own. It's slower, warmer, a touch more dangerous. "Gives us a little time together."

"Aye," he rumbles, leaning in close, brushing his lips right against my cheek in a gesture that's more possessive than tender. "A little time to make that baby."

A flush blooms low and heavy in my belly, heat spreading like honey on hot skin, thick and unhurried. I match his grin without hesitation.

"Aye," I whisper back, letting the word roll from my tongue just like I know he loves it, soft and Irish and laced with something more than just affection.

He chuckles, a gravelly sound that stirs something primal in my chest.

"But first," he says, stepping back just enough to flash me a look. "Let's eat. I'm famished. Let me cook for you this time," he offers, a little too eager, like he's trying to prove something. There's affection behind the offer, sure, but also mischief.

I try, god, I try, not to grimace. But my face betrays me, and he sees it, clear as day.

He throws his head back and laughs. A real one, deep, rich, and unfiltered. It fills the room and warms the air.

"Come on now. You can teach me, can't you? Just rest a bit, love. I can handle pasta. Who can fuck up pasta?"

"Who indeed?" I mutter under my breath, smirking. I swat his ass as he turns toward the kitchen, and he yelps, grinning like a lunatic.

He pulls out a box of pasta, some off-brand thing I've never seen before, chucks it in a pot, and sets it to boil.

Five minutes later, it's chaos.

Somehow, he burns it. I don't even know how. One minute, the water's simmering like it should be, and the next, the fire alarm is wailing. And right in the middle of the madness, he grabs me and kisses me like the world's ending, and our food isn't ruined.

I double over laughing, uncontrollably, nearly wheezing. I almost pee myself from how baffled he looks, standing there with a wooden spoon like it's betrayed him.

"What the hell did I do wrong?" he says, dragging a hand through his hair.

"You let yourself get distracted by your new wife." I giggle, still catching my breath.

He groans like a man suffering in silence. "Fine. We'll come to an agreement. You cook, I clean, for all the meals, eh?"

"I like that deal," I say, my lips curling into something sly.

He pops open a bottle of red, something dark and probably expensive, and pours us each a glass. I rummage through his cabinets, find some meat in the fridge, a can of tomatoes, and a head of garlic that looks half alive. The basics. A few minutes later, the kitchen is thick with the smell of onions sautéing in butter, the beef browning in a swirl of herbs and cracked pepper.

"Simple food's the best food," I tell him, stirring the sauce.

"It is," he agrees, watching me like I've conjured some form of edible magic.

I find a crusty loaf of bread in the fridge, smear it with garlic and butter, sprinkle it with herbs, and toss it under the broiler until it's golden, crisp, and perfect.

"This looks incredible," he says, his eyes wide and reverent. "Forget having kids. Maybe you should just cook for me, love."

I laugh, but there's something under it, something smaller and quieter that doesn't quite go away.

"I've heard stories about Keenan McCarthy," I say softly, not looking at him. "I hope what you said is true, that your mother can soften him."

"My da's not a bad sort, Zoya," he says, setting his fork down. "We've talked about this, aye? His issue with me… It's because he listens to his best mate's advice."

"Why would he do that?" I ask, frustration creeping into my voice. "You seem reliable."

"I am reliable. But not manipulative. And his friend is. There's a difference."

"It makes sense," I murmur. "I'm glad Rafail's never had to deal with anything like that."

"My father's old now. Tired. He's ruled the family for a long time. But when his friend promised him a kingdom, he took the bait."

"I know it," I say, and I do. I feel it, how old men still dream of crowns, even when their hands are shaking.

He eats with focus, like he's thinking between every bite. But when we talk, he's fully present. He sets his utensils down. He gestures, expressive, telling me stories of his youth, of Belfast summers and family dinners. Of loyalty and loss. I tell him mine in return, pieces I've never given anyone else.

We fit, somehow.

"We're oddly suited for each other, aren't we?" he says with a wistful kind of grin.

"Definitely," I say.

"Now, all that's left is convincing our families to see it too."

"I wouldn't say it's our only problem," he sighs, rubbing the back of his neck. "But it's definitely the biggest, isn't it?"

"I don't know," I say, rising from the table and sweeping the dishes into my arms. I don't meet his eyes, not yet. I walk to the sink, and the sound of plates clinking against stainless steel fills the silence between us.

Then, without thinking, my mouth curls into a smirk, sharp and teasing. I glance over my shoulder, just enough to catch him watching.

"I think our biggest problem might be that my husband thinks he can cook."

I don't even finish the sentence before he's on me. His arms wrap around my waist, warm and impossibly solid. I burst into laughter, wild, breathless, uncontained, as he pins me between his body and the counter. His hands find my sides, relentless, tickling until I'm writhing and gasping for air.

And then he kisses me, right at the curve of my neck, where his beard scrapes and burns in all the right ways. I swear I feel him breathe me in, like I'm something vital. Like I'm the only air he needs.

"You're a firecracker," he mutters against my skin, his voice frayed with want.

"Leave the damn dishes," he says next, and there's heat behind it. "I think the real problem is my wife still hasn't learned how to obey me."

An involuntary breath catches in my throat. My body hums with it.

"Okay," I whisper. I don't know if that's what he wants to hear, or if he's just going to toy with me more and draw it out like he always does.

"Is that the right thing to say?" he murmurs, one hand drifting lower, fingers sinking in and squeezing my ass like it belongs to him.

"Yes, sir."

He lifts me like I weigh nothing, turns me, and sets me down on the counter. The granite is cool under my thighs, but he's blazing. He leans in, forehead to mine, and his voice, god, I love his voice.

"Say it again, Zoya."

"Seamus," I breathe out, more of a whimper than a name. But that's not what he asked for. That's not what he wants.

"Yes, sir," I whisper, this time with more certainty.

My eyelids flutter shut as his mouth captures mine. Then my cheek. The softest parts of me. He kisses me like a man starved, like he's memorizing the shape of me with every press of his lips. Worshipping me, like I'm something rare and sacred.

"One night left," he says, quiet but resolute, like a vow wrapped in steel. "Let's make it count. Let's do everything we can to bring our families together."

He kisses me like time isn't running out. Like we're not on the brink of something terrible. Like this isn't the eve of war and we aren't teetering at the edge of a cliff, one step away from plummeting to our deaths.

Our lives, mine and his, are balanced on the edge of a blade.

And yet, when he speaks to me, it's reverent, as if I'm his sanctuary in a world set on fire.

His mouth drifts lower, to my shoulder. The top of my breast. My nipple. My belly. Every kiss is a benediction.

I answer only with trembling fingers, clutching his shirt, and breath that breaks from me in shuddering bursts.

"Go to bed, darling," he says, his voice darker now, thick with that same authority that makes my knees weak. "I want you to edge yourself. Slide your fingers between your thighs. But don't come. Not until I get there."

"But I'm cleaning the kitchen," I try, my protest soft, uncertain. I like pushing just a little.

He leans in, his voice like smoke curling around my ear.

"That's not your job anymore, and you know it."

I nod, swallowing hard. "Yes, sir."

"And if you make yourself come before I get there, Zoya…" His voice drops even lower. It's dark, sinful… full of promises I'm half-certain I want him to keep. "I'll take my belt to your arse before I fuck you."

The words sear into me. Brand me. Heat flashes up my spine like a live wire. I've never been spanked with a belt. But the way he says it, possessive, certain, commanding, makes my body tense with the urge to disobey. Just to know what it feels like.

"Yes, sir," I whisper, and I mean it.

So I do exactly what he said.

I go to the bedroom, take off my clothes, and lie back on the bed, sheets cool beneath me and my skin already flushed with need. I'm naked, aching, my nerves strung tight. I slip a hand between my thighs and gasp. I'm soaked. Slick. Swollen. *Starving.*

I think of him. His hands. His voice. His weight pinning me down. His belt.

I'm closer, chasing the edge, until I'm right there, right on the precipice.

Do I want to fall? Do I want to tempt him, tempt that punishment? Taste the wrath he promised?

No. Not yet.

Where is he? *Seamuuus...*

I pull my hand away, and my body trembles. Every nerve is on fire, desperate. I lie there, straining to hear. A dish clinks. Water runs. His voice floats in from the kitchen.

My heart leaps, but it's just a phone call.

Frustrated, I roll onto my side. I touch myself again, fingers slipping into a rhythm fast, deep, and devastating. My other hand grips my breast, pinching, tugging, trying to hold on.

I think about the belt. The weight of it. The leather. The crack of it against skin.

And just like that, I fall.

I come hard. Too hard. My body jerks, wracked with wave after wave that refuses to stop. I try. I swear I try to stop.

But I can't.

And then I see him.

He's standing in the doorway.

His arms are crossed, his eyes dark, unreadable, but dangerous.

"You didn't," he growls.

"I..." I start, but the words die in my throat.

"Tell me you didn't disobey me and make yourself come." The hard line of his cock in his jeans tells me he might want me to admit my failing.

"Um, I didn't mean to," I whisper, like it'll make a difference. Like maybe if we both lost control, it balances out.

But it doesn't.

"It just happened, Seamus. I swear, I didn't mean to make that happen."

"But you did," he growls, stepping forward. "You had control. I told you what to do. I told you not to come. And you chose to come anyway."

He stalks across the room, and suddenly, he's not just Seamus anymore.

He's The Undertaker.

The man who makes grown men piss themselves.

The most feared man in Europe.

And now I see why.

I scramble back on the bed, more out of instinct than real fear. Because underneath the terror, I want this. I want him.

Because this is Seamus. *My* Seamus.

He wouldn't really hurt me.

Would he?

"Let me ask you something, angel," he says.

The way the word *angel* slips from his lips, it should sound sweet. Soft, like affection. But it doesn't. There's a steel thread running through it, laced with warning. It tells me not to get too comfortable. Not to mistake tenderness for mercy.

"Am I a man of my word?"

He told me he'd marry me. Swore he'd come back for me. Promised that the only reason he ever left at all was because someone else took him, ripped him away, and locked him up, like I didn't matter. Like we didn't matter.

There was a time I would've said no… that he wasn't a man of anything.

But now?

Now, I know better.

"Yes, sir," I whisper. The words barely leave my lips, like they're afraid to make themself known. Saying the truth out loud feels like it might cost me something I won't be able to get back.

He watches me.

"What did I tell you would happen if you came without permission?"

My mouth is dry.

"You said you'd spank me," I murmur, looking down, wishing I hadn't come here. Wishing I had. Wanting everything and nothing all at once.

"In detail, Zoya. That's not what I said."

Oh god.

"You said you'd take your belt to my ass," I whisper, my face burning. The shame rolls through me like a wave of fire, but underneath it, something else pulses—hotter and more dangerous.

It's humiliating. It's terrifying.

It's arousing.

He's so massive. So dominant. Every movement is careful, calculated. There's no hesitation in him, no second-guessing. He doesn't bluff. He executes.

"I did, didn't I?"

His voice is soft now, almost amused. "And it seems like my new wife needs to learn how to obey her husband."

He's in jeans and a tight white T-shirt, and the fabric clings to his chest and arms like it was made to showcase how lethal he is. He reaches down, unbuckles the belt at his waist, and slides it free with a long, slow pull that makes my stomach drop.

The sound is loud. Final. Like a door slamming shut. Rain pours outside. It's warm in here, though, and I'm on *fire*.

He shakes his head once, deliberately, then stomps toward me.

"Hands above your head, where I can see them."

I obey without thinking.

My arms fly up. I'm trembling. Every instinct in me is screaming *run*, but every nerve is screaming *stay*.

"Good," he says.

But he doesn't say good girl.

And that, god, it hurts. Like a phantom limb, like I've been denied something vital. I ache for it. I crave him telling me I'm his good girl.

His gaze stays locked on mine. His eyes are dark and unreadable, but there's something behind them. Something dangerous. Something certain.

He loops the belt in his hands and snaps it once with a flick of his wrist.

The sound cracks through the room.

I flinch.

He walks to the bed and sits down slow, spreading his legs wide. He looks completely relaxed, like this is routine for him. Like punishing me is just another part of loving me.

He pats his lap.

"Anytime I have to punish you, it'll be over my lap," he says calmly. Like this isn't a negotiation, it's doctrine.

"If you're not being punished, I'll use my hand. If you are…
something else."

Oh god.

He's thought this through. He has a plan he's ready to
execute.

"Okay," I whisper. The word is barely there.

He points.

"Now. Over."

My legs feel like liquid, but I obey. Trembling, I move
forward and slide across his thighs. His lap is sturdy, warm,
and immovable. My hair falls forward, curtain-like, hiding
my face from the world. My hands scrabble for balance, but
I can't find anything solid except for him.

He places one firm, heavy hand on the small of my back.

He lifts the belt.

And brings it down.

The leather strikes the crease between my thighs and the
curve of my ass. The sound is loud, the sting sharp. I cry
out, my breath caught in my throat.

"*Ow.*"

It doesn't exactly hurt, not in the way pain is supposed to. It
startles me more than anything. It steals my breath and
leaves something else behind. Arousal. Electricity.

"Good," he murmurs.

Then he brings it down again.

Two.

Three.

He flicks the leather strap across each cheek, a measured, controlled rhythm that feels more like a seduction than a strike. Each one lands with purpose, not violence, not punishment. Not yet. It's like he's drawing heat into me, teasing the edge of pain, coaxing my body to respond, to yield.

He's not even using half his strength; I know that.

He's playing with me. Testing my limits.

Warming me up for something darker.

Something I can't yet see, but I can feel it coming, like a storm on the horizon.

"There," he says, after six deliberate lashes.

He sets the belt down like it's something sacred, something he treasures, not just a tool, but a ritual. Then his hands, warm and possessive, cup my ass, his palms pressing firm against the sting, soothing and branding me all at once.

"You're a good girl, Zoya."

I sigh. There it is.

His voice is almost too soft, deceptively gentle. It slides over my skin like silk, wrapping around me.

"I don't think you need a severe punishment, do you?"

But oh, something inside me wants it.

Wants the punishment.

Wants to earn it.

Wants to see exactly how far he'll go.

Wants to feel everything he's capable of giving.

Still, I shake my head, my voice barely above a breath.

"No, sir." I swallow. "I really didn't mean to disobey you. I'm sorry."

The words come out quiet and broken, fragile like glass on tile.

A tear slips down and hits the floor before I even know it's there. My chest tightens.

"There," he says again, softer this time, smoothing his palm over me, again and again. Each pass is reassurance and claim, comfort and control.

"That's a good girl."

The way he says it... god, the way those words wash over me.

Then his hand shifts and slides between my thighs, nudging them apart with the back of his fingers. A subtle command.

His fingers find me wet, throbbing, and desperate, and he groans low, like the sound was pulled from somewhere deep in his chest.

"Just as I thought," he murmurs, his voice thick now, heavy with knowing. "You're aroused again, aren't you?"

I nod, almost ashamed by how badly I need him.

The desire climbs through me like fire, licking every nerve and demanding more.

It's shocking how fast it returns. How much harder it hits.

I've never come more than once in a night, but with him? With Seamus?

Everything is more.

Every breath is sharper.

Every part of me is lit up like he's flipped some hidden switch.

I used to think about him when I touched myself in the dark.

Sometimes I'd let myself come. Sometimes I'd stop at the edge, then fall asleep aching for him.

He's pulled every string in me, tuned me to the brink of madness.

"Good girl," he whispers reverently, like he's promising something only I get to hear.

"There you go, baby. On your back. I want to taste you."

"Seamus…" I'm already trembling, as he pinches the heat of my ass cheek, grounding me.

"What do you call me?" His tone is sharper now.

"Sir," I choke out, my pulse hammering.

"Do you really plan on talking back to me just after I strapped you?"

I gulp and move to obey.

He moves with quiet purpose, going to the drawer. Metal cuffs gleam in his hands.

When he snaps them around my wrists, they click into place, my arms stretched above my head.

I'm held. I'm open. I'm his.

"Oh god…"

"Spread your legs."

He kneels and settles between my thighs like he belongs there, and he does.

Then his tongue drags slowly, maddeningly, over my clit.

I cry out. My hips jerk, chasing the feeling, already trembling under the weight of his mouth.

I didn't know it could feel like this.

Didn't know I could want again so fast.

Didn't know I could need this way.

But I do. God, I do.

He sucks. Licks. Flicks. Over and over.

I rise from the bed, straining for him, moaning for him, aching.

Then… he stops.

A kiss to my thigh, maddening in its gentleness.

"You'll stay like that," he says quietly. "Your punishment isn't over."

Then he stands.

"I need to do a few things."

"Seamus," I gasp. "My god, you can't. Please… Seamus."

"What's my name?"

"Sir," I breathe out, wrecked.

"Don't leave me like this. Please. I'm sorry, I promise I—"

"And I promise you," he cuts in coldly.

"I'll let you come. You'll love it when I do. But you'll learn to obey me, Zoya. First, because I love it. Second, because it'll keep you alive."

Then he walks away, leaving me cuffed, wet, exposed.

Burning.

I squeeze my thighs together, seeking relief, anything, but it's useless.

The ache only grows.

Even if I had the key, I wouldn't use it.

I wouldn't move.

I want to obey him.

I want to please him.

I want to be perfect for him.

I want to be his good girl.

God, I love when he calls me that.

So I wait.

I count. Ten. Fifty. Two hundred. Three hundred.

The storm outside rages, rain slamming the glass, thunder shaking the sky, but inside, it's still warm. Still him. Still us.

Then he appears in the doorway.

"Still here, my love?"

His voice sends a shiver through me.

I nod.

"Spread your legs again," he says, rough now, full of hunger.

"Seamus, sir, please…"

"That's what I like to hear," he growls. "I love to hear you beg."

He drops to the floor again and licks me with purpose, his tongue flicking just where I crave it.

I cry out, my hips lifting off the bed like I've been shocked.

I want him.

I need him.

"Tell me you want me," he says, low and commanding, his lips brushing against my thigh like a brand. It's not a question, it's a demand. A dark, brutal need.

"I want you," I whisper, broken open. "God, I want you so bad."

He exhales, slow and heavy, like he's been holding his breath underwater. He reaches up, and his hand finds my throat, not choking, not tight, just resting. Possessive.

A reminder.

"You're mine," he growls. "This body. This mouth. This fucking sweetness between your legs. Mine."

I nod frantically, my eyes wide, panting. "Yes, sir. I'm yours."

"Say it again," he commands, his palm tightening slightly, not enough to hurt, but enough to remind me who's in control.

"I'm yours," I say louder, trembling. "Every inch. Every part of me."

"Good girl," he purrs. "Now you can come." He slides his tongue lazily over my clit.

The permission crashes into me like a wave breaking against stone.

I come undone.

The orgasm tears through me, wild and punishing. It doesn't ask, it takes. My body bows against the restraints, my muscles seizing and my vision going white at the edges.

He watches the whole thing, still worshipping me between my legs, like this moment belongs to him.

It does.

"Beautiful," he whispers, moving up and brushing a kiss over my temple. "So fucking beautiful when you break for me."

"I want you. I want this. All of it, Seamus."

I freeze. My breath catches in my throat, suspended like a thread stretched too tight.

"No," he says softly, a low command wrapped in velvet. "Say it again. I want to hear my name again."

"Seamus," I whisper, the word barely more than breath now, a sigh, a surrender.

"That's it. Oh, good girl. You deserve a reward for that, don't you?"

"Please, Seamus," I whisper again, need curling like smoke around my voice, pulling it taut. "If you touch me again, it's too much—"

"Trust me."

He bends down, and his mouth is hot, dangerous, as his tongue flicks across my nipple again, teasing and tormenting until my hips rise of their own accord. My body is no longer mine. It's his. All his. I buck, begging without words, drowning in the ache.

"Beg me," he orders, a gravelly threat laced with desire. "I want to hear you beg."

"Please," I gasp. "Please let me. I need to, please, let me…"

"Will you obey me?"

"Yes," I cry, trembling under the weight of how badly I need him. "I promise. I'll be good. I'll be so good for you."

Tears slip down my cheeks, hot, unrelenting. I'm undone, raw as he fingers me. I'm so close to the edge already. I've lost count of how many times I've come, but my body knows what to do now.

"Seamus, *please.*"

"That's my girl," he murmurs, licking the other nipple with reverence that borders on worship.

"That's my angel girl. I give you permission to come, love," he says, his lips brushing against the swell of my breast like a vow. "You have my permission."

He suckles. He strokes my cheek with fingers that almost feel gentle. And then I shatter.

Pleasure detonates through me, violent, blinding, a firestorm I couldn't stop even if I wanted to.

Blood pounds in my ears. Nerves light up like fireworks, bright and merciless.

I moan, my hips writhing, every part of me begging for more as he strokes my pussy, fingers my clit, plunges two fingers deep, curling them until they hit that perfect place, my G-spot, again and again, with ruthless precision.

He licks and sucks and presses until I can't take it, until I dissolve into something boneless and breathless beneath him.

And then he's kneeling above me. Watching.

"I want you on your knees," he says, calm and controlled, as he unfastens the cuffs from my wrists. "I want to take you, love."

I scramble to obey, eager and desperate, but he shakes his head slowly, the movement deliberate.

"No," he murmurs. "I need to ease you into this, don't I? We need time. More time."

Then he shifts, pressing the thick head of his cock against me, and I gasp.

My arms wrap around his neck as he slides inside.

This time, it doesn't hurt. This time, it's nothing but plea-sure, pure, indulgent pleasure.

He did this to me.

He broke me open, made me come so hard I shattered, made me wet and swollen and ready for him. And now I take him easily. Willingly.

He moves inside me, slow and careful, his control razor-sharp. His kisses are soft, almost reverent.

He thrusts again, and I feel it, that he's holding back.

He's not the kind of man who ever holds back, but right now, for me, he is.

He's giving me care. Respect. Maybe even love.

Again and again, he moves inside me, each thrust deeper, more deliberate. My pleasure builds slowly this time, a slow burn, a climb toward something inevitable.

"I'm going to come again, sir," I whisper against his neck, trembling.

"Call me by name now," he growls.

"Seamus," I moan, my breath hitching. "Seamus, I'm going to, please."

"Go on, Zoya," he whispers. "Come as many times as you want."

Then he drives deep, and I splinter again, but this climax is different, less sharp, more consuming. Deeper. It fills me to the edges.

I press my chest to his, moving with his thrusts, feeling the tremble in his body as he nears his own release.

When he comes, his body jerks, and his forehead falls against mine.

"God, this is so goddamn sweet." He groans. "God, I love you, Zoya."

He pulls out slowly, carefully, his every movement tender.

And then he's back, inside me again, but not just physically. Emotionally. Entirely.

I'm so tired.

My eyes flutter shut as he gently cleans me. Like I'm precious. Like I matter.

My head finds its place on his shoulder, and my limbs go weightless, floating in the afterglow.

I want him. God, I want him.

I don't know what he's done to me.

I close my eyes and drift toward what I hope is dreamless peace.

CHAPTER 19

SEAMUS

SHE FALLS ASLEEP BESIDE ME.

But I can't sleep. I hold her against me, feeling her soft breathing. While she sleeps, I think about what's coming next.

Then she wakes and rolls over, one eye open.

"We should run," she says quietly. "Hide. Go somewhere no one can ever find us again. *No one.* Just us, Seamus."

"Zoya," I whisper.

"If we left now, we could run to the ends of the earth. Somewhere far, where they'd never suspect we'd go."

I hate to disappoint her, god knows I do, but I have to. Not that I don't want exactly what she's suggesting.

She sighs like she already knew. Like she was just waiting for me to admit it.

"I knew you'd say no."

"There are too many people depending on us," I tell her, and it's the truest thing I've ever said.

I think of them all, my brothers, my sisters, my men. My dad. My mom. Her family too. Even if she doesn't know it yet, they're part of this. Part of us.

I have to end the tyranny. I have to bring peace.

We have to end this war and break the chains we were both born into.

Our families, hers and mine, stand a better chance if I succeed.

I press a kiss to her shoulder.

"I need to put my baby in you, Zoya. And I need to protect you, now more than ever."

"Do you think you'll get arrested again?" she asks, her voice small and quiet.

"I'm wanted by the Russian mob," I say, flat, deadpan. "So yeah. We're not the kind of people who get to escape easily."

"No," she agrees softly.

I run my fingers through her hair, maybe to soothe her. Maybe to calm myself.

"I want you," I tell her. "No matter what."

"Where would you go," she asks, "if we could?"

But she doesn't wait for me to answer.

"Me, I'd go somewhere tropical," she says, her voice turning wistful. "I've never had a tropical vacation. I think I'm due for one."

I smile at that, at how fast she answered.

"And what would you do on this vacation?"

"I'd lie on a white sand beach and soak in the sun," she murmurs, her eyes distant. "Then, when I got too hot, I'd dive into crystal-clear water. I'd collect seashells and make crafts. I'd drink pretty cocktails with little umbrellas."

She pauses.

"I'd buy gifts for everyone. For my family. For the little ones. Jewelry, probably. Jewelry I'd never wear to anything fancy, but I'd have it, and it would sparkle."

She trails off.

The weight of it all lands heavy on her chest and mine too. The reality claws its way in, cold and merciless. If we run... there's no beach waiting for us at the end. No fruity drinks with tiny umbrellas. No family to get dumb souvenirs we would laugh about later.

"I'd eat food I've never tried before," she adds, quieter now.

"What about you?" she asks.

"Oh, I don't know." I smile, soft and crooked, dragging my hand slowly across the warm, bare skin of her back.

"As long as I was with you, I think I'd be happy. I'd be a lucky bloke."

She smiles, then lets out a yawn so delicate it tugs at something deep in me.

"You're tired, love."

"I am," she whispers. "So tired."

"All right," I murmur, brushing her hair back. "Then what I want you to do is close those pretty eyes and try to sleep some more, okay? We've got a busy day ahead of us, and I want you to get your beauty sleep. Be my good girl who rests when she's told."

"All right," she says, the words already slurred, fading fast. "I will."

"We've got that tropical beach in our sights," I whisper against her temple, pressing a soft kiss to her skin like a promise I can't guarantee.

"Okay," she breathes out, a sleepy smile tugging at her lips. "Done."

And a few minutes later, I know she's really out this time.

And god help me, I want to believe in that dream right along with her.

"Zoya," I whisper... but she doesn't answer.

No response, no movement, not even the twitch of a finger. Just the slow, steady rhythm of her breathing, heavy and deep. Her body finally letting go, finally giving itself permission to rest.

I stay right where I am, wrapped around her like armor, letting her warmth seep into me, like maybe it'll fill all the cold, cracked places I've kept hidden.

And as I hold her, I start to make my plan.

My plan to secure what's mine.

To lock down my kingdom, brick by bloody brick.

To protect her from everything that's ever tried to break me.

To save us both, no matter the cost.

I bring her hand to my lips, one knuckle at a time, kissing each one with the reverence of a vow I'm too much of a coward to speak aloud.

She softens even more, her body melting into mine like some part of her already knows. Already trusts. Already believes I'll do it.

She sleeps.

I close my eyes and try to follow her into that quiet place, but I can't.

Not yet.

My thoughts are a storm, wild and restless. Schemes twist through my mind like smoke from something already burning. So instead of sleeping, I plot. I prepare.

I wait for the sun to rise.

So I can finally move.

So I can finally begin.

CHAPTER 20

ZOYA

I wake to warmth. His warmth.

The early light spills through the curtains, soft and blinding. His arm is draped over my waist, heavy and grounding. His breath brushes the back of my neck in soft, even bursts.

For a fleeting second, I keep my eyes closed and let myself believe we're normal.

Ordinary.

We're newlyweds on a honeymoon.

We had a beautiful wedding.

There's no one chasing us, no shadows clawing at our heels.

No enemies who want us dead.

Just peace. Just us.

Safe, finally. Blessedly safe.

But then the memories come flooding back. Dreams that felt too real to just be dreams.

I saw an angry Irishman dragging him away from me.

I screamed, reached for him, and begged, but they wouldn't let me.

Rafail. Stern, stone-faced, and shaking his head like I'd disappointed him. Like he was already mourning something inevitable.

Seamus sighs and moves. It's just a small shift, the slow drag of his thick, calloused palm down the curve of my hip, but it starts something in me.

A chain reaction.

My body remembers his touch. Remembers everything we did. And I respond before I can think.

He kisses the base of my neck softly, and I tilt my head back without thinking. My eyes flutter shut.

We don't speak.

We don't need to.

We move like this isn't new, as if he didn't take my virginity just two nights ago.

Like our bodies already know each other, like they've always known.

He rolls me onto my back, his body covering mine like a shield. I feel the weight of him, the length of his erection pressing against my belly. He cups my face, so gently, it's like he's scared to break me.

And then he presses down, slow and deep, his cock throbbing against me.

This isn't about power or control or domination.

This isn't a lesson in obedience.

This is something else entirely.

Something sweet, aching and wordless.

We say everything with our bodies because the words would shatter the moment.

I love you.

You are my safe place.

You complete me.

We breathe in tandem.

His mouth finds mine, his tongue sweeps inside, and we kiss like we've got forever.

But we both know we don't.

I'm naked from the night before, nothing between us now but his boxers. I reach for the waistband. He shifts his hips to help me, and then he's bare—hot, thick, ready.

He spreads my legs gently with his knee and settles between them. Then he positions himself at my entrance and pushes in.

There's no pain this time. Just heat. Pressure.

I'm full. Stretched, but ready.

So ready.

He glides in and out with ease, slick with how wet I am. We move together in a slow, sacred rhythm. His left hand finds mine, fingers lacing tight, palm to palm.

We make love like this might be the last time. Like we'll never get another morning like this.

"Seamus," I whisper, my breath catching. "I'm going to—"

"Come, lass," he finishes for me. "Come. I want to feel you."

And I do. I come apart around him. And as I do, he follows, groaning against my skin.

It's not as rough or frenzied as the night before, but it's just as sweet. Just as intimate.

I love being connected to him like this.

I love having him inside me.

I love the heat of his body, the weight of him.

And in that moment, I imagine a future.

A baby.

Maybe this time...

This time, maybe I'll get pregnant.

And maybe, just maybe, that could end this war.

By the time we're done, the sun has crested the horizon, painting the world in soft gold.

He rests his forehead against my shoulder, almost boyish in the way he clings to me. His skin is damp, his heartbeat still racing beneath it.

I trace the tattoos on his shoulders with the tip of my finger. Memorizing. Holding on.

He whispers something, a confession, a plea.

I nod… because I understand.

Time is slipping away.

The silence from my family is too sharp. It's not peace.

It's a pause before a strike.

Like his—too quiet, too still.

"They're watching," he whispers.

"I know," I say.

We lie there, tangled in each other, saying nothing more.

"What do you want me to do, Seamus?" I ask, even though I already know the answer. He won't put me on the front lines, never that. But maybe he'll let me contribute in some small way, let me in on whatever they're planning behind closed doors.

"They're planning something," he says, his eyes hard as ice and just as cutting.

"Be ready. Stay close. And Zoya…" His voice drops. It's serious now, a warning, maybe. A promise. Maybe both.

He props himself up on his elbow, those brilliant blue eyes catching mine. "When I say move, you move. No questions. Do you understand me?" He says the words firmly but almost gently, like he doesn't want to frighten me but needs me to know this is not a request. "I'm not joking, love."

"Yes, sir," I whisper, and he blinks once, slow and dark. A wicked smile curls at the corners of his mouth.

"Careful with that, love." But I know he likes it. The control. The reverence. The way I yield without truly yielding.

I like it too.

Still, something cold curls in my stomach, a slither of fear that won't go away no matter how warm his touch is. "We're going back to your family home in Ballyhock?"

He doesn't answer right away. Just studies me, silent and still, like he's deciding what version of the truth I can survive. Finally, he nods. "Yes."

A beat passes.

"The more you know, the more danger you're in. So please" —he reaches for me, brushing my hand—"forgive me for not telling you everything."

That should terrify me more than it does. But I nod anyway. I trust him. I don't know why. I just do.

He sits up and throws the blanket off like he's shedding something. "Time for some training."

"Training?" I blink, still drowsy and tangled in warmth and confusion. "Now? What do you mean training? Are you going to..." But I don't finish the question.

He grins, that rare, feral grin that says I'm in trouble in the best possible way. And despite myself, I feel that answering tug low in my belly, even though I should be too exhausted to feel anything.

"Come," he says. "You're helping."

Helping, as it turns out, means lying on the bed like a human dumbbell while Seamus uses me for strength training. I yelp the first time he lifts me straight into the air like I weigh nothing. But his grip is steady, his palms flat on my waist, locked like steel. I'm not a person to him in that moment. I'm resistance. Challenge.

And I'm laughing. It's absurd. Ridiculous. "You're out of your mind! Seamus, what are you even doing?"

"Quiet, love," he says, furrowing his brow like he's trying to scold me, but his lips are twitching, threatening another grin.

"I need to keep my strength up, don't you know? You see a gym around here?"

I laugh out loud, breathless. "You love this."

He doesn't deny it. Just keeps lifting me, keeps moving. It's wild, reckless and intimate in the strangest way—the way his muscles bunch beneath me, the way his eyes stay locked on mine like I'm all that matters, the way sweat glistens on his chest and neck.

First, he bench-presses me, before he squats with me on his shoulders, then does some bizarre tricep dip that feels like a ride at a theme park. But I never feel unsafe. I never feel like I'll fall.

"Seamus," I gasp, giggling as he lifts me straight over his head and squats again.

"I can squat more than your weight, darling," he says, all smug and flushed and glistening.

"I bet you can." But still, it's impressive. His body is carved from strength, legs like tree trunks, chest wide and powerful. It's mesmerizing to watch.

I bend to kiss the crown of his damp hair. "I love you."

"Don't distract me," he says lightly, but his voice is warm and soft. Everything about him in that moment says he feels it too.

Eventually, he lays me on the bed and collapses beside me in a breathless, half-naked heap. "Let's get changed."

Every second that ticks by now is one less we have before whatever is coming next. The showdown.

Later, in the shower, the silence is different, thicker and heavier, like we're standing in the eye of the storm and pretending it's calm. I wash his back. He rinses my hair. When he turns me to face him, the water running over his stubble and dripping down his chest, he says it.

"It's time to go."

I nod. I don't ask where.

I just follow. Always. It feels natural and right.

He leans down, kisses the side of my mouth. "Whatever happens, Zoya... remember this. I love you."

Then he adds, "Trust me," and that's how I know it's serious. Seamus McCarthy isn't a man who deals in hope. He doesn't peddle promises he can't keep. So if he says trust me, it's because there's no other choice.

I expected the drive to the McCarthy home to be longer. I

don't know why. Maybe I thought if it were this close, someone would've come for him sooner.

"Are we here already?" I ask as gravel crunches under the tires and the car stops.

Outside my window, the McCarthy estate looms, perched on a cliff that looks like something out of a dream. Craggy rocks jut from the shore below, seafoam-green waves crashing against them. It's breathtaking. But my heart is pounding.

We're here.

The mansion sprawls wide and proud, unapologetic in its wealth and weight. I wish I were coming here for different reasons. I wish he were proud to show me this place.

I wish I didn't feel like a weapon. A trophy. A warning.

He claimed me.

We made love. Said things people like us don't say without blood on our hands. *Stay. Mine. Forever. I love you.*

But as we cross the threshold, the air thickens, like it knows I don't belong. Like it's warning me.

His hand tightens on mine for just a moment before he lets go.

"We may be separated for a bit," he murmurs, right before anyone else enters the hallway.

"What?" I ask, but then he's here.

Keenan McCarthy.

I don't need to be told who he is. I know. He looks like Seamus but with silver at his temples, a bearded jawline with hints of salt and pepper. The kind of man who doesn't need to raise his voice.

His eyes narrow on Seamus.

Seamus pulls me a little closer.

"Whatever happens next," he whispers, barely audible, "I will come for you. You'll be safe. Hold your own, Zoya. I know you can."

Then he looks at me, steady and clear.

"You were Zoya Kopolova when I met you. You're Zoya McCarthy now. No one stands in your way, lass."

Keenan plants his hands on his hips. "Zoya, my father. Keenan McCarthy. Dad—" Seamus starts, but Keenan cuts him off with a look.

"You brought a fucking Kopolov into my house," Keenan says. Not loud. Just final.

Seamus stiffens. I see the tightness in his jaw, the fight he wants to wage. But he says nothing. This is still his father's kingdom, and even the heir has to bow.

Keenan flicks his fingers at Seamus. "You. With me." Then his eyes cut to me. "You. With the women."

No goodbye. No kiss. No look back.

Seamus lets go of my hand and walks.

And I feel the echo of every lonely night I waited for him in that damn pub, when he didn't show. The ache of wanting someone who might not want you back. But now I hear his voice like steel in my mind: *You are Zoya McCarthy now.*

And I know what that means.

"Come. This way, please, ma'am."

A woman with bright eyes and a sharp ponytail leads me away without introducing herself. Hired help. Efficient. Cold.

She opens a door, and I step into a room with three women. They don't look alike, not really, but for the eyes. Those are McCarthy eyes, just not Seamus's.

"And you are?" one of them says, sizing me up.

She's tall, though not as tall as Seamus, but commanding in her own way. I remember what he told me about his sisters. Bronwyn and Kyla. One sweet. One savage.

"Nice to meet you," the tall one says, but her smile is pure venom. "How did you manage to trick my brother into marrying you?"

Well, that sorts out who's sweet and who's savage.

Bronwyn, the younger one with a rounder face, flushes pink as Kyla continues. "You fucked him, didn't you? Smart girl. Use your body to get what you need, eh?"

I flinch, shocked. My mouth opens, but I can't speak.

"That's enough," Bronwyn says quietly, her cheeks flushed with embarrassment. But Kyla keeps circling.

I finally smile and find my voice. "Ah. You must be Kyla. Seamus spoke so highly of you."

Her lips press together, and she doesn't respond, not yet.

Her clothes scream money. Power. Precision. She's thin, dressed in tailored designer from head to toe. And every inch of her says, *You don't belong here.*

Meh. *Not yet*, I think.

But I sure as fuck will.

"Do you have any idea what *you've* done?"

"What *I've* done?" I blink slowly, take a breath. "It seems to me, you and I have a very different take on what happened between me and Seamus."

"*Seamus?*" She spits the name like it's poison.

She turns and looks at her younger sister, Bronwyn.

"You call him Seamus? *No one* outside our family fucking calls him Seamus."

"Well, apparently his wife does," I say calmly, holding my ground, squaring my shoulders like I've been trained for this moment my whole life. I don't flinch. I don't blink.

Bronwyn just smiles, like she's already decided how this is going to end. "Oooh," she whispers.

"If you'd care to be kind enough to me," I say, not flinching, not folding, "you might learn a thing or two. You don't have to throw me a family welcome party, but why don't you at least listen to the actual story?"

Kyla glares. "I know he betrayed us," she says bitterly. "That he took a Kopolov by name. That he's been holed up in that goddamn house of his, and he came back and put every-thing at risk."

"Did he?" I ask softly, evenly, deliberately not answering any of it. Not giving her a single piece of ammo. I can't risk it. Not right now. She keeps circling, predator slow.

"We bleed for our family here. We marry for them. We kill for them." Her words fall heavy. "You think a warm pussy and big eyes like yours got you a seat at this table?"

I shake my head and let out a short, dry laugh.

"I'm so pleased to meet you too," I tell her. "As far as the warmth of my pussy and size of my eyes, I think that's something you'd best take up with your brother."

I flash her something that could almost pass for a smile if you didn't know better. It's tight and polite. "Interesting," I say while shaking my head. "Seamus speaks so highly of *you*."

And for a second, just a beat, her face shifts. There's a flicker in her eyes. Regret, maybe. Sadness.

She straightens and crosses her arms over her chest. "Why don't you tell me your side of the story then?" she says, quieter now.

"Sure," I say with a shrug. "Might as well hope for the best."

I tell her everything, bare bones but honest. "We met in a pub. I fell in love. So did he. He went to jail, and I thought he was gone." I let that hang there for a second. "While he was away, my oldest brother arranged for me to be married to someone else. It seems Seamus wasn't having it." I shrug. "He broke out of jail to come and get me because, apparently, I mattered to him."

Their eyes widen.

And then, softly, "It was actually on my wedding day that Seamus killed him and took his place."

A beat.

"And now we're married."

I give her a sweet smile that doesn't touch my eyes.

Her jaw drops. "He did *what?*"

"How does that match with your version?"

But before she can answer, the kitchen air shifts when someone else walks in.

She has long, dark hair streaked with silver. A woman, still beautiful though aged, in that timeless, maternal kind of way. Her presence is calm but unyielding. Her eyes land on me, and her voice is soft, laced in velvet but backed with steel.

"Kyla," she says sharply, and her tone alone demands silence. "Your argument is not with Zoya. Leave her. Please. Be kind. Just because you're bitter about your life doesn't mean you get to take it out on your new sister-in-law."

Kyla visibly bristles. But she obeys. Barely.

"Sweet girl," the woman says gently, walking over to me, her hand out. "Come. You're shaken. Let me make you some tea. I'm so sorry for your welcome here," she adds, almost in a whisper. "I think if you understood... It's been a rough few days."

She trails off, eyes flicking away like she isn't sure herself how to finish.

"Maybe you will. Maybe you won't. But let's have a cup of tea, shall we?"

I nod slowly, my throat tight. "And you are…?"

"Oh, lass," she says with a soft chuckle, "I forgot myself. It's a shame things happened the way they did. You'd have already known me by now."

She gives me a smile that's all warmth.

"My name is Caitlin McCarthy," she says, like it's the easiest thing in the world. "I'm Seamus's mother. Your mother-in-law. Welcome."

She kisses me on both cheeks, soft and gentle and real. It's the kindest thing anyone has done since I got to Ireland, and I nearly cry from the sheer tenderness of it.

Almost.

"I like her," Bronwyn pipes up, stepping back into the kitchen like she hadn't just vanished. She's younger, bright-eyed and mischievous.

She's got a round face, curves like her mother's, and thick hair hanging all the way to her waist. She's young, but there's wisdom in her eyes.

"We're all still reeling, Zoya," she says gently, offering me her hand. "My name's Bronwyn."

I take her hand, and she squeezes lightly. "This wasn't what we expected. My dad… oof." She grimaces. "He's been fuming for days. It's only 'cause of Mom he didn't storm Seamus's house."

"Mmm," Caitlin says with a sigh. "My husband has a way about him." Her eyes meet mine, soft and regretful.

"But you'll see. He's just very... What's the American term? Ride or die?" She smiles. "Loyal, you know. Protective. I imagine you and Seamus had time to... catch up?"

She looks away as if the reality of what her son has done just landed. That he took me. Brought me here. Kept me.

Like a beast and his beauty, locked away for three days and counting.

I clear my throat. "Obviously, we've had some time to... catch up."

I glance around the kitchen, needing something to ground me. It's old, but looks recently updated, chrome fixtures gleaming, beautiful tilework glowing in the light. It's homey. Smells like coffee and cookies.

I kind of want both right now.

But my eyes keep drifting to the door. I'm waiting for him.

Wondering how things are going with him and his father. Wondering if that fire in his eyes met steel. He's told me his father is a good man, loyal and ruthless, like Rafail. That he loves fiercely, protects without question.

But will he hurt him? Shame him?

Oh god.

Then the door opens, and I lift my eyes, my breath hitching, hoping to see my husband.

But it's not him.

A man steps in. Tall and broad, with scars that twist across his knuckles. Tattoos snake up his neck. His head is shaved clean, and a jagged but thin silver scar splits his cheekbone in two. Ink crawls down both arms like vines, and his eyes are gunmetal gray.

He stops dead when he sees me.

Doesn't blink. Doesn't snarl. Just stills.

Two long seconds stretch.

"And who's this?"

"Ash," Caitlin says tightly. "Meet Zoya. Seamus's wife. Zoya, this is Seamus's cousin, Ashland."

Something shifts in his jaw before his face goes blank.

"So the traitor's brought home his feckin' pet," he says.

Kyla smirks, like she's enjoying this.

Bronwyn gasps. "You can't say that. Honestly, Ash!"

But I'm already moving.

I rise slowly, every inch of my spine straightening, one vertebrae at a time.

I set my tea down gently, both hands flat on the table.

"You can watch your mouth," I say, my voice as calm as winter ice. "I've already had a lovely welcome from the sisters, you see." I smile at him, dead-eyed.

He smirks back, small, cruel, unkind. He's watching me, measuring me. I don't trust him. Not one bit.

Seamus married *me*. We took vows. I love that man.

I've had just about enough of this cold welcome.

I nod to Caitlin. "Thank you." Then Bronwyn. "Thank you."

"But the next person with something nasty to say?" I smile again. "They can hold their tongue until they're brave enough to say it in front of my husband."

Caitlin blinks, then sits back slowly. "Good girl," she says. "Mmm. He chose well, didn't he? I see now why he loves you."

And I nearly melt under that.

Because none of them would dare say these things in front of Seamus.

"Ash," Bronwyn snaps. "Stop being a feckin' cunt."

"Bronwyn," Caitlin says, like a warning.

But I can tell she's already lost the battle against the foul mouths in this house.

"It's family dinner." Kyla shrugs. "What did you expect?"

"Not a goddamn interrogation. Let her breathe already. And she's right. Say that in front of Seamus and I'll eat my damn hat."

Ashland doesn't move. Doesn't blink. Just steps aside, shakes his head like it isn't worth the effort, and turns to leave.

"Excuse me," I say, quiet but firm.

He pauses and turns back, then faces me fully. All eyes are

on me now, but I don't flinch. I don't blush. I don't stammer. I stand rooted in place.

"And that's the last time any of you call your Seamus McCarthy a traitor," I say. "He's as loyal to this family as they come, and you'll see soon enough what he's meant to do. What he's *called* to do."

I don't say more. I can't. I'm already toeing the line. But I won't let them disrespect my husband.

"Is that right?" he mutters calmly, as if challenging me.

I bare my teeth at him, a hiss catching between them. "You'll speak of my husband and *your boss* with respect."

Bronwyn and Caitlin share a glance, a loaded one. I see it. I feel it.

Bronwyn smiles wide. Caitlin, calm as ever, tops off her tea. Ashland exhales like the weight of the room is too heavy for him and walks out with Kyla close behind.

Good. Let them leave.

I release a breath.

"Sit down, darling," Caitlin says gently, tapping the table like she's summoning a cat to her lap. "You did well. So did my son," she continues, smiling. "Let's figure out dinner."

The room smells like cloves and sugar, thick and sweet, a kind of comfort that makes me ache with memories of home. The teapot is already steaming again as Caitlin moves like she's done this a thousand times... because she has. She pours two cups like we're just two women catching up after brunch.

"Would you take sugar, Zoya? Or are you one of those purists who likes the taste of bitterness in their cup?"

I blink, then smile. It's impossible not to.

"Two sugars, please. Not a purist. No milk."

"Good girl," she says, like she's proud. "That's how I raised my boys, you know, sweet enough to kill you, strong enough to burn."

She sets the cup in front of me, then pushes the tin of biscuits closer like it's an offering.

"Go on. Try the shortbread. Store-bought, but let's pretend I've been slaving away in this boiling heat. I love this kitchen, but the whole damn thing feels like an oven sometimes."

The kitchen is stunning but hot, with warm-toned wood, black marble counters, and hanging copper pots.

I take a piece of shortbread. It's good, not as good as the honey-drenched ones Rodion and I used to make back home or Anya's flaky masterpieces.

"Do you cook?" she asks, her head tilted. The diamond on her ring catches the light. I look down at my hand with only a slim gold band. I'm not used to the feel of it yet.

"I do," I say, softer. "And baking too. My brother's favorite is honey cake. It sort of became my thing at home."

"Did it?" Her eyes light up, full of practiced interest. "Goodness, I'd love some honey cake. Can't say I've had it, but I'd love to try. We'll have to get you in the kitchen." She leans back a little, and her voice drops. "We had a cook. But she left. Her husband got another offer too far from here. It was time for them to go." A pause. "She was with us for thirty years."

Thirty years, longer than I've been alive. My chest tightens.

"She must've known Seamus almost his whole life. When will I see him?" I ask, trying to keep the tremble from my voice.

Caitlin's eyes flicker. She stirs her nearly empty cup, like buying herself time. "Soon, sweetheart. We've been through quite a lot."

"I understand," I say with a nod, even though it punches the breath from my lungs. "But how long can one conversation be?"

She exhales slowly. "Oh, you'd be surprised. But there's been an uproar since you married my son."

She meets my eyes. And in that moment, I see her, really see her. The power behind the softness. The storm she's holding back.

"Let things settle, Zoya," she says gently. "We'll get to know you." She leans forward. "I promise you're safe here with me, but stay close to my son, alright, love?"

But I can't help but wonder: Am I safe with anyone else?

CHAPTER 21

SEAMUS

I STAND IN THE COURTYARD. The afternoon sun slants down between ancient stones, golden light slicing through the silence. He didn't bring me to his office. He brought me outside, like I'm some sort of offering.

And my fists clench because this feels too much like another time. Another version of me, years ago, standing in front of my father after doing something stupid.

So fucking stupid.

I stole his race car. Took it for a joyride like a cocky little bastard. I might've gotten away with it if I hadn't forgotten to wash the mud from the tires.

And then, worse: When I was furious with a rival gang, riding the high of recklessness, I stole one of their cars too. One mistake stacked on top of another.

But this? What I've done now? This wasn't some teenage impulse.

No.

This was cold. Deliberate. This was war.

I took Zoya Kopolova and murdered her betrothed.

I dragged chaos through our front gate and planted it in the garden.

My father's voice slices the quiet.

"You disobeyed the fucking code, Seamus. What the *fuck* were you thinking?"

He's shaking from fury and grief and the weight of betrayal.

"You took her. You touched her. You chose her."

A pause. A breath.

"A *Kopolov*."

I keep my face still, unreadable, even as my chest cracks wide open.

"She's not the enemy."

His eyes flash. "Oh no? Then *you* are."

The words hit like a gavel. Final.

"This syndicate is splintering because of you. Because of this. You're sleeping, literally sleeping, with the enemy."

He throws a hand in the air, pacing the way he always does when he's balancing on the edge of losing control. His voice grows louder.

"This family is teetering. I could be exiled for this. Killed."

"I need you to trust me," I say. The words don't tremble. They vibrate with threat. With conviction and truth.

The study flashes behind my eyes, dusty books, cracked leather, the smell of stale cigars. I remember what it felt like to be called reckless. To be punished.

But I'm not that boy anymore.

"I've told you before, and I'll tell you again. Your friend, your golden boy Branson? He's a fucking traitor." My words are a loaded gun.

His jaw tightens, and his eyes lock on mine.

"You've said that," he spits. "You don't know how loyal he is. You don't know what he's done for this family."

"Why don't I, then?" I say, shrugging one shoulder. "Why was I, the one meant to inherit this throne, kept in the dark?"

He scoffs. "Jealousy," he says, pointing a finger at me like it's a curse. "That's what this is."

But it's not.

I shake my head slowly. "No. The Irish aren't splintering because *I* married a Kopolov. They're splintering because of *him*."

But he won't see it. Not yet. Maybe not ever.

Because Branson showed up when I was too young. Too impulsive. And my father never looked back.

My father has a hard time letting go of control. Always has. He allowed just this one friend in, just one, because that man proved himself. In my father's eyes, loyalty is everything.

In that moment, standing across from him, he is as immovable as the stone pillars surrounding us. "I'm ashamed of you," he says, shaking his head.

It burns. It stings.

A sharper blow than any blade. Sharper than any strike I've taken to the ribs or jaw. I taste bile and swallow it down like poison.

"I need you to trust me," I say, softer this time, almost pleading. He leans in close.

His whisper is deeper than his threats. "You murdered her betrothed, Seamus. They'll come for blood, son."

I shake my head. "Not if I can help it."

My breathing evens out, steady now. Every lesson he taught me, every scar he gave me, I'll use them all. I'll make them my armor.

I know she's being held somewhere secure. I pray she is. Somewhere close. I tell myself maybe my mother is near, maybe Bronwyn's with her, two women with hearts made of iron and gold. Maybe they'll protect her for now, shield the rest.

But I didn't marry a stranger. Not some woman dragged off the street.

She was raised by Rafail Kopolov himself. She knows how

to survive under fire. She was forged in it. And yet... I hate this. I hate the pain of being apart.

I haven't felt like this in years. Not since the last time I made a reckless, desperate move. I've spent years crawling back into my father's good graces. Rebuilding the broken bridge of his trust, brick by agonizing brick.

And now, here I am.

His phone chimes, and he glances down. "Your mother says it's time for dinner," he says, clipped.

Annoyance flickers in his eyes. Probably not at me, at her. Maybe both.

I guess she's calling for him. I push up to my feet, exhale hard, and nod. A silent reprieve. A moment to breathe.

An escape. Dinner's early tonight. We don't usually eat this early. It feels off.

I know I'm not finished here, not by a long shot. But I'll take the moment anyway.

"I'll go," I say.

"Aye, you will. And you'll behave in front of your mother."

He snaps the words at me like an order. I stop and turn toward him.

"I'm not a child anymore."

For the first time, we meet eye to eye. I look down at him and realize... he's shorter than I remember.

Time has taken something from him. He's still strong, still

built like the soldier he once was. He still trains, still lifts, still carries the weight of the past on his shoulders.

But I've grown. I'm in my prime. And he knows he can't overpower me now.

I see it in his eyes, the flicker of something like fear. "Da," I say softly. "Please. Trust me."

His jaw locks as his gaze bores into mine. "You've left me no choice."

"I know," I whisper, letting go of his wrist.

"Let's go to dinner."

I step past him, across the threshold. His glare lingers behind me. But I have other priorities.

I need to get back to Zoya.

I'm not letting the hammer drop. Not tonight.

But tonight, it's time for a call to Matvei Kopolov.

CHAPTER 22

ZOYA

"Aren't you a wonder," Caitlin says, her voice warm as she places a hand on my shoulder and pulls me into a quick hug. "No wonder Seamus loves you so much."

Her words catch me off guard. Make me ache. I think of my mother.

"Did your mother teach you to cook like this?" she asks, her eyes bright, looking at the honey cake cooling on the counter.

I shake my head, looking away. "No. She's been gone a long time. I was just a child when she died."

"Oh, sweet girl, I'm sorry," Caitlin says.

I breathe out slowly. "Thank you. I taught myself. I'm pretty good at it."

"Are you?" she asks, smiling. "I'm not very good myself. I

304

had a sheltered life. Maybe I'll tell you about it someday. Not now." She winks.

"My son likes to eat. They all do. Tonight's a little celebration," she says with a smile. "Doesn't feel right asking the bride to cook though! I hope Seamus isn't put out. Do you like wine?"

"Yes." I nod eagerly.

"White or red?"

"Either's fine."

"It's all right, lass. You can pick."

"I actually like both," I admit.

She chuckles. "Good. My son needs someone agreeable."

I shrug. "Only one person can be in charge, I guess."

"Oh, I know how that goes." She laughs again. "Now let's see. You teach me how to cook, and maybe I'll teach you how to survive a McCarthy man, eh?"

I shake her hand with a laugh. "Deal."

We start pulling things together for the meal, her guidance easy and practiced. The ingredients are simple but fresh. Roasted chicken with garlic and lemon. Buttered green beans. Honey-glazed carrots. Fresh bread, baked earlier in the day.

And for dessert, a honey cake, light, golden, and fragrant.

"This is amazing," Caitlin says, watching me mix and move. "Seamus will scold me for putting you to work."

"I'd rather stay busy," I reply. "I cooked for him back at the cabin."

She grimaces. "Oh dear. Tell me he didn't try?"

I laugh. "He did."

"No. Oh, I'm sorry." She grimaces. "Not his strong suit."

"Definitely not."

We laugh again, and I catch Kyla watching us from the doorway, coming and going with plates.

Ashland's in the background too. Observing, quiet.

Bronwyn enters just in time to admire the honey cake. "It only takes thirty minutes," I tell her. "Fresh food doesn't have to take forever."

"Let's bring this out," Caitlin says, and leads me into a large formal dining room.

"We don't eat in here much anymore," she says. "It's gone out of style, hasn't it? The old tradition of the family table."

I nod. "We eat in the kitchen too."

"Yes," she agrees. "But tonight is special."

Bronwyn walks in. "Bronwyn, darling, wine glasses, please. Kyla, fetch your dad his drink."

They move quietly, obediently. But I notice Seamus isn't here yet.

It twists in my gut.

"So," Caitlin says, pouring a glass of white wine. "Tell us about yourself."

I take a sip, fruity, sweet. I like it.

"I'm the youngest in my family. Three older brothers, one sister. She lives in South Africa with her husband. My brothers are all married. I stayed close to home."

"How'd you meet my brother then, staying so close to home?" Kyla asks boldly, tearing into a roll.

My cheeks burn.

"She gets snappy when she's hungry," Bronwyn says.

"Eat, Kyla," she says calmly. "And maybe shut up."

"Girls," Caitlin warns, sharp-eyed. "Go on, Zoya."

I clear my throat. "I got tired of my brothers' rules. Took a little trip to a pub one night. Met Seamus there. He's always been good to me."

"When was this?" Kyla presses.

"A while ago," I say, dodging the trap.

Seamus said I was safe here. But am I?

"If only he didn't act the feckin' traitor," Ash mutters.

I set my wine glass down, hard. My gaze slices to Ash. "I told you. Don't call him a traitor."

He scoffs. "You can defend him if you want, but it won't work."

"No," I snap. "You want to go at him, do it to his face. But I'm telling you right now, my husband is not a traitor."

I jab my finger into the table, my fury rising.

"Is that right?" Ash gets up.

"That's right," I say, standing.

"That's my girl," I hear Seamus say behind me. Relief floods through me.

I exhale at the sound of his voice, like a warm tide cutting through the chaos.

"So brave. That's my good girl. Ashland, sit *down*. You want to call me a traitor to my face, lad?"

Ashland scowls, his jaw tight. "You brought a fucking Kopolov into the house."

"I did." Seamus's voice is calm, but there's steel underneath. "Obviously. I did more than that, actually. I put the man she was about to marry into the ground." He turns to face Ashland directly, like he's challenging him to argue. "Does that say anything about my decision?"

Then he steps to my side, fingers weaving through mine like it's second nature. He bends down, kisses my temple, slow and deliberate, and says, "I love her." Then, eyes back on Ashland, "You want to take this outside?"

A shiver runs through me at the tone of his voice.

Ashland hesitates. Then, quietly, "No, sir."

He sits down.

"Kyla?" Seamus asks, narrowing his eyes at his sister. "I heard a tone I don't care for when you were speaking to my wife. Want to try that again in front of me?"

She answers softly, looking down at the table. "No. But give us a minute, Seamus. I've given you several."

But he snaps, sharp. "My decisions are between me and Dad. I'll demand nothing but respect from the rest of you. Zoya is one of us. She's Zoya McCarthy now."

"She'll *never* be Zoya McCarthy," Kyla hisses. She pushes back her chair with a loud scrape, tosses her napkin on the table like it burned her, and storms out.

Caitlin lets out a breath like she's been holding it for minutes. "Oh dear," she mutters.

Seamus moves half a step like he's about to go after her, but Caitlin reaches out, gently pressing a hand to his arm.

"No, son. Leave it. I'll have a word with her."

My heart thuds.

I don't want them to fight over me though. That's not what I came here for. That's not what love is.

"Now, lad, come and sit. Eat. Have some of this delicious food your wife made for us."

"My wife?" he echoes, looking at me with a kind of wonder, like the word tastes new and sweet on his tongue. "They put you to work already?" he asks, taking a seat.

"Mm-hmm," I say, a little sheepishly. "The housekeeper had to leave."

Caitlin chuckles, then turns to him. "You know how I am at cooking?"

"I do know how you are at cooking," he replies, grinning apologetically, and I stifle a giggle.

"This looks delicious, Zoya," he says, his eyes scanning the table.

Bronwyn leans in, smirking. "See? Now I know why he married you. You know how to cook. The rest of us are absolute shite at it."

"Bronwyn," Caitlin warns, giving her a look. "Language."

Seamus scowls at his sister. "You heard mam. Watch your mouth," he adds.

"Sorry," Bronwyn mumbles, her cheeks flushed. She doesn't meet my eyes.

Bossy, overbearing brother is awfully familiar to me, only this time I'm *married* to him.

Yikes.

Just then, a hush falls over the room like a curtain being drawn. The door at the far end creaks open, and with it, the air shifts, charged now, like the static hum before a storm. Caitlin sits up straighter, and her eyes instinctively sweep over each of her children at the table, assessing, anchoring.

Keenan McCarthy steps into the room, moving with a quiet, unspoken authority that bends the room to his will without a single word. It's the kind of presence that makes spines straighten and conversation die mid-breath. Seamus rises immediately, a reflex, a sign of deference that runs deeper than mere politeness. I follow a breath later, his cue, my instinct.

His fingers find mine, a grounding point in the chaos, warm and sure. "Da," Seamus murmurs, his chin tipping toward the door in a subtle signal. Keenan nods, his gaze gliding across the room.

And when it lands on me, it holds. No flicker of anger, no hint of warmth either. Just a cold, clinical assessment, like I'm another piece in a puzzle he's trying to fit into place.

"Zoya," he says, deep and almost unnervingly smooth. "Welcome. I apologize for my earlier behavior. I'm sure you're well aware your family and mine... have not exactly seen eye to eye for some time now."

His civility is unnerving. Not kindness. Not warmth. Just razor-sharp composure.

"Thank you," I say carefully. "Yes, I'm aware."

Better to stay quiet, let my silence speak for me. He doesn't press. Just claims the seat at the head of the table like it's a throne. Every movement is deliberate, surgical.

"This looks delicious," he says, his tone appreciative but distant. Caitlin starts to rise to serve him, but he stops her with a raised hand.

"No, thank you, lass. I'll get it myself."

He reaches, helping himself. Caitlin nods toward me. "Zoya cooked for us," she says gently.

"Is that right?" His brows lift with mild curiosity, eyes swinging to me again. "You like to cook?"

"I do," I answer, the words catching slightly on my tongue. I feel exposed, as if my ability to prepare a meal somehow makes me more likable.

"We're not much for cooking since our head chef left," Keenan offers, his tone neutral.

"Yes... Caitlin told me." My cheeks warm. I'm not sure what to say, or where I belong here, how I fit in this hierarchy, in this family that's not mine. Do I call her mom? Mrs. McCarthy? She introduced herself as Caitlin...

Seamus's large, warm hand finds my knee under the table, grounding me again with a soft, steady squeeze.

"Bronwyn," he says, affectionately.

"How'd your driving go?"

"Very well," Bronwyn answers proudly.

"Aye. She only knocked over two streetlights," Caitlin chimes in with a mischievous grin.

Keenan's eyebrows shoot up to his hairline before everyone breaks into quiet laughter.

"Just kidding," Caitlin adds, winking at Bronwyn. "Just one."

"I didn't knock it over," Bronwyn mutters, her cheeks flushing pink. "It was just... wobbly." She shrugs, looking away, embarrassed.

Then to Seamus, "Take Bronwyn out again tomorrow, will you?"

Seamus agrees.

I'm mildly surprised Bronwyn doesn't have her license yet. She must be around nineteen, old enough, surely, but maybe she's cautious. Or maybe Seamus has been protecting her. Maybe both.

"How's the city?" Seamus asks Keenan.

"All right," Keenan replies smoothly, cutting into his chicken with almost clinical precision. "Branson swept the warehouse on the coast."

The table quiets. "It's clean," he continues. "Shipment came in. Easter arms, just like the specs." He sets his knife down, wipes his mouth.

For a moment, we all eat in companionable silence, the kind that feels worn-in, familiar. And just like that, homesickness claws at my chest.

It was like this at home—Rafail at the head of the table, the rest of us gathered around. Now that we're scattered and married and rarely home, Rafail has instituted once-a-month Sunday dinners. No excuses. It's the highlight of my month.

Bronwyn leans in, her eyes sharp and unapologetic. "Now that Seamus is back... any chance Russia could come after him? He escaped custody, right? Would they want him returned?"

A chill trickles down my spine. Oh god. Why hasn't that ever occurred to me? That the Russian government might still want to reclaim him?

My eyes dart to Seamus, but he doesn't flinch. Unshaken. His fingers curl around mine again, a soft, steady pat. Reassurance without words.

Keenan answers instead. "The likelihood of extradition is low. Political climates have shifted. Our alliances are mostly intact, for now." He cuts Seamus a look. "Keep a low profile. No headlines, no fireworks. Nothing flashy until the dust settles. Yeah?"

"Yes, sir," Seamus says, his jaw locked.

I can't help but think: *No headlines, no fireworks*, that might just be his preferred method of ruling. Quiet, effective, ruthless.

Keenan turns his attention back to his plate, the conversation shifting again. And I start to see it, how Seamus learned to rule not by raising his voice, but by speaking only when he had to.

His eyes find mine as if to say: I'm not afraid. You don't have to be either.

Am I afraid? Maybe. Maybe I'm just lost, like a fish out of water. But fear doesn't feel quite right. Not exactly.

"This is really delicious," Bronwyn says, sweet and earnest. "Leave it to Seamus to find a woman who can cook when we actually need one."

Her cheerfulness is infectious. I smile. "Thank you. I do like to cook."

"Can you teach me?" she asks.

Ash snorts. Caitlin gently smacks his arm. "Ash, be nice."

But he just shakes his head. "If you can teach Bronwyn to cook, we'll call you a miracle worker."

I chuckle, placing a bite of chicken into my mouth. "We'll start small. Maybe toast."

Seamus winks at me. My heart doesn't flutter, it somersaults. We may be married, we may have spent months tangled in each other's lives, but somehow he still does this to me.

And I want him. God, I want him.

Wine is passed around, and the conversation softens. It feels normal, almost.

"Where is everyone else?" Seamus asks, his voice lowering slightly. He turns to me. "I have brothers, too, you know."

"I'll introduce you shortly," Keenan says. "After your absence, I had to send them on a bit of a recon. I'll fill you in later. Tomorrow," he continues. "By then, we'll have the full family together. Here."

Yay.

"I can hire a caterer," Caitlin begins.

But Keenan interrupts, his eyes locking with mine.

"You could. Or you could give Zoya another opportunity to cook."

A challenge. His smile doesn't reach his eyes.

"Would you like that?"

He's testing me. I meet his gaze, unflinching. "I'd love that. I cook for my family at home all the time."

Silence. No one responds. And once again, I feel my cheeks burn.

My family. Their enemies.

Seamus leans in, his lips brushing my ear. "I've had enough of the social life now. Let's go." He stands. "Thank you for dinner," he says, reaching for my hand.

"I prepared your old room for you, son," Caitlin says,

standing to embrace him. "It's good to see you. Good to have you back."

Keenan nods at Seamus but doesn't rise. "I'll see you tonight. I'd like to go over what you missed in your absence."

"Yes, sir," Seamus replies.

He heads for the door.

"Well, that went well," I murmur to him, my voice a little wry, a little surprised, like maybe I hadn't expected it to.

Seamus gives me a smile, slow and tight, but full of something private. Something just for me.

Once we're in the hallway alone, the door clicks shut behind us, sealing off the muffled voices and lingering tension on the other side. It's quieter here. Dimmer. The kind of quiet that lets truths come out.

He reaches for me without hesitation, like he needs the contact, and cups the back of my head, his palm warm and steady against my scalp. Then his forehead touches mine, our breaths mingling in the space between us.

"I love you, Zoya," he whispers, and the weight of it lands softly but undeniably in my chest. "I'm sorry."

"Sorry for what?" I ask him, already knowing it's not just one thing. It's never just one thing.

"I'm sorry this had to be your entrance into my family," he says. "I wish they'd done better. I wish it had been easier."

I exhale softly. "I knew what I was walking into, Seamus. You think if we sat down to dinner with my family, they'd be any friendlier?"

I can't help but smile as I shake my head. "If anything, I think your family's probably nicer than mine would've been."

He gives a soft, rough chuckle, the sound vibrating in his chest.

"You forgive too easily, Zoya," he murmurs huskily.

"Do I?" I ask, tilting my head.

But he's not wrong. I forgave him for leaving me, for good reason, maybe, but still. And I've forgiven many things in my life. Things most people would never even consider forgiving. I've made peace with monsters.

"Come," he says, his tone shifting, want threaded beneath the word. His mouth to my ear, "I want you alone."

My heartbeat stutters in my chest.

The corridor is dim, lit only by the moonlight slanting through narrow windows. The house is beautiful in a way that feels both old and curated, an Irish estate that's witnessed many come and go. He leads me to the second floor, then turns left, guiding me down a long, hushed hallway. Our footsteps are swallowed by thick gray carpet, soft beneath my feet.

"We've had many families in here," he says. "There was a time when we were bursting at the seams. My father had to add a whole extra floor. A lot of remodeling."

I can almost see it in my mind, children racing down these halls, thick accents and big tempers, rough affection and fierce loyalty.

"This one," he says, stopping in front of a black door. "This room's mine. Has been since I was a small lad."

He opens the door, no lock, unlike the heavy, bolted ones back at my house, and closes it softly behind me. I inhale slowly.

My heart slows as I take in the space. It's stark. Masculine. Impeccably clean. Like his house, everything about the room is so intensely him, though a simple vase with red roses on a shelf tells me Caitlin was here.

Once the door clicks shut, he turns to me and reaches for my chin. The kiss he gives me isn't rushed. It's not wild or needy, but gentle, intentional. A quiet claim.

I melt into it.

The heat between us builds, not fire, but something slower. Smoldering. An intimacy that feels like comfort and danger all at once. His touch is reverent, like he's reminding me this is us now. This space. This night.

"Tonight, we rest," he whispers. Then, after a beat, "Or... perhaps tonight we try for that baby."

I blink. "Try for a baby..."

"Aye," he says. "Your idea, wasn't it?"

"Mmm." I nod. I still think it's a solid strategy that neither his father nor my brother could argue with.

He kisses me again, but this time it's softer.

"Seamus."

He pulls away a touch. "Aye?"

"I... don't want our lovemaking to become a duty."

He shakes his head, brushing his thumb over my cheek. "Neither do I, love."

"I'm not on birth control," I tell him gently. "And by my calculations... I'm definitely ovulating."

His brow quirks up, amused. Interested. Dangerous.

"Are you?" he says.

"Yes," I answer, fingers threading together as I watch him watch me.

And that's when I note his hard length. He's already hard. The idea of making love to me, of claiming me like that, is enough to undo him.

"Maybe it doesn't have to be a duty," I whisper, thinking aloud. "Maybe it doesn't have to be because someone else told us what to do. Maybe it's just because we love each other... and we want this."

"Hush, lass," he nearly growls.

And then I'm in his arms. My legs wrap instinctively around his waist. I hear the solid click of the lock behind me, and he's already striding toward the bed like a man on a mission.

My body heats with every step. I feel his erection pressing against me, solid and demanding. When he lays me down, I remember. I remember the way he's spanked me, the way he's made me burn with need, the way he's never let me forget how much he wants me.

"You're a good lass," he murmurs against my ear. "Such a good girl, aren't you?"

I nod. Yes. I'm his good girl. Maybe the only time in my life I've wanted to be one.

"I want you on your back, legs spread, darlin'," he whispers, his accent thick and seductive. "Let's get you stripped."

Our clothes fall away like wrapping paper, each layer peeling back to reveal the gift underneath. Naked. Vulnerable. Open.

He kisses every inch of my body like it's sacred.

When he finally finds my pussy, his tongue strokes me in one perfect lick. My hips jerk of their own accord.

"You like that, don't you?" he murmurs against me.

"You're good at it," I whisper, and oh god, yes, I do.

"No rules tonight," he says, his breath hot on my inner thigh. "Do whatever your heart desires, angel."

And I do.

I spread my legs for him, shameless and aching, and his tongue finds my clit. My head tips back, my fingers curling into his hair like it's the only thing keeping me tethered. His inked shoulders are strong, a vision of masculine power. I grind into his mouth, overwhelmed.

He tongues my core. Licks. Suckles. Nips, until I'm nearly screaming.

"Please, Seamus," I beg. "Please. I want to come."

"Come, love," he says. "Tonight's yours, lass. Tonight's your reward."

The scruff of his beard scratches my thighs before he gives one last, wicked lick, and I break. My orgasm tears through me. My hips rise off the bed, and I stifle a scream as he licks me through every last wave of pleasure.

Then he's on me. His weight, his heat. His need.

He pins my wrists gently, his breath ragged. "On your knees," he growls. "I want you on your knees."

I'm a little scared; it's still new. We've only done this a few times, though each time has gotten easier. Better.

He spreads my legs. My chest hits the bed, my palms flat, bracing.

"Back down," he whispers, pressing his hand to the small of my back. His voice is rough silk. "Good girl."

It's different here, not like home. At home, I feel free, reckless. Here, the walls feel like they have eyes. Watching. Judging.

And yet... I kind of like it. Maybe I have a touch of voyeur in me after all.

Fuck whoever wants to take us apart. This? This is my husband. This is us. I *want* him.

He positions himself behind me, the head of his cock nudging my entrance.

"If it's too much... tell me," he says softly. "I don't want to hurt you, Zoya."

"Please," I whisper, trembling. "I want you in me. I want you, Seamus."

And then he pushes into me, and it's not pain, it's perfection. Full, deep, right.

It's everything.

I shatter. My pussy hugs his cock, contracting in ecstasy. I stifle a scream, loath to be overheard, as he fists my hair and pounds into me. I rock with him, riding the waves of pleasure, until we're both spent and boneless.

It's been a long night. Every inch of me aches in that delicious, spent way. He cleans me up tenderly, his touch reverent, then I collapse onto the bed, my body giving out.

My eyes are half-lidded, floating somewhere between consciousness and sleep. "You're so tired, darling," he murmurs, brushing hair from my cheek. I give him a soft, lazy smile.

"The wine's hit me. It makes me sleepy," I add, barely above a whisper.

"I'll keep that in mind," he says, a teasing glint in his eyes as he winks.

I drag myself to the bathroom, moving like a half-dead zombie. My limbs feel like they're moving through syrup, but I want to be clean before I crawl into bed for real. Once I'm done, I slide under the covers, and he's there, lifting them gently, tucking me in.

No one's tucked me in since I was a little girl. I didn't know I missed that. It feels... warm. Safe.

"Thank you," I whisper, and I mean it.

He bends down, presses a kiss to my forehead, and there's something sacred in the gesture. "Thank *you*," he says back. He doesn't tell me what he's thanking me for. But he means it too. I can feel it.

"Are you coming to bed?" I ask, surprised when he doesn't join me. I want him behind me, his warmth, his weight, his breath on my neck. My oversized teddy bear, lethal and all mine.

"Not yet," he replies. "I have some work to do."

He walks to the sliding glass doors that lead to the balcony, phone in hand, wearing nothing but a pair of black boxers. His body is ridiculous, cut like stone, and mine to worship. But there's something in the set of his shoulders that tightens my chest. Something's wrong.

"Do you want to talk about it?" I ask gently, hoping, praying, he says no because I'm too tired to carry anything heavy tonight.

"Not yet," he says, turning to glance at me. "I will. Get some rest, Zoya."

I grab my phone, check for messages from home. Nothing. Why has no one reached out again? It's unlike them.

I scroll aimlessly, letting the blue light lull me. But I can feel it, the tension pulsing in the room. I wonder if the code he swears by is fraying at the edges. If the whispers have started weaving their way through his ranks. I know they don't trust me. Our families are at war, and I'm the enemy in their eyes.

Thank god that Keenan said it's unlikely Seamus will be

picked up by Russia. Though he did say unlikely... not impossible.

His phone buzzes. Again. And again. He scowls down at it, thumb tapping the screen. "Branson," he mutters.

I drift off to the low hum of voices. His voice, serious and sharp. I don't know how long I sleep. An hour? Two? When I wake, I can tell it's the dead of night by the inky blackness out the window.

He sits beside me, gently shaking my shoulder. "I'm sorry to wake you, lass. You awake, love?"

I sit up fast, heart pounding. "Yes."

"I got a call," he says quietly. "And I need to go. Makes me nervous leaving you here, darling. You remember what I said about you accompanying me. I trust my family, but they aren't the only ones in and out of this house."

"You want me to come with you?" I ask, already throwing the covers off. I remember how he said he'd come with me wherever I go.

I'm your shadow, your bloody shield, your man for every damn thing.

He hesitates. "I'm just meeting with my men. They have updates. My father wants me there."

I nod. "I understand."

"But aye. I want you there."

I throw on clothes just before he hands me a gun.

"Here. Take this."

My heart pounds harder. "Of course," I say. "But... why? It's just your men?"

His expression darkens. "Do you remember what happened at the bar in Russia, darling?"

I nod slowly. I remember. He killed his own men... because not all of them were loyal.

"Right," I whisper. "Got it."

We walk downstairs. The house is quiet, heavy with sleep. The voices we heard earlier are gone, swallowed into private rooms. If anyone's awake, they're not making their presence known.

Outside, two cars are idling, headlights casting long shadows across the driveway. Seamus nods to a man who opens the passenger door for me, helps me in, and then slides into the driver's seat.

"You remember the rules, Zoya," Seamus says as we pull away, giving me a sharp side glance. "Stay quiet. I don't want to hear a word. Do what I say. This is not the time to fucking push me. Understand? It's for your own safety."

"Yes," I answer quickly. "Of course. I'm not going to disobey you."

"Because you're loyal. And brave," he says. "And sometimes the loyal and brave do fearless things to protect people."

My stomach drops. "Oh god. Seamus... are you in trouble?"

He shakes his head. "No. I'm reclaiming what's mine and bringing you with me."

I wonder what his father told him. "Does your father know you're going?"

"Aye."

The warehouse we pull up to is nothing more than a nondescript rectangular box on the edge of town. No lights. No signs. If Seamus hadn't stopped the car, I would've missed it completely.

I follow close behind him, every step echoing in my chest. I whisper a prayer, though I don't know the words. I just need someone, anyone, to keep him safe. My husband.

Inside, the ceiling yawns high above us. Figures linger in shadows, flickering in and out of view under dim, buzzing bulbs.

They stop when we enter. No one speaks.

Seamus doesn't hesitate. Doesn't flinch. He stands tall, still, a living monument to danger and dominance.

He looks around. "This is my wife. Zoya. *Respect*," he says flatly.

One by one, they rise to their feet, except for one.

He stays seated. Defiant.

Seamus's gaze locks on him, and the whole room tenses. The air stills. The moment stretches long and sharp before he draws his gun. Fires.

The man drops, crimson blooming on dark hair. No warning. No explanation. His head lolls forward.

I clamp a hand over my mouth, the scream silent behind my fingers. But I don't move.

Seamus looks around. "Anybody else want to disrespect my wife?" he asks, lethal and calm.

"No, sir," comes the chorus. A wave of reverence. Fear. Submission.

He turns to me. "This is Zoya McCarthy now. She's mine."

Then, like nothing just happened, he walks to the head of the table and pulls out a chair for me. I sit, every nerve still screaming, but steady.

He takes the seat beside me.

"Now," he says, folding his hands. "Where were we?"

CHAPTER 23

SEAMUS

To Zoya's CREDIT, she doesn't even flinch when I pull the trigger.

I knew it was only a matter of time. Sooner or later, I'd have to deal with the rot. There've been whispers and rumors circling like vultures among my men, and I never believed for a second that I'd cleaned house entirely back at the bar in Russia.

And when I spoke to Da, he didn't need to say much, just enough to confirm what I already knew in my gut. There were whispers I'd made a mistake. That marrying Zoya was a weakness. The only men who thought that? Branson's loyalists. The old guard who'd rather see the past reign than step into the future. I suspected he assured their loyalty with empty promises or threats against their families.

Our feud, Branson's and mine, isn't something I've taken lightly. I haven't shared the details with anyone. No one but

Da. And up until now, even he's leaned toward Branson's side.

That'll change. In a few days, once the truth surfaces, it will change.

So when I made every man in that room stand, when I watched their eyes slide over to Zoya, the woman I've crowned my queen, I knew. I knew exactly who'd betrayed me.

I didn't hesitate. I pulled the trigger with the ease of someone who's done it before. Who knows when justice must be swift.

Another woman might've screamed, might've run from the room in horror.

But not my lass.

No, not my beautiful, brave lass. She stayed standing beside me, spine straight as an arrow, eyes sharp and calculating. She's kind, yes. Gentle, sometimes. But beneath that soft veneer is a core of steel.

It's what I love about her.

Back to the task at hand. Ah. Introductions.

I gesture to my left. "You've met Ashland, love," I say. "My first cousin."

Next to Ashland sits Lorcan, Nolan's lad. He's got the same dirty-blond hair and piercing blue eyes as his cousin. The same lean build and restless energy, always scanning, always calculating.

"And Cavin, my brother. Would've been at dinner tonight if he hadn't had business to handle." Thick with muscle, he has my father's build and my mother's eyes. He's got that quiet power, the kind that doesn't need to posture. "Cavin runs guns out of Belfast. Loyal as hell to our family."

He might see Zoya as a threat to the Irish legacy. That'll change too.

"Daire," I say, nodding my head to the youngest at the table. Twenty-five. Reckless. Scarred knuckles. Bitter mouth. Eyes that have looked up to me since he could walk. He'd do anything I asked.

"Now," I say coldly, "why the fuck did you pull me out of my bed in the middle of the goddamn night?"

I've walked into the warehouse mid-meeting, summoned by Ashland.

I jerk my head at the cooling body on the floor. "Lorcan. Clean it up. Fast."

I don't like killing. But I hate my wife being disrespected even more.

This meeting wasn't mine. They called it. They tested me. It wasn't subtle, and it wasn't smart. Orchestrated by Da and Branson's old guard, no doubt. They wanted to see if I'd gone soft. If marriage, if love, had weakened me. They wanted to prod the heir and see if he'd bite.

Well, I did.

And the blood's still fresh.

The body's still bleeding out, and I keep my voice calm, like

I'm discussing wine instead of murder. "Now, men," I say, "why the hell are we all here?"

No one answers right away. Cavin leans forward eventually, slow and deliberate. He's built like a brick wall, thick arms covered in ink. When he speaks, people listen.

"Wasn't meant to be a test, sir," he says, flicking his eyes toward the body without flinching. "But... there's been talk."

I don't blink. I wait. "Hmm?"

He clears his throat. "Some of the younger lads... ones who don't remember what it took to build this empire... they've been wondering. Whispering. They see you married. Gone for days at a time. Think you've gone soft."

"I'd like to think I've proven I haven't," I say.

Cavin nods once. "Maybe they just needed a reminder. Bit of a culling, aye?"

Definitely.

The silence after that is thick. Nobody breathes too loud. They all just learned that proximity won't save you.

"Now," I say, resting my hands on the cold metal table, knuckles wide and scarred. "Let's make one thing clear."

Every man straightens. Nobody speaks.

"I'm the heir. Not Branson. If any of you are loyal to him, you tell me now. I've made it clear I don't trust him. I'm loyal to my father."

I draw my gun and place it on the table. "I won't shoot you. But this is your only chance to walk away."

They stay still.

"Where've I been?" I ask, scanning the room. "Cleaning up the messes none of you could stomach. Making deals your fathers never dared dream of. And I married a woman strong enough to stand beside me while I build something bigger."

I nod to Zoya.

"She is not a weakness. She is your queen. And you will treat her as such."

Cavin gives a slow, understanding nod. He's always understood the bigger picture.

"You think I'm distracted?" I ask. "No. I've been focused. Belfast is ours. Dublin's folding. And there are men across the sea waiting to kneel at our table."

I scan the room again. "But if any of you want to play petty kingdom, whisper behind my back, test me, I'll bury every last one of you and rebuild from the ground up."

Another silence.

And this time, they know it's their test.

I start pointing.

"You," I say to Daire. "Ride out. Reinforce Belfast. Cavin runs point. No movement without his say-so."

"Aye. Yes, sir," comes instantly.

I round the table and stop behind Zoya's chair, placing both hands on her shoulders. She doesn't flinch.

"My wife will be protected. And anyone who forgets that won't get a second chance."

A chorus of "Yes, sir" follows.

But one voice cuts through. "And the Russians, sir?"

I turn my eyes on him. "What about them?"

"They murdered half our crew. You're saying there's no retribution?"

I press my lips into a thin, bloodless line. "Those responsible will pay. That's a promise. But if you trust me, I will not lead you astray." My voice cuts through the silence. "Do you understand?"

"Yes, sir."

"Good." I nod. "Then we're done here. For now."

I glance down at Zoya. "You ready, love?"

She stands. And together, we walk out of the warehouse, leaving behind silence, a body cooling on the floor, and a room full of men with questions I'm not ready to answer.

Not yet.

CHAPTER 24

THE NEXT MORNING, when I wake, the house is already quiet. Seamus is gone. No note. No sound. I sit up, frowning, wondering where he's gone. Did he even go to bed last night?

I pad downstairs barefoot, slowly, half hoping I don't run into anyone else. This isn't my home, not really. Not yet. But I need to start treating it like it is, at least for now. We'll be here a while, I think.

From the corridor, I glance out the wide window facing east. The sun is unforgiving, blazing and relentless, and there on the lawn, I see him. Seamus. With... I squint. Ashland? Their heads are bowed close together.

They don't see me.

Their posture is intimate, conspiratorial. Ashland laughs, tossing his head back like he just heard something hysterical. But Seamus? He doesn't laugh. His hands are jammed deep into his pockets, his jaw set, his mouth a hard, grim line.

Strange. Why would he be talking to Ashland? He killed a man last night for disrespecting me, and Ashland's been the absolute worst.

I keep walking, refusing to linger. This isn't my business. Is it? But either way, I don't want to know. I don't want to have to know. Seamus turns then, catching sight of me from across the lawn. Our eyes lock for a second. But he doesn't come after me. Doesn't explain. Just nods. A single, dismissive nod.

Like that's enough.

It's not.

I head toward the kitchen. Caitlin and I had made plans. Well, I promised her I'd show her how to make pirozhki this morning. Something simple, sweet and familiar.

She's already busy when I walk in, humming softly to herself, her hands moving with the kind of ease only years of practice bring. She looks up, sees me, and offers a warm, easy smile.

"Good morning, lovely," she says, placing a mug in front of me, steam curling into the air. "How are you today?"

"I'm good," I answer automatically. But there's weight at the end of that sentence, a silent question hanging in the space between us.

She sits beside me. "Here's your tea. Just like you like it." Her smile is soft, maternal.

"You know, at home I was always the one who put the kettle on for everyone else."

She smiles. "Helps, doesn't it? Listen, I know we don't know each other very well," she begins, "but when I moved here, Keenan's mam, Maeve, was an absolute joy to me. She's been gone a couple of years now. God, I loved her. She made me feel like I belonged."

She glances down for a beat, her fingers tightening around her mug. "She was like a mother to me, you know."

I nod, swallowing hard. "I lost mine young," I manage, my throat tightening with the memory.

"And your sister's... far, yes? Complicated history?"

"She's in South Africa," I reply softly. "We haven't been close for a while. There's no problem between us, we're just distant."

She nods, gentle, but doesn't pry. "I don't want to overstep, love. I just want you to know, I'm here. For whatever you need. You don't have to do it alone."

I smile at her, small but genuine. "Thank you. I mean it. I appreciate it."

I glance away, uncomfortable with how kind she is. "I just... I don't like that our families are feuding. I don't like the fighting. I like peace. I hate conflict."

She raises a brow, grinning. "Yet here you are. Russian Bratva, married into the Irish mob. Sounds like conflict might be our middle names, huh?"

I laugh, in spite of myself. "Apparently."

She winks and takes a long sip of her tea. "I find it helps if you add a splash of Jack Daniels to the tea. Calms the nerves."

"For breakfast?"

"Oh, what they don't know won't kill them, eh?"

I shake my head, laughing. I sigh. Now it's my turn to tread carefully. "I don't want to overstep, but... I think your husband doesn't like me?"

"Oh, love, no. Keenan and I talk about everything. He keeps nothing from me after all these years. Been married for decades now. Raised all these kids together. And I can promise you, it's nothing personal. Give him time, love."

She sighs, nostalgic. "Though it was different for us at first. His dad died the same day we got married. So he took the reins while grieving. He's been through it, believe me. And it's worn on him. His health, his mind... it takes a toll running a crew like this."

I nod. "I imagine it does. Rafail had gray hair before he hit thirty."

"Rafail's your oldest brother, aye?"

"Yes," I say. "He became my guardian when my parents died. He was eighteen."

She leans in slightly, her voice softer. "If I can tell you anything, Zoya, it's this: Our pain and our loyalty, that's what binds us. My husband, he doesn't *dislike* you. He wants peace, too, just like you and I do. But he doesn't agree with how Seamus went about all this."

"I get that," I murmur. "So does Rafail. I just wish I could make them talk. It's like one of those romance novels, where you just scream at the pages, 'Just talk to each other already!' But they never do."

"Romance novels?" she asks with a sparkle in her eye.

I shrug. "My sister-in-law's obsessed. She gives me all her recommendations."

"Oh, fascinating," Caitlin says, grinning. "I read them too. My daughters got me into them." She winks again. "Now. I'm starving. And I wish I could cook better because, let's be honest, the way to a man's heart is absolutely through his stomach, no?"

I laugh. "So they say."

We pull the first round of pirozhki out of the oven, warm and fragrant. "Sometimes we fill them with sweetened cheese and vanilla, sometimes apple or berry jam, or a poppyseed paste."

"Oh, Zoya. These look divine," she says, beaming. "I don't care what my husband says. My son made a good choice."

We laugh, and her words warm me. But they don't settle the gnawing unease in my gut.

But here, in Caitlin's kitchen, stirring batter beside her steady presence, it almost fades.

Almost.

"Kyla went into town to pick up some clothes for you," she tells me. "I would've taken you myself, but Seamus asked you to stay nearby. Bronwyn's at school."

"Right."

"I was very young when I had Seamus, you know. He's a bit older than the others."

I nod.

"Now, maybe you can help me put together a plan to cook this week?"

"I'd love to." I help her plan while keeping half an eye on the door, waiting for my husband.

We plan the week's meals together. I show her my family's favorite Russian dishes, pelmeni, borscht, pirozhki, and stuffed cabbage. She suggests Irish classics, soda bread, colcannon, and corned beef.

"It'll be a mix of both, then," I say, jotting down ideas on a pad of paper. It feels almost symbolic.

"There's a website I use for these recipes." I reach for my phone to look up a recipe, when I realize I didn't bring my phone, but Seamus's by accident.

I must've grabbed the wrong one off the bedside table. "Oops," I murmur with an apologetic smile. "Wrong phone."

"It's all right," Caitlin says, reaching over. "We all have access in case of emergency. I can turn it on to get the recipes."

She presses her thumb to the screen. It unlocks.

Interesting. His mother can access his phone, but I can't.

I scroll through for the recipe, trying to ignore the three

unread message notifications blinking at the top. But finally, when Caitlin's back is turned, curiosity gets the best of me.

A preview of the message catches my eye.

Rafail Kopolov.

My blood turns cold.

Trembling, I swipe down to read the preview.

> **Rafail**
> You deceived her. Release Zoya or we're coming for you.

What?

Oh god.

My stomach knots, and my skin goes cold.

I drop the phone like it burns. "I need to grab mine," I say, already on my feet.

"Be right back."

I dart through the house, my heart pounding, panic rising. He's not in the kitchen. Not on the lawn.

Where is Seamus?

I race to our bedroom, slide his phone back onto the table like it never moved, and grab my own.

Then I search for him.

Desperately.

I shouldn't have looked at his phone. I know that. Maybe the message meant something different. Maybe I misread it, saw only what I feared. But still, why would Rafail think

I'm here against my will? What exactly happened to make him question that? Oh god.

I need to talk to him.

I turn, and just like that, I walk straight into Seamus. "Whoa, easy there, love." He catches me without hesitation, wrapping his arms firmly around my waist, his chest warm and solid.

"Zoya," he murmurs. "Y'alright?"

"I'm all right," I say quickly. "I was just cooking in the kitchen with your mom."

He smiles and strokes slow, deliberate circles down my spine, fingers trailing heat and grounding me in the moment. "Are you? I love that. She's a good woman. You're like her," he adds, softer now.

Then he bends, brushing a kiss to my cheek, tender, possessive, familiar.

"Seamus," I whisper, barely trusting my voice, "tell me what's going on."

He falls silent. And my heart starts pounding like a drum trapped in my ribs. That kind of silence speaks louder than words.

"Do you... Do you regret taking me?"

His arms tighten just slightly, not enough to hurt, but just enough to say he's hiding something. Enough to make me feel like there's something heavy weighing him down.

"Of course not."

"All right," I say quietly, not entirely convinced. "You left your phone on the bedside table."

"Oh, I wondered," he replies. "Christ, my father would've had my head if he sent a message and I missed it."

He strides across the room and grabs his phone. I watch him as he unlocks it, scrolls through it, and frowns. His brows knit together. Scrolls again. Then, nothing. He pockets the phone like it's nothing.

"What's going on?" I ask, softly but firmly.

"My father didn't text," he says with a smile. Too fast. Too smooth. Like it's rehearsed. Either he's hiding something, or he really doesn't want me to know what Rafail said.

"Go back to mam if you'd like," he says, his tone shifting. "I have business to tend to, love."

Business. A word that could mean a thousand things. I can't stop thinking: Does this business have anything to do with hurting my family?

"I'm just uneasy, Seamus," I tell him gently. "I wish there could be peace between our families."

"I know," he replies, almost sharply. "Don't you know I know that? I promise. I'm doing everything I can to make that happen."

"Are you sure you don't regret marrying me?" I repeat again.

He turns to me slowly, and there's a warning glint in his eyes. "Ask me that again, and I'll put you right over my knee."

I blink.

"Regret taking you?" he says, his voice rising. "Jesus freaking Christ, woman. It was the proudest moment of my life."

Then he turns, and just like that, he's gone.

I shower, dress, and get ready. I return to the kitchen, but I'm still stuck on everything we just said... and everything we didn't.

I text Rafail.

> Hey how are you? Things are good here. I met Caitlin McCarthy and I love her.

The response comes back quickly.

> **Rafail**
> He treating you well?

> So well

I wonder if my response is too canned, too rapid. Will he believe me?

All he writes back is:

> **Rafail**
> Glad you're doing okay.

Nothing else.

He doesn't believe me. He thinks I'm pretending. But why? What happened to make him think I'm lying?

What are my brothers thinking? What are they planning? Don't they know that half the men in this house blame them for the bloodshed, for the men they lost? I was the one who saw it all. I was there. I watched Seamus take them down.

What if I'm the reason Seamus loses everything?

What if they turn on him because of me?

What if he dies, and it's *my* fault?

My eyes flutter closed, and I force a deep breath. Sometimes this estate feels like a fortress. Other times, it's a prison.

Over the next few days, Kyla brings me clothes. She doesn't bother with pleasantries. She's polite in the way a soldier is: brisk, impersonal, calculated.

Bronwyn, though, she's different. She makes it easy to talk. I end up showing her and Caitlin how to make some of our family's favorite dishes, and in just a few days, they're making them almost as well as I can.

That night, I prepare dinner, something special. One of my family's signature Russian dishes: steaming pelmeni with sour cream and butter, fresh dill chopped fine, and black bread on the side. Comfort food from home. For dessert, I try something Irish I found online, a whiskey-laced bread pudding soaked in cream. A bridge between worlds, I think.

At the table, Keenan eyes the plate in front of him with curiosity. His mouth quirks up.

"Is this some sort of ploy?" he asks, amusement dancing in his voice.

"What do you mean?" I say.

"Pairing the Russian food with the Irish?" He arches a brow. "Are you trying to get me to literally swallow peace, Zoya?"

Heat flushes up my cheeks. I look away.

"Da," Seamus mutters, frowning. "She's an expert at cooking Russian food, and she's learning to cook Irish. What's your point?"

Dinner is a little stilted after that. A little too quiet, too careful.

Later, alone in the sitting room, with the fire low, the light casting soft shadows on the walls, I finally say it.

"I want to go back to our house." My voice is soft. Not demanding, just aching. "Why do we have to stay here?"

"It's safest for now," he says. "Unfortunately."

"Will they talk about me behind closed doors?" I ask. "They don't want me here, Seamus."

He sighs and runs a hand over his face. "I'm trying to protect you, Zoya."

"You're hiding things."

"I'm keeping you safe," he snaps.

"From what?" I press. "The truth?"

He doesn't deny it.

I stand. The ache in my chest spreads like a bruise under my ribs.

"Are you sure you don't regret this?" I whisper.
"Regret *me*?"

He doesn't answer right away. That pause, it shatters something.

"No," he says at last. "Of course I don't. Zoya, I wish I could tell you more, but I'm working on this. Every second. I promise."

"I don't belong here," I say, the words painful to even say. "I don't belong with the Irish. I'm a fish out of water. A square peg in a round hole."

He reaches for me, but I pull away. I can't stay. Not right now.

I leave the room before I break down because the one thing I can't say out loud is the one thing I can't stop thinking:

What if he dies because of me?

What if they turn on him, and it's my fault?

That night, I fall asleep long before he does. He paces on the balcony, phone in his hand, fingers flying across the screen, sending texts like he's trying to fight a war with words.

I think about the moments he made me believe in us. Every kiss, every whispered promise. Every time he held me, like I was his anchor. The months that kept us apart.

But now... what if love isn't enough to survive a war?

CHAPTER 25

SEAMUS

I knew I was being watched. That wasn't paranoia, it was instinct. It's why I kept Zoya right beside me, as close as I could without chaining her to me.

Because I don't trust Branson. Not for a goddamn second.

He's been my boss since before I was of age. A kingmaker in a crumbling empire, hiding behind my father's trust. And I was too young back then to see what he was doing. Too loyal. But the veil dropped in recent years. I finally saw the power play for what it was—he's been usurping the throne under my father's nose. And now, he knows. He knows I married her. That Zoya's not just mine, she's family now.

He's coming. I felt it in my bones before he called. Before that burner phone lit up at midnight with a single word:

Come.

To my father's office.

I went downstairs, barefoot and boiling. Zoya stirred as I moved, lifting her head from the pillow, hair spilling everywhere.

"Is everything okay?" she asked, her voice soft, heavy with sleep.

"It will be," I tell her, kissing her cheek. "Sleep, love."

I wanted to believe that. God, I did. But I knew what I was about to do would rip her apart. I only hoped the foundation we'd built, stone by stone, was strong enough to hold.

Now I'm here, sitting across from Branson in my father's office. The man's draped across the leather like he owns the place, swirling his drink with that same smirk he always wears when he thinks he has the upper hand. His red hair's gone gray with age, but his eyes are as sharp and conniving as ever.

"Tell me something, Seamus," he says lazily, like we're old friends. "How long've you been keeping secrets from me?"

I don't move. Don't blink. Don't let him see me breathe. I have secrets he's yet to unearth, so I need to play it safe.

I smile and shrug. "'Bout as long as you've been betraying my father," I reply coldly.

He just laughs, shaking his head like I'm a child he's amused by.

"You say that," he muses, "but you've got no proof."

That's what he thinks.

He doesn't wait for me to answer.

"She's pretty, that Russian girl, isn't she? The Kopolov girl." His tone is mocking. "Sweet voice. Pretty little mouth. I bet you put that to good use, don't you?"

He's baiting me, and he's good at it—gets away with saying shite I wouldn't tolerate from anyone else. My pulse kicks hard, but I don't take the bait. Not yet.

He leans forward, grinning like the devil.

"Rafail Kopolov's sister," he says. "You've been fucking her."

My jaw tightens. Still, I say nothing.

"You think we didn't see you?" he continues, talking like this is casual. "Think I didn't know you were holed up at that little bar in Moscow? You think my eyes don't stretch that far?"

He tosses something across the table. Photos, grainy but clear enough. Zoya and me, her head against my shoulder, her smile soft and real. Us in my car. Us outside my flat.

Fuck.

My father sits still, frowning, his eyes flitting from me to Branson, then back to the pictures on the table.

I don't look away.

"I married her for a good reason," I say, steady. "We've had enough bloodshed."

"You should've told me, son."

"No," I shoot back, holding his stare. "Because you haven't believed a damn thing I've said, have you?"

He flinches. Doesn't speak.

"Seamus," he says hoarsely, "you're my firstborn son."

"But blood isn't thicker than water," Branson cuts in, his voice oily. "I've got evidence. He's been betraying us for years, Keenan. And then he brings her into our home?" He scoffs. "What's next? Invite the Russians in? Give them a seat at our table? Brought that little Russian girl in so she could relay everything to her family? I'd bet my fucking eye teeth that's what he's planning."

"I'm loyal to this family." I slam my fist on the desk. "She's kept quiet."

Branson snarls. "For how long? You think she'll keep her mouth shut when we bleed someone in front of her? We're not in the business of sentiment, McCarthy. She's a problem. And you,"—he jabs a finger at me—"you're mine. You're *The Undertaker*. You don't get to play house with the fucking enemy."

"She's not a threat," I snap.

"She's a liability," he spits back. "And if you're vulnerable, you're useless to me."

"To you?" I turn to my father. "Do you hear him? He doesn't care about you. Or this family. It's about him. His legacy."

I breathe in through my nose, long and steady. Controlled.

"You lied to me," my father says bitterly.

Fuck it.

"I did," I admit. "Because when I told you the truth, you shut me down."

Branson leans back, smiling like he's already won.

My father gets to his feet and stalks to the door. "We're done here, Seamus. Do what he says."

The door slams with finality behind him. I've lost all credibility.

Fuck.

"You want to prove you're still loyal?" he says calmly. Deadly. "There's only one way."

I know what's coming. I still shake my head as if that will somehow ward him off.

"Kill her."

My heart slams against my ribs.

"You said you were loyal," he goes on, smarmy as fuck. I hate the feckin' bastard. "Said your code meant something. *Show* me."

I meet his eyes.

"She trusts me," I whisper. "I'm not going to kill her. She's my *wife*."

"She's not family," he says flatly.

"She is now."

"Right," he says, standing, buttoning his jacket. "You've got one chance, McCarthy. One. Make her disappear. Quiet. No mess. And we go back to normal."

"Like fuck we do," I snarl.

His smile hardens into something cold and brutal.

"If you don't, you know what happens next." He heads for the door. "You heard your father. The syndicate's splintering. We won't allow that to happen." His eyes narrow. "Do it."

He turns away.

Conversation over.

God help me.

CHAPTER 26

ZOYA

I STARE AT THE CALENDAR, the app on my phone that tracks my cycles.

Not pregnant.

My heart sinks, heavy and low.

Why did I think it would happen the first month? That I could just will a baby into existence, manifest it, like it was magic, and everything would neatly fall into place. That somehow, this chaos could alchemize into something whole and new. No. That's not how this works. Life doesn't bend to dreams. It's not a fairy tale.

But I don't cry. I don't even feel the sting of tears. I just sit on the edge of the bed, staring down at my phone like it's a verdict. A sentence. Another month of trying. Another month of hope unraveled.

Another month of trying to be perfect. Another month of trying to keep the peace with my own body, trying to soothe the ache of being too much and not enough at once. I shake my head, the motion small, bitter.

I can almost hear Yana in my head, her voice dry and sharp. *"Stop trying to be the one who holds everything together. Just let it go. Things will sort themselves out."* But I can't. I don't. Because I let myself hope. I let the dream in, for just a breath, that maybe... maybe I could be more than the burden. Little Zoya, whom everyone had to shield and protect and manage. Maybe this time, *I* could be the one who changed things for the better, rather than serving a cup of tea and a hot biscuit.

Maybe this centuries-old war between our families could end... with me.

I walk to the bathroom, my steps slow and silent. I feel Seamus behind me.

I pick up my toothbrush and begin to brush my teeth, trying to ignore the weight of his presence. But I see his eyes flicker to my phone, to the mark on the app. He sees it. The little red drop.

"Your period started?"

I nod. He nods back, then turns away. Just like that.

It's the silence that lands hardest.

Have I let him down?

He's been distant since yesterday. Cold. Not cruel, just... gone. He barely touched me. When I asked what was wrong, he wouldn't tell me. I don't like this. This not-knowing. This shift.

He leaves the room without a word, and I feel it like a slap. The sting of failure, low in my belly. I'm not stupid.

I know what pregnancy would've meant. It would've been a tether. A bridge. A reason. It would've proved this was more than obsession and madness and forced proximity. That there was something real, something secret and blooming beneath it all.

Without it... what am I? A hostage. A complication too dangerous to set free. A liability.

But then, why did he look almost relieved? Why did his shoulders sink, his jaw unclench, as if a burden had been lifted?

He's relieved I'm not pregnant.

Why?

I wrap my arms around myself, aching. And I follow him.

It's late afternoon. The sky's dipped in gold, the kind of light that clings to your skin and makes the world feel too sharp, too vivid. The cliffs stretch out wide before us, open and wild. My god, it's gorgeous.

And I hate how much I love it here.

It makes me feel like a traitor. Like I've traded in Moscow. Like this place has worked its way under my skin, and I've denied who I am.

I hate that I love walking beside him, even when the silence between us feels heavy with all the things we're not saying.

He glances over his shoulder at me, then reaches out a hand. And I take it. Quietly.

We don't speak as we walk. Just the sound of gravel crunching beneath our boots and the distant cries of gulls overhead.

"I'm sorry, little Zoya," he murmurs. "My sweet lass."

I don't ask what he's sorry for. I already know.

Sorry for the distance. Sorry for dragging me into this storm. Sorry it's all so tangled, so damn complicated.

I feel eyes on me. Cold. Measuring.

When I turn, I catch the flick of a curtain in the window behind us. Kyla. She's always watching.

"She doesn't like me," I say softly. "Why?"

He doesn't look at me. "I suspect she reports to Branson."

My stomach twists. "And you let her?"

"I don't have a choice," he bites out. "Not now that he's back. There are eyes and ears everywhere, Zoya. One wrong breath and it all goes back to him."

"I don't understand," I whisper. "Why doesn't your father believe you, Seamus? After everything?"

"I was close," he says, his eyes shadowed. "So bloody close. He was just beginning to trust me again."

He pulls his hand from mine and shoves both into his coat pockets. The absence is sharp. It feels like rejection.

"Taking you... they didn't understand. My family didn't.

And maybe now, I don't either." He stops himself, then shakes his head and doesn't finish.

I frown. "But why Branson? Why him?"

"When I was a child," Seamus says, "he saved my father's life. He's earned my father's loyalty. And my father, he wants the easier truth. That Branson isn't a threat. That I'm just young and naive."

It stings, hearing him call himself young. He's nearly a generation older than me.

"But wasn't your father your age when he took the throne?"

"Aye," he says. "Because his father died."

His gaze drifts out over the waves. "And I would've had it. I would've had his trust. But then Branson showed evidence, you and me. Moscow. Us sneaking around. And just like that, I lost every ounce of credibility I'd built."

"Oh god," I breathe out, shaking my head. "Let's go. Please, Seamus. We can still run."

I've been thinking about it for days. Obsessing. Whispering it into the dark when he's asleep beside me.

"We can leave tonight," I say. "Take a car, drive away, just keep going. Disappear. Just you and me. We don't need this. We could become nothing, no names. Just... free."

He stops walking and slowly turns.

"Run where, Zoya?"

"Anywhere."

"There's nowhere he won't find me," he says. "You don't understand."

"I do."

"No." He cuts me off. "If I go now, I hand over every man who's ever followed me. I hand over my brothers and sisters. My father. Everyone. To that traitor." His jaw clenches. "If I run, it's over."

He sighs. "I'm sorry."

And I know he means it.

"I wish we could," he says, his fingers lacing through mine.

We walk until we reach the edge of the cliff. The drop is steep. The sea below, wild and endless. A thousand shades of blue and green and black.

He sits. I follow, my knees pulled to my chest. The wind catches my hair and tangles it, but I don't care.

"It's beautiful," I say, almost reverent.

He pulls a bottle of Guinness from his coat and holds it out. "'Tis. Fancy a drink?"

I arch a brow. "Now?"

He winks, but there's sorrow behind it. "It's not drugged, lass."

I snort. Then I take a sip... and grimace. He chuckles.

"Too strong?"

"No," I say. "I was raised on vodka."

He gives me a crooked smile. "Fair."

The silence stretches, but now it feels a little softer.

"Do you ever swim down there?" I ask.

"Aye. Even this time of year. It's cold but clear. Gorgeous."

"You ever jump off the cliff?"

"When we were lads. My father nearly murdered us when he found out. But the water's deep. You can make the jump if you know how."

"I used to swim too," I tell him. "Back home. There was a lake near our summer house. I'd sneak out before dawn. Dive in while the world was still asleep."

"Of course you did," he says, teasing. "Little brat."

I laugh. "Like your father, Rafail wasn't too happy when he found out."

His expression softens. And for a moment, there's something in his eyes I can't name.

"I loved it," I whisper. "Being under the water. Quiet. Moving without thought. It felt free. Like I could be anyone. I used to pretend I was a mermaid."

"Do you still swim?" he asks.

I nod. "Not like I did when I was younger, but I can."

He looks out at the water like it's whispering something to him that I can't hear.

"I reached out to my family again," I say softly. "They haven't responded."

I see his shoulders stiffen.

"Not even Rodion," I add. "Not one word."

"They think you're here against your will, love," he tells me softly.

I look at him, my chest tightening. "Why doesn't anybody ever believe me?" I whisper. "It's frustrating... being the youngest."

He sighs. "It's frustrating being the oldest."

I glance away, and his voice follows. "Because you're the peacekeeper, Zoya," he says gently. Then even softer, "They think you're still the good girl, trying to make things right."

"God, I know, but I'm not, and I can't." I swallow. "Just now, I was frustrated with myself for not being pregnant. Can you even imagine that?" I shake my head. "Being mad at yourself for something like that. Like children are puzzle pieces to fill a void."

"They're not," he murmurs. "Don't be so hard on yourself."

I swallow and lean back against him. The silence settles over us while he sips his drink, and I take a pass. He slips an arm around me, and when I shiver, he says nothing, just shrugs out of his jacket and drapes it over me. It's warm and smells like him.

"I just wish they would all understand. Listen."

"It's more complicated than that, isn't it, love?" he says. "Way more complicated. I'm sorry you're stuck in the middle of all this. But I'm not sorry I married you. Goddammit, I'm not."

I turn and meet his gaze. His blue eyes burn, cheeks flushed with heat and heartbreak.

"I'm not either," I tell him honestly.

He cups my cheek in his palm. "You're my good girl," he says. "And nobody's going to take that away. Do you understand me?"

I nod, my throat tight.

"Listen to me, lass. No matter what happens, no matter what, you need to trust me. You need to know that I love you. Do you understand?"

"Yes," I say, my breath catching. "Yes, I do."

I reach for him. "And I love you, Seamus. Please… tell me what happens next."

"I wish I could," he whispers.

"Would you hurt me?" I ask quietly.

He hesitates. "I'm afraid even the rocks have eyes and ears now that Branson's here. He's going to try to kill me, you know."

"What?"

"He'll make it look like an accident," Seamus says with weight. "That's how he works. He wouldn't dare kill me outright. My father would never forgive him, but an accident? That, he can do."

"What are you going to do?"

"I have a plan," he says softly. "Like I said. You have to trust me. Will you?"

"Okay," I whisper. "I trust you. Let's head in. It's getting late." He kisses my cheek. "I love this dress on you, love."

I smile. "You like everything you pick out for me?"

He shrugs, even though his eyes are sad. "What can I say?" He tugs a lock of my hair. "I have good taste."

The family's seated for a late dinner. Seamus pulls out my chair without looking at me. We eat in silence. I barely taste anything.

Caitlin tries to speak, to make something of the stillness, but finally gives up.

Seamus won't look at me.

He's gone stone-cold. The man from outside, who held me, who asked me to trust him, feels like someone I imagined.

He clears the dishes like a machine. I follow him.

"What's wrong?" I ask.

His jaw ticks. "I think you should go upstairs, Zoya. Go to bed. I don't want to talk right now."

I blink. What?

I linger, staring, hoping something in him will soften. Finally, I go upstairs. My chest is a knot.

I try to read but can't stay focused. But I don't sleep. I wander the house, then slip out the back door. The sea air is bitter.

Outside, the cliffside is slick with salt and spray. The ocean yawns black and endless below.

And then, I see them.

Branson, standing at the edge.

Ashland, beside him.

No Seamus.

"You there," Branson barks. "What are you doing out here alone? Does your husband know?"

I don't answer.

Ashland's voice snaps like a whip. "Speak when you're spoken to, lass. Don't you fucking walk away."

I hear heavy footsteps behind me.

Seamus.

He takes me in with one glance, then he looks to Branson and Ash. The setting sun throws shadows across his face.

"Zoya." His voice is low, a warning.

"Why do they hate me?" I whisper.

"You know why," he says. "You shouldn't be here."

I am *over* the coldness. "I'm not leaving."

He steps closer. But the cold in the air shifts, becomes something else. It's in him. In his eyes. They're empty. Shuttered. Dead.

"You disobeyed me," he says. His hand closes around my arm, tightly. It hurts.

And he walks me toward them.

Toward Branson. Toward Ashland.

What the hell is he doing?

"I told you to go inside," he says. "You disobeyed. So I can punish you right here."

This isn't like before. This isn't play. This isn't *him*.

"Seamus," I plead. "No, you can't—"

He doesn't stop.

"Did you really think this was all about you? That you could do whatever you wanted?"

He waits for me to answer. But I can't. I'm frozen. I can't speak.

"You know why you're here," he says sharply. "You were convenient." His mouth twists, and he doesn't meet my eyes.

"I don't need you anymore, Zoya. You can't even give me a child."

The words are like a fist. I suck in a breath.

"Seamus... you're lying. This isn't you. What are you doing?"

He steps closer. Drops his voice.

"No, Zoya. This *is* me. You just fell for a fantasy. You fell in love with what you wanted me to be."

"Why are you saying this?" I whisper. "Seamus—"

But then I remember what he said.

Trust me.

No matter what happens.

But I can't. *I can't.*

"This is over," he says. "I must choose loyalty to my family."

"What?" My voice breaks. "What are you—?"

We're at the edge of the cliff now. The wind howls. My feet slip on wet stone.

"Your family doesn't want you anymore," he says, leaning in. "You betrayed them."

His breath touches my cheek. "And I don't want you anymore either. I used you to get to them. Now that I have access, this is over. I'm a McCarthy... loyalty to blood comes first, regardless of what you think this charade was about, regardless of what you want or how you feel about me."

Then his hands are on my shoulders.

And suddenly, I'm teetering. I blink, trying to wake myself from this horrid dream, but it's real, and it's all happening too fast.

For one wild second, when he leans in close to me, I think he's going to kiss me, that this is all some nightmare, and I'll blink and wake up.

That he'll say sorry.

But he doesn't.

He pushes.

And the world rushes by me as I plummet downward.

Sky, sea, and screams blur together.

The icy mouth of the dark Irish Sea swallows me whole.

CHAPTER 27

MY HANDS ARE SHAKING, but I don't let it show. I stand at the cliff's edge, and I swear to fucking Christ, I'll hear the sound of her scream being swallowed by the wind and water for the rest of my life. It's carved into me now, the sound of her voice breaking as the sea opened up beneath her.

The wind bites at my arms. She was wearing the little dress I picked out for her, loose and lightweight on purpose.

The sea crashes below like it's mourning her, but I don't look down. I can't. Instead, I turn toward my crew. Toward Branson.

My heart is in my throat, pounding so loud it might crack my fucking ribs. "Are you happy now?" I snap, venom lacing my voice. "You fucking traitor."

He doesn't flinch. Doesn't blink. Just smiles, sharp and cruel.

There was a time I looked up to Branson. He was almost a hero to me. My father's best mate. Loyal to our family. Powerful. Strong and ruthless. A man to fear, a man to follow. But now…

"I didn't know you had it in you," he mutters.

He turns away from me, bored already, and faces Ashland. "Find the body," he says. "I want evidence that she's gone. Call me when you have it," he adds, like he's talking about a broken vase, and not a person.

Ashland nods. There's something in his eyes, almost a glint of glee. I don't meet his stare, don't want to give anything away.

"Yes, sir," he says and walks toward the narrow stone steps cut into the cliffside, leading down to the rocky beach below.

The sea is rising. The tide will wash everything away soon. We're at high tide as the minutes drag.

The salt wind stings my eyes, but I don't wipe it away. I don't say a damn thing while I wait for Ashland's call. I just stand there. Still. Numb. Until the phone rings.

Branson puts it on speaker, staring at me like this is a show he's been waiting years to watch.

I turn, my breath catching.

Ashland's voice comes through, clear and cold. "I've got her," he says. "There's no pulse. Looks like she broke her neck."

A pause.

"She's gone."

I close my eyes. Even hearing those words makes pain lance through me, bright and vivid.

Branson smiles. "Well done, Seamus," he says quietly, like he's proud. "Let's go tell your father."

We march into the house, and my stomach twists and churns. I feel like I might vomit, but I don't reach for my phone. I don't do anything except move.

Kyla stands by the front door. Her face is pale, stricken, her mouth open in disbelief. "Seamus, what did you do? What have you *done*?"

My mother is behind her, one hand pressed to her mouth like she's seen a monster. Fuck me. She looks at me as if I've drowned a fucking basket of puppies. "Seamus," she whispers, her eyes wide.

"I don't want to hear it," I say, my jaw clenched. "I had to prove my loyalty. You know that."

I turn and face them both fully. "I did it for you. To protect you. All of this, it's always been for you."

"I never asked you to," my mother whispers. Her voice breaks on the words. "Is she...?"

"She's gone," I say, turning away again. It's the only answer I can give.

Branson walks victorious. Triumphant. Smug.

My father's waiting in his office. When we walk in, he looks up, surprised.

"What happened?"

"He did it," Branson says, clapping me on the shoulder like I'm a boy who just lost his virginity. "Pushed her right off the goddamn cliff. Leave it to Seamus to kill and still make it a show, eh?"

My father blinks, then stares at me.

"You pushed Zoya off the cliff, son? You killed your wife?"

"*You* fucking told me to do what Branson ordered," I snarl. Rage flares in my chest. I will never forgive him for this. Not ever.

I turn away and drop into the nearest chair.

"Did you have confirmation of it?" my father asks flatly, his voice hollow, his eyes wide.

Does he regret the order?

Branson nods. "Ash looked at the body himself. Said there was no pulse. She's gone."

"Who else witnessed it?" he presses.

"Me. Ashland," Branson says. "Caitlin and Kyla saw from the window too."

"*Jesus,*" my dad mutters. He runs a hand down his face. He's not thinking about Zoya, not really. He's thinking about my mother. About the emotional fallout. She's seen him do terrible, wicked things, and she's always forgiven him.

But this?

Will she forgive this?

I hate it. My whole fucking life, I've been trying to make him proud. To make him happy. And he's been a good father, in his own cold, brutal way. Loyal. Strong. Brave.

But now...

"Now we prepare for the blowback from the Kopolovs," he says. "They're already here."

I sit up straighter. "I've been tracking them. They're already in the city?"

My father nods. "Assemble everyone. You know what to do."

Yeah, I know exactly what to do.

But it's got nothing to do with what my father has planned.

CHAPTER 28

ZOYA

THE COLD WATER hits like knives, sharp, slicing, merciless. My lungs burn as I break the surface, coughing up seawater and gasping for breath. It hurts. It stings. Not just the water. Not just the impact. But the words. What he said.

What he *did.*

I'm so cold I can't think straight. I can't feel. I can't even scream. The waves drag me like some discarded toy, bobbing me up and down, crashing over my shoulders, yanking me under again, slamming me into jagged rocks, and then dragging me out just to do it all over again.

But I fight. I swim. I've always been strong in the water, quick and graceful. The tide is high tonight, so it's easier to float, to surface. I push back against the pull of the sea, the waves breaking in the distance like applause for my survival.

I can feel eyes on me, watching. But I can't see through the blur of salt and wind and desperation. I fight harder. I swim with everything I've got left in me, and after what feels like an eternity, but must be just minutes, I reach the shore. My fingers claw into wet sand like it's salvation. My whole body trembles violently.

There's blood. Something's cut my leg, but I don't care. I'm alive.

He pushed me.

Seamus pushed me.

The thought hits me like a second impact. The memory of his voice, those words, the chill in his eyes, colder than the ocean.

How could I trust someone who would look me in the eye and then push me off a cliff? What if the sea had taken me for good? What if I had been pulled under and never surfaced?

To my right, there's a blinking light, red and rhythmic. Some kind of beacon, a rescue maybe, but it doesn't move. Doesn't come closer. Is it even for me?

I drag myself to my knees in the shallow surf. The water is fresher here, mixing with the tears I won't let fall. My hair is plastered to my face, soaked in salt. The wind howls like it's mourning. My thin dress clings to me like a second skin. Thankfully, it's light, unlike the jeans I wore earlier.

Thank god, Seamus told me to change.

The sky presses heavy above me, gray and angry. There's a silhouette on the rocky path above the beach. Watching.

I freeze.

Why isn't anyone helping me? I just survived being thrown from a cliff, swam to shore through god-knows-what, and nobody's moving. No one's running to help. I blink hard against the salt stinging my eyes.

"Somebody help," I croak, my voice broken and raw. Still, no one moves. They just stand there.

I double over and wretch again. A sob claws its way up my throat but never escapes. I sit back on my heels, numb and shaking. What do I do now?

I can't go back up to Ballyhock.

He left me. Discarded me like I was nothing. Was he told to kill me? Was that the plan all along?

Then someone steps forward. My heart stutters. I don't want to be seen. I want to disappear, but I also want answers.

I have to get out of here. I have to go home. But even that thought feels like a lie now. Is home even safe anymore?

The figure steps closer, tall and calm. Too calm.

Ashland.

Shit.

I freeze. My heart is beating in my throat. He raises a finger to his lips, *Shhh*, like I'm supposed to be quiet. Then he gestures for me to lie down in the sand.

My instincts scream no. I don't move. I don't trust him. I don't trust anyone anymore, not even Seamus.

Ashland pulls a gun.

Cocks it.

Points to the ground again. "Lie down," he whispers.

I obey. My spine hits the wet sand. The wind steals the breath from my lungs. Ashland kneels beside me. His fingers reach for my neck.

I slap at him, trying to shove him away. He bats my hands aside like they're nothing and pins my wrist to the ground. His fingers find my pulse point again.

"Aye," he mutters, not looking at my eyes. "That's what I thought. No pulse."

Wait—what?

He pulls out a phone. Finger to his lips.

When I don't move, he dials. "I've got her," he says, calm and flat, like a man commenting on the weather. His fingers trail down my neck. I shiver.

"There's no pulse. Looks like she broke her neck."

Oh my god.

"She's gone."

He's *staging* it. Faking my death. He's in on it. *With Seamus?*

Then, without another word, he stands and disappears around the bend in the cliff. "Stay there," he says, like it's nothing.

The second he's gone, everything changes.

The silent watchers from before suddenly surge forward. Too fast. Too many. I scream, or try to. Hands clamp down on my mouth, my arms, my legs. I fight like hell. Kick, claw, bite.

But it's no use.

A gag goes across my mouth. A bag over my head. Darkness.

I can't see them, but I can feel something—something about them is familiar. A smell. A breath. A whisper I half remember.

They wrap me in a thick towel and carry me like I'm nothing. I'm shoved into the back of a car. I thrash and scream against the gag, but my body's still too weak. My adrenaline's raging, but it's not enough.

Then I hear it.

Russian.

A familiar voice, rough and sure. The bag is pulled off my head.

Relief hits me so fast it knocks the breath out of me.

The driver turns. Our eyes meet in the rearview mirror. Matvei.

My cousin.

"Hold on, Zoya," he says, voice gravelly with emotion. "I'm sorry you had to go through this. You're okay. You're not safe yet, but will be."

My teeth are chattering. "Wh-what happened?" I ask, shaking. I'm freezing even wrapped in the towel. Still wet. Still raw.

He sighs. "I'll tell you everything. I've been working with Seamus."

My eyes widen.

"You know my parents fled after their betrayal, don't you?"

I nod.

"They've been plotting with Branson," Matvei continues. "And now it's time. Seamus is making his move to take the throne. The only way to do that... was to cut Branson out. For good."

"My fucking god, is he going to apologize?" My voice cracks. "Apologize for breaking my heart? For pushing me off a fucking *cliff*?"

Matvei's jaw tightens. "He'd better. He planned it all. He called me. I was already in town, waiting for this. The others are coming. I had to make sure they don't kill him." He sighs.

My blood turns to ice.

"So yeah," I mutter, "he'll be lucky if *I* don't get to him first."

I feel it, the rage, the betrayal, and the wild, awful love still buried somewhere in me.

Matvei's lips curl. "Attagirl," he says, proud.

"I'm not joking!"

"Oh, you'll love him again," he says softly. "You'll see. He feigned your death. Ash was in on it."

"*Ash*, like you're best mates?"

"Aw. Mates, like you're Irish already."

"Of all the fucking—"

"And that dress," he says, nodding to me. "He made you wear that?"

"Yes," I spit. "Said I looked pretty in it."

"It's because it was light," Matvei says. "So you'd surface. He checked the tides too. Made sure they were high."

I blink. "Did you see the Coast Guard?"

"Yeah," he says, eyes dark. "He had four crews on standby. So no, there was no way he was gonna hurt you. He pushed you far enough to fall, but not enough to break anything. Not enough to risk anything, really."

I'm speechless.

"I waited on the shore," he finishes. "While Ashland reported your death to Branson."

"So... Ashland's on Seamus's side?"

"Yes," Matvei confirms. "They all are now."

CHAPTER 29

SEAMUS

I FEEL DETACHED. Half-alive. A walking fucking ghost. There's this slow burn under my skin, rage mixed with dread, and all of it points to Branson. He forced my hand, pushed me into this. And now? Now I have no choice but to follow through. I have to. There's no going back.

The grand front hall is too quiet. Unnaturally still, like the house itself is holding its breath. The only sound is the faint shuffle of expensive shoes on polished hardwood. I lean against the doorway, arms crossed, and watch as my mother glides past the base of the staircase. She moves like she's haunted, slow and careful, like she might shatter if she steps too hard.

She won't meet my eyes. I don't blame her.

Behind her, my sisters drift, clothed in muted tones, heads down, not saying a word. They won't talk to me. Again, I get it. They're scared, maybe even disgusted. But none of that matters now. Because the clock's ticking. And if everything unfolds the way I've planned…

My father stands off to the side near the staircase. Shoulders broad. Back straight. The very image of a king too stubborn to kneel. But he won't speak. He won't look at me. Doesn't have to. They all know.

I glance away, exhaling slow through my nose, trying to steady the churn inside. The night air presses in, thick with tension, with expectation. This is it. No more lies.

"It's time," I say, stepping forward, letting my voice fill the silence. "I've brought you all in here for a reason. Please. Sit."

From upstairs, I hear the steady, unmistakable clank of boots on wood. My men. Loyal, brutal, armed, and ready. Ashland's across the room, eyes locking with mine. Branson's next to him, still spewing whispers, still believing he's got Ash on his side.

Idiot. He doesn't see the noose tightening.

My people pour in behind me, spilling into the hall with military precision. Every single man and woman who serves me knows what this moment means. This is the reckoning. We've spent years building up to this one moment.

I glance at my phone. Still nothing. Branson hasn't caught wind. Good.

I lift my head and step forward. My voice is ice cold.

"I did what you fucking told me to," I say, staring straight at my father. My words cut through the silence like a blade. "I don't know if I'll ever forgive you for what you made me do."

They don't know yet. But they're about to.

"I have an announcement to make," I continue, louder now. My words echo up the stairwell. My boots hit each step with weight as I head toward the living room.

Ashland nods. He lifts his phone, starts recording. Branson lingers just behind, his expression shifting. My men step into position, fanning out like wolves. They surround him, silent and still.

My father follows, his eyes unreadable. Curious.

I press a button on the remote. Years ago, Da had this place rigged, family movie nights, they called it. Now I'll put it to use.

The screen flickers to life, casting a cold glow across the space. First slide: the beginning of the end.

"You asked. You followed," I say. "You believed a traitor."

Branson shifts in his seat. "What the hell is this?"

"Quiet," I snap. "I'm in charge now."

He starts to rise—wrong move. Four hands shove him back down. His face twists. "Get your hands off—"

"Sit still."

I turn to my father. "Give me ten minutes. Just ten fucking minutes. To show you why I did what I did. Why I had to."

My voice breaks just slightly. "You asked me to kill my wife."

Silence. Then, my father: "You have it. Branson. Sit."

I nod. "Branson betrayed you. All of you. And I have the proof."

The screen changes, and now it's footage. Conversations caught on hidden cameras. Handshakes in shadows. Money exchanged. Envelopes. Whispers. Tells.

"You don't know. You can't—"

"Ah. I can. Quiet," I snap, furious that he made me do what I did. He'll pay for that.

The men in the room shift, the weight of the truth starting to press down. Guns slowly rise, eyes narrowing.

There are codes. Timestamps. Locations. Names. Lines connecting him to Russia. To the rogue Kopolovs.

"Matvei Kopolov's parents," I say. "They've been working with Branson. Trying to steal the crown from within. They failed to claim the Kopolov throne. So they came here to take ours."

My mother covers her mouth. The screen keeps cycling... documents, intercepted calls, blueprints.

"This is the coup plot," I say. "This was the plan to take everything from us. Including Kyla."

A final slide hits the screen: Branson's handwriting. A note, short and scrawled in ink.

Take her.

Kyla.

Gasps. Kyla's scream pierces through the silence.

My father draws his gun, aiming at Branson, held in check only by discipline.

I step forward again, my eyes locked on the screen. "You wanted proof. Now you have it."

My voice is steady and calm, even when I want to scream. My fist clenches.

"I went to Moscow when I found out about the Kopolov betrayal. I met with Matvei. Risked everything. And I brought it back."

More slides. Text messages. Photos. Flight logs. Weapons stashes. All of it.

My phone buzzes. A message.

> **Matvei**
> They're here. I can't stop them. You have
> five minutes.

Shit. My chest tightens. I glance at my father. "That night, at the Wolf and Moon, it wasn't the Russians who pulled the trigger. *I* killed them for their betrayal, which I've shown you clear as day. I made sure no one was left alive."

A pause.

"Except one," I add. "Zoya Kopolova. She saw everything. I took her. Made her my wife. And I did it for this. For you. Because they were trying to overthrow you."

I look around. Eyes are wide. Weapons are drawn. The gravity hits.

"I need you to hold Branson. Keep him alive. Punish him with Matvei's parents. But we don't have time. The Kopolovs are at our door."

Gasps rise around me.

I spin to the guard. "Where's Matvei?"

"We lost contact."

I squeeze the remote. Boots on gravel. Outside.

My father steps up beside me, his face grim. "This goes deeper than betrayal. This is war."

But it isn't who I expected. It isn't Rafail Kopolov or one of his men.

We both turn as the front door creaks open, and Matvei enters the room.

"I tried to hold her back," he says, pleading. "But she says she has something important to tell you."

"You have her, then?" I ask, my voice hoarse.

Zoya steps out of the shadow behind him and into the light.

CHAPTER 30

"Zoya." Seamus stares at me across the room. They all do. Caitlin cries quietly. Even Kyla wipes at her eyes. But everyone's still.

"I'm sorry," he whispers hoarsely. "I'm so sorry." He faces the room.

"I never—"

A sound cuts him off. A sharp click. Then another.

Too late.

The windows explode inward.

Smoke. Screaming. Gunfire. A blur of black-clad bodies. I'm on the ground. Someone grabs my arm. Seamus screams my name, then everything goes black.

I KNOW the minute my eyes fly open that I'm not alone. I look over my shoulder and immediately recognize Seamus's profile. His head lolls to the side. I quickly assess the situation. We're in a room that looks like a cell, one window to the left, a single bulb overhead, and concrete beneath us. I shiver. It's freezing in here.

My head throbs from a hit I must've taken, but I force myself to breathe slow, to remain present. My hands are tied behind me, with Seamus bound next to me. We're here. Alive.

For now.

It can't be my family because obviously they wouldn't have taken me like this. Maybe him, but not both of us. He suspected an ambush from my family. Who is this, then?

We haven't gone far. It's still night out, still inky black. I inch my shoulder toward him. "Seamus?"

With a gasp, his head snaps up. He blinks. "Zoya?"

"I'm here. We're tied up. Shh, I'm trying to figure out where we are and who took us."

"Jesus," he growls. "What the fuck?"

"I don't— This can't be my family," I whisper. "They wouldn't do this to me."

"Nor mine."

"It can't be yours. You slaughtered every traitor already, didn't you?"

"Save Branson, aye." Out of the corner of my eye, I note his wrist is askew, at an odd angle.

"Oh my god, what happened to you?" I ask quietly, but I can't turn to look at him.

"I tried to stop them from taking you. They broke my wrist."

I wince. Goddamn, that must hurt.

"Who took us?"

Our question is answered when a heavy door scrapes open.

"You killed my brother for this little girl?" a voice sounds, loud and gravelly. "Isn't that nice. You'll both be punished then."

Shit. Pavel's brother. The Morozovs have come to collect. Payback.

My knees tremble, and I can feel Seamus's tight body next to mine, coiled, ready to spring. If only he could.

Morozov's gaze sweeps over me, a silent accusation. I see the brutal slouch of Seamus's stance in my peripheral vision. Ready. Always ready.

"You put him up to it, didn't you?" He paces in front of me, his eyes angry slits. "You were plotting. Our sources say you were there the night of the slaughter at the Wolf and Moon. You plotted with him, didn't you?"

I shake my head, and he raises his hand to strike me. On instinct, I flinch, but I feel Seamus move as he presses himself between us.

"She didn't know a fucking thing. Leave her out of this. Your battle is with *me*."

I choke out a gasp as he strikes Seamus hard on the cheek.

Oh *god*. I hate seeing him hurt, hate seeing him suffer like this.

Another blow lands, and this time he's thrown off balance. My breath is erratic. I'm rooted in place. Blood swells on his lip. He grunts, and my belly flips seeing him brutalized, but he shifts back to brace his body over mine. Protecting me even now.

Then we feel the vibration: distant gunfire. Footsteps. The unmistakable sound of someone approaching. Morozov rises and curses.

"Zoya," Seamus whispers, his fingers on my wrists. "The loose end, love. Tug it." I give it a pull, and his wrists spring free, then he loosens mine. Seamus is instantly on his feet and just as quickly puts his body between me and Morozov.

THEN CLOSER, boots hammer concrete, a warning shout. The *snap-snap* of a gun. Morozov turns, fury twisting his features. He barks a command, but it's too late. A click followed by a *boom*!

Smoke fills the small room instantly.

Morozov shrieks something indecipherable in Russian, but his plans splinter as he's ambushed. And then I see them— *my brothers*—Rodion, Rafail, Semyon. They've come all this way.

I can hardly see in here. Seamus yanks me to the side as a gunshot fires and a bullet wedges into the wall just beside me.

Oh god.

I'm screaming, deafened by the sound of ringing in my ears. Rodion's eyes are wild, a blood stain on his shirt, his or someone else's. He fires twice, cold and exacting, before calling my name.

"Zoya! Where is she?"

"I'm here!" I say, waving my hand, but in the dense fog of smoke, he can't see me.

"Are y'alright?" an Irish voice rings out.

"Yes!"

"Oh, thank fuck."

Is that… one of Seamus' men?

Then I hear Seamus in my ear. "Down, love." I fall to my knees just as Morozov points his gun at me, but before he can pull the trigger…

Bang.

Seamus shoots Morozov and hits him, straight between the eyes.

Moments slow. I stumble and drop to my knees, behind Seamus, covered by his body. Then I realize it isn't just my brothers who have come—his are here, too, along with his cousins. Cavin and Ashland, Colm and Daire surround the Morozovs as one.

Our families. United in their efforts to save us.

I watch as things begin to slow. We exit the room, smoke billowing around us, gasping for air in the dark night, lit only by the moon.

Rafail stares at me and Seamus. Blinks.

"He protected you," he says, bewildered. He blinks again.

"That's what husbands are meant to do," I say, looking him in the eye. My anger at Seamus is momentarily forgotten now. "Aren't they?"

My brothers stand shoulder-to-shoulder, their weapons now lowered. Cavin stands, blade in hand, beside Colm, barking orders into a phone, and Daire, wiping blood from his face with the back of his sleeve.

Russian and Irish. Side by side.

"Come, lass," Seamus whispers to me, offering a hand. "It's time I get you home."

CHAPTER 31

ZOYA

THE KITCHEN SMELLS FAINTLY of antiseptic. Someone's dumped half a med kit on the counter. Caitlin's on a stool, her long hair tied back, patching up Seamus's arm like she's done it a hundred times. Maybe she has.

Her eyes meet Seamus', then Rafail. "Listen to me and listen well, lads," she says softly, and somehow I get the distinct feeling she's every bit as in charge of this family as Keenan is. "You'll not have any more bloodshed in my home. If you must fight, leave. Not here. Not in Ballyhock. We've worked for decades to have peace with the locals, Mr. Kopolov. I hope you understand."

I watch as Kyla wipes blood off Daire's cheek, swatting his hand when he tries to do it himself. Everyone's passing around the same dented flask.

No one's fighting.

No one in either family suffered more than a superficial wound.

Branson's secured somewhere in holding, and Matvei's talking emphatically on the phone in the corner of the room. It's hard to adjust to seeing my family here, right here, in the McCarthy family kitchen.

I lean against the door and watch. There's something surreal about it. Our families, side by side.

Rafail walks toward Keenan. For a second, I brace myself on instinct, but Rafail sticks his hand out. Keenan doesn't even hesitate.

They shake.

I blink. No guns. No shouting. Just... peace.

"So we had to get kidnapped and almost murdered for you two to make peace?" I ask, half-amused.

"Aye," Keenan says. "Leave it to Seamus to have a bit of flair about him." He turns to me. "I'm sorry, lass. So very sorry."

And somehow... that's it. The fire's gone. The war is over. I watch it happen like waking from a dream. My brother, the one I was raised to follow, and Seamus, sitting in the same room. Still breathing.

I let out a shuddering breath. Kyla comes to me. "My god, what you've been through," she says. "I'm so sorry. And I'm sorry for how I treated you." She grimaces. "I just—" She sighs. "No, there's no excuse for it. I'm sorry, Zoya. Forgive me?"

I nod. "Of course. This has been messy and unconventional. I get it."

"Aye," she says with a sigh. "Hasn't it though?"

Rafail and Seamus sit side by side. Seamus sits up tall. "Matvei sent me the footage," Rafail says. "And I saw you save Zoya in there. You took the blows meant for her."

"Of course," Seamus says. "I'll always protect her, Kopolov. Because I love her."

Rafail looks at me across the room and smiles.

I breathe a sigh of relief.

"Alright, then," I say, my voice carrying across the room. "If we're at peace, can we please agree to get along without another damn fight? I'm still not pleased with my husband for what he did, and it's hard keeping track of who the hell I'm angry with."

Seamus gives me a sheepish smile. Rafail nods. Keenan opens another bottle and pours us another round.

Seamus walks up to me and wraps his arms around me. "I'll make it up to you, lass. I give you my word, I'll make it up to you."

He kisses me in front of all of them, long and slow and claiming.

I kiss him back. Somewhere, far in the distance, church bells ring, hearkening the break of dawn. It feels symbolic.

For a moment, I fancy they're wedding bells.

Welcoming a new era.

EPILOGUE

ZOYA

Maybe he left it at the top of my bedside table so I would find it, but it was slightly buried beneath a few pieces of paper. So I'm not sure if he left it on purpose, or if he forgot. But Seamus doesn't forget anything.

He doesn't make mistakes. He doesn't do anything accidentally. His mind is a vault.

Every decision, calculated with precision.

So when I see that key and find myself alone in the house the next morning, I know exactly what I need to do. Still, I wait.

I wait until the sun sets and the motion sensors around the property come on—signaling someone is getting close, even Seamus. I wait until I'm surrounded in darkness, then flick on the hallway light and hold the key in the palm of my hand. It feels symbolic somehow.

After everything we've been through, after everything we've done, this key feels like the beginning of understanding my husband. Even now, a tiny part of me wonders if I'll find something that will make me want to turn away.

But the second that question surfaces, I know the answer.

There is nothing—nothing—that could ever keep me away from him.

No demon he could unearth. No secret he could confess. Nothing that could keep me away from the man I love. The man I've given my life to. The man I've vowed to.

He owns every piece of my heart. And no matter what I find beyond that door, nothing is going to change.

Not now. Not ever.

Warmth floods my chest with that certainty, and I clutch the key tighter, smiling to myself in the darkness.

Really, this is it.

This is the moment.

This is what I've been waiting for.

I take a deep breath, slide the key into the lock, and turn.

At first, it seems like nothing. An office?

He kept an office for me? There's a desk and a few things in the corner of the room.

Did I really build this all up in my mind just to find...

Oh. Wait.

I walk over to the desk—it's flimsy. This chair wouldn't hold Seamus's weight for anything.

Is this a prop?

I move the chair aside gingerly, waiting. Behind the desk, there's a wall. A wall that isn't just a wall. I tap it gently, and it gives way.

I cover my mouth when dust rises, revealing a hidden sanctuary.

If you opened the door and glanced in, all you'd see is an old, unused desk and nothing else.

But here...

Oh, God.

My knees give out and I sink into a chair.

There are boxes upon boxes, all labeled with dates.

With trembling hands, I open the first one.

A pair of pearl earrings. Dated over a year ago.

> You said you loved pearls but never bought them because you feared only old ladies wore them. No. Pearls are classy—like you. I bought these after the first day I met you. They're freshwater, gold setting—perfect for classy women like you, my sweet angel.

They're the most gorgeous, luminescent pearls I've ever seen.

Oh, God. Seamus.

I put them back carefully and reach for another box—dated the following week.

A French press? I laugh.

You said you wanted to try coffee made in a French press, so here you go, lass. I'm not sure when you'll get this, so give it a good wash first, eh?

Another box, heavier. I nearly drop it. Inside: three hardcover books.

You said your brothers read these to you when you were little. That they made you feel safe and calm. I look forward to the day I can read them to you.

Tears sting my eyes. He didn't. He did.

I finger the pages, transported back to my childhood bedtimes.

I put them down and pick up another.

Every item is curated. Thoughtful. Precise.

Some wrapped in paper, some bare. Everything labeled.

"Thursday the 23rd. The first time she wore that blue scarf."

"*One-year anniversary of her showing up again.*"

There are notes.

One velvet ribbon I once wore in my braid—pressed between tissue.

She smiled today. I remembered how to breathe.

My knees nearly buckle.

There's a pastry tin from a Moscow bakery I once said I missed. Empty, but inside: a gift card.

Jewelry—delicate, symbolic.

Photographs.

Polaroids. Letters.

They're all addressed to me.

Letters I'll read and savor.

One shelf at eye level. I open it. My breath catches.

Two children's books.

One in Russian. One in Gaelic.

As if he already thought of children.

I swipe at my eyes. God, Seamus.

Unlocking this room really did feel like unlocking his heart. And I was not wrong.

Seamus McCarthy loves me with everything he has.

I think I've cried enough—until I find the last box.

I pull it down. Open it. Sniff hard, trying to stay composed.

But I can't.

I bury my face in my arms and weep.

When I finally lift my head, I wipe my eyes and look again.

It's a framed photo of my parents' wedding day.

He found them.

He forgave my family.

We're forging ahead.

I stare at the picture—at my father, who looks like Rafail, with a touch of Semyon and Rodion.

At my mother. My god, my mother.

Now I understand why Rafail protected me so fiercely.

Because this is the first time I've ever seen her like this— young, glowing.

She looks just like me.

I'm a miniature version of her.

I've only ever seen pictures taken after Rafail's birth, when they already looked older. But this was before the heart- break, before the war.

They had years of infertility before they had Rafail. They were practically children when they married. I've never seen them so vibrant. So alive.

My God, how did he find this?

There's a soft click behind me. I don't turn.

"You found them," he says. His voice proud but hesitant.

I feel him behind me, a man who's never lost a fight, now worried about my reaction.

I hold the photo.

"Where did you get this?" I ask. "Oh, Seamus."

"Your aunt and uncle worked for us. You know that, right?"

"Yes."

"I paid a pretty price for that picture," he says with a smile. "Never the cost of betrayal. No, they just wanted money. Who knew an old photo could cost so much? It was worth every penny lass, wasn't it?"

My throat tightens. "Thank you," I whisper. But the words feel too small.

How do you thank someone for giving you a piece of yourself you never knew was missing?

"Why did you... why did you hide all these? *Did* you hide them?"

He shifts, hands in his pockets. Looks almost... bashful and boyish.

"I wanted to wait until the time was right," he says softly. "Until the war ended. Until we were at peace. Until you already knew that I loved you—before I gave you even more proof."

"Oh, you exasperating man," I say, laughing through tears. "I love you so much."

He takes me in his arms and kisses me. Hand to cheek. Lip to lip. Heart to heart.

"I love you, Zoya McCarthy," he says.

"I love you, Seamus."

His arms wrap around me. And in the silence, I stand with him. Comforted, hopeful. Loved.

THE END

BONUS EPILOGUE

Want to read more of Seamus and Zoya's story? Scan the QR Code below to get the free Bonus Epilogue for Unrequited: A Dark Mafia Age Gap Romance!

PREVIEW

IRISH KING: A DARK IRISH MAFIA ARRANGED MARRIAGE ROMANCE

Fans of Jane Henry's best-selling Irish mafia series **_Dangerous Doms_** get ready, because in 2026 the McCarthy clan is back with a vengeance!

All your favorite McCarthy men have been **_VERY_** busy with the loves of their lives and there is an entirely new generation of McCarthy men ready to melt your heart and set your knickers ablaze! All your favorites characters from _Dangerous Doms_ also make appearances. A new generation of Jane's trademark feisty heroines also awaits you with all the wit, snark and strength you've come to expect from her!

Catch the next chapter in the McCarthy Clan's generational epic... coming January 31, 2026!

Pre-order the first book in the Jane's new McCarthy Family Legacy series "Irish King: A Dark Irish Mafia Arranged Marriage Romance" by scanning the QR code below. Available on January 31st, 2026 -> FREE to read in Kindle Unlimited!

What's that? You don't want to wait until January 31st next year to read about the McCarthy clan? I've got you covered! Scan the QR code below and get my best selling series ***Dangerous Doms - The Complete Collection*** (FREE to read in Kindle Unlimited). All seven books from the epic original McCarthy clan story... ***Keenan, Cormac, Nolan, Carson, Lachlan, Tiernan & Tully***... Learn how Seamus's father, Keenan & his brothers conquered the Irish mafia world and woo'd the women they love. Get all backstory that lead up to Seamus and Zoya so you're ready for the next chapter in the McCarthy clan's generational epic!

Fueled by dark chocolate and even darker coffee, USA Today bestselling author Jane Henry writes what she loves to read – character-driven, unputdownable romance featuring dominant alpha males and the powerful heroines who bring them to their knees. She's believed in the power of love and romance since Belle won over the beast, and finally decided to write love stories of her own.

Scan the QR Code below to receive Jane's Newsletter & be notified of upcoming new releases & special offers!

Be sure to visit me at www.janehenryromance.com, too!

www.ingramcontent.com/pod-product-compliance
Lightning Source LLC
Chambersburg PA
CBHW060612300726
48975CB00005B/1544